OCT 1 6 2012

"Look at this," KiKi said, waving her hand over the shoppers in the dining room. "Murder truly is good for business. I never knew people could be so ghoulish. Everyone wants to know every gory little detail about Cupcake and the body. I suppose it's like Cher said: 'There is no such thing as bad publicity.'"

"Cher said that?"

"She would have if she'd thought of it first. We've been busy as ants at a picnic. I'm thinking it's all because of the body in the Lexus, but now we are getting clothes to sell. I took in some costume jewelry that looked kind of nice, and maybe we should start to do furniture. While you were gone, I went and named your store the Prissy Fox."

Iced Chiffon

DUFFY BROWN

BERKLEY PRIME CRIME, NEW YORK

THE BERKLEY PUBLISHING GROUP
Published by the Penguin Group
Penguin Group (USA) Inc.
375 Hudson Street, New York, New York 10014, USA

Penguin Group (Canada), 90 Eglinton Avenue East, Suite 700, Toronto, Ontario M4P 2Y3, Canada
(a division of Pearson Penguin Canada Inc.) • Penguin Books Ltd., 80 Strand, London WC2R 0RL,
England • Penguin Group Ireland, 25 St. Stephen's Green, Dublin 2, Ireland (a division of Penguin
Books Ltd.) • Penguin Group (Australia), 250 Camberwell Road, Camberwell, Victoria 3124, Australia
(a division of Pearson Australia Group Pty. Ltd.) • Penguin Books India Pvt. Ltd., 11 Community
Centre, Panchsheel Park, New Delhi—110 017, India • Penguin Group (NZ), 67 Apollo Drive,
Rosedale, Auckland 0632, New Zealand (a division of Pearson New Zealand Ltd.) • Penguin Books
(South Africa) (Pty.) Ltd., 24 Sturdee Avenue, Rosebank, Johannesburg 2196, South Africa

Penguin Books Ltd., Registered Offices: 80 Strand, London WC2R 0RL, England

This is a work of fiction. Names, characters, places, and incidents either are the product of the author's
imagination or are used fictitiously, and any resemblance to actual persons, living or dead, business
establishments, events, or locales is entirely coincidental. The publisher does not have any control over
and does not assume any responsibility for author or third-party websites or their content.

ICED CHIFFON

A Berkley Prime Crime Book / published by arrangement with the author

PUBLISHING HISTORY
Berkley Prime Crime mass-market edition / October 2012

Copyright © 2012 by Dianne Kruetzkamp.
Cover illustration by Julia Green.
Cover design by Diana Kolsky.
Interior text design by Kristin del Rosario.

ISBN: 978-0-425-25160-7

BERKLEY® PRIME CRIME
Berkley Prime Crime Books are published by The Berkley Publishing Group,
a division of Penguin Group (USA) Inc.,
375 Hudson Street, New York, New York 10014.
BERKLEY® PRIME CRIME and the PRIME CRIME logo are trademarks of
Penguin Group (USA) Inc.

PRINTED IN THE UNITED STATES OF AMERICA

10 9 8 7 6 5 4 3 2 1

ALWAYS LEARNING   **PEARSON**

~Acknowledgments~

Thanks to Faith Black and Roberta Brown for believing in this series. A new author is always a gamble; I won't let you down.

Thanks to my kids—Emily, Gina, Ann, and David—for believing in me and to the gals at the real Fox, the Snooty Fox. Working with Donna Spigel, Michelle Webber, Emily Gildea, and Trish Goodman is always an adventure and a bit of a mystery. Is that Gucci bag real or a knockoff?

Chapter One

I POURED out the last of the pinot and lifted my glass as I gazed around the dining-room table. "Good-bye, Louis, Donna, Diane, and Ralph." A vintage Armani cocktail dress and Kate Spade pantsuit were draped over the table, sad and abandoned. "To friends. We've been through luncheons together, dinners, weddings, and funerals. You made me feel good when I was PMS-ing and bloated or put on five pounds from a Godiva bender. You've been there for me, from country-club dances to the Hobart bar mitzvah, and I appreciate it; I truly do."

I gulped down another toast as Auntie KiKi, my mother's only sibling, sashayed in through the back door from her house, next to mine. "Reagan, honey, don't you think it's a mite early in the day for tying one on, even by Savannah standards?"

Today KiKi's hair was frizzed out from the humidity,

and she had on her favorite red floral skirt. When she was born, the angels hovered over her crib chanting "cha-cha-cha" and turned her into a dance instructor. For Mamma, they'd chanted, "Follow the elephant," which led to her becoming a staunch Republican, which is how I ended up with the name Reagan.

"Who in the world are you talking to, anyway?" Auntie KiKi asked.

I cut my eyes to the grandfather clock in the living room, the only thing left in there since I'd sold off the Chippendale davenport, Oriental rug, two matching chairs, and the Tiffany lamp, which had been a wedding present seven years ago. "Don't you have fox-trot lessons at nine on Wednesdays?" I blurted, feeling a little stupid for talking to a bunch of designer clothes. "The future beaus and belles of Savannah need to be up to dancing speed for the spring cotillion, or their mammas and daddies will be deeply upset, and that is not good for business."

"I threatened to play my Sinatra collection if they didn't keep practicing while I ran over here to see what was happening. Your lights were blazing all night long. Why are your nice things laid out like a Sunday buffet?"

"Hollis Beaumont the third had the social connections in our marriage," I told KiKi. "Now that we're divorced, I'm back to being Reagan Summerside the first. I have no need for designer clothes, and I'm taking them to that consignment shop on Broughton."

I waved my hand over the Ralph Lauren slacks with the cute red trim. "I put this wardrobe together from resale shops and eBay. I did it for Hollis. He said *we* had to look successful so *he* could be successful. Being a real-estate broker in these times, the man needed every advantage." I sighed. "Now he's dancing in the high cotton, and I have overdue bills."

"And the moral of that particular story is never sign a prenup. Like Cher used to say, 'If you put everything you know about men on the head of a pin, there'd still be room for the Lord's Prayer.' " In college Auntie KiKi had been a roadie for Cher, and she'd never quite left the tour. "There's just no figuring men," she continued. "Especially the one you happened to pick."

"Seven years ago, I was young, knew everything, and believed love conquered all. Now I'm thirty-two, divorced, broke, living in a half-restored Victorian, and have learned that overdue bills conquer all." I gazed up at the crack across the dining-room ceiling, which seemed to be getting wider— or maybe that was one of the aftereffects of cheap wine at nine in the morning. Nope, there was white plaster dust on the Donna Karan navy silk blouse. "Least I got Cherry House."

"You're the one who's done all the work on this place since buying it five years ago. You had your eye on Cherry House since you were a kid, and the only reason Hollis bought it was that he knew it was a good investment and that you'd do all the rehab work. He finally agreed to give you the place so he wouldn't look like a total horse's patoot for taking up with that platinum-blonde cupcake fifteen years younger than he is. If he looks bad, no one will list a house from him ever again, and he knows it."

"The cupcake is twenty years younger." I hiccupped, feeling a little woozy from bad wine and a lot woozy from being kicked to the curb and having cracks in my ceiling. "Hollis turns forty-five next week."

The clock chimed, and KiKi swiped the glass from my hand. "Gotta go. The real problem is that Hollis has terminal MLCS—midlife crisis syndrome." She downed the last sip before heading for the door. "I'll take that white Christian Dior suit if you're sure you're getting rid of it," she called over her shoulder. "It's just the thing to get me going on a diet, and you should keep the pink chiffon, Reagan; it's a killer dress." KiKi two-stepped across the yard to her stately Queen Anne, which had been in the Vanderpool family since 1888.

KiKi had married the perfect Southern gentleman.

I'd married the perfect Southern philanderer.

I picked up the white Dior and tried to picture my fiftish auntie of ample proportions in a size eight, but my gaze drifted back to the pink chiffon. Maybe I should keep it. Maybe I'd go somewhere snazzy someday. I wasn't dead yet.

"Yoo-hoo, Reagan, are you in there?" came a voice from the back door. "I have that wallpaper you've been waiting on."

Restoring an old Victorian meant I ordered cornices, entablatures, and other ornate gingerbread pieces online because I couldn't find them anyplace in Savannah. They always cost the earth, and I'd gotten to be real good friends with my UPS delivery crew.

"Well, butter my butt and call me a biscuit, is this a real Louis Vuitton?" Chantilly Parker breezed into the hall and entered the dining room wearing her brown company uniform, her long curly hair tucked under the official UPS hat. She laid the double rolls on the table and picked up the azure canvas tote I'd gotten at a resale shop in Atlanta.

"You can have it. It suits you," I told her.

"Girlfriend, I don't deliver wallpaper for free, and you've no reason to hand over a nice purse for nothing either." Chantilly's eyes wandered. "Are you selling all this stuff?"

"See that pile of bills?" I nodded to the second step of the stairway, where I'd stacked everything marked "overdue." I'd sold the mahogany hall table, where I usually put the mail and parked my big yellow purse I thought of as Old Yeller, my best friend and constant companion. The historic walking tours I led around Savannah didn't make a dent in what it took to keep this old house going. Being a guide was a great outlet for my Southern-history degree, but now I had to either find a new source of income or sell the place.

"Been to the steps myself a time or two," Chantilly offered. "Then I got this job. I love UPS but don't much care for the uniform. When I get a tan in the summer, I look like a tree trunk. I fear someday a dog's going to pee on my leg." She pulled out a checkbook.

"Think UPS would hire me?" I asked. I could drive a truck and make deliveries.

"They're laying off, just like everyone else these days, but I'll keep an eye out for you," Chantilly promised as she passed me her check.

I waved it off. "That's too much."

She shook her head and dropped it on the table. "You should keep that pink chiffon, sugar. That is a to-die-for dress with your blonde hair—when you don't have three inches of roots showing—your green eyes, and skinny behind." Chantilly left through the back door with her new tote slung over her shoulder. It looked better on her than it ever did on me.

The front door opened, and Hollis and Janelle (the

cupcake) strolled in, holding hands. Some days it was just me, the rotting timbers, and the cracking plaster around here; other days, like today, it was Grand Central Station. Hollis and Cupcake didn't even knock but stood there in the hallway looking as if they owned the place. Well, technically, Hollis did own half the house until his no-count, low-rent, conniving, scum-sucking, sleazebag lawyer transferred the deed to me. I forced a smile. The divorce was final six months ago but the house wasn't officially mine yet. I had to play nice.

Hollis was fit, handsome as always, and looked thirty-five. Were those blond highlights in his hair? I raked back my curls to try and hide the roots. Janelle truly did look like a cupcake today in her yellow silk blouse, white slacks, and a hundred-dollar mani-pedi in creamy peach. I put my hands behind my back to hide nails ragged from stripping wallpaper. At least I didn't have to suck in my stomach, the upside of an empty fridge.

Hollis laughed at something Cupcake said, his bleached teeth a bit blinding. "We were showing a house over on Bolton and came to get your key to my Lexus while we were in the area," he informed me as he picked out his own car key from his ring and held it up.

This was Hollis rubbing his success in my face. He and Cupcake were always in the area. The real-estate office was three blocks away, and they worked there together. They did other things there together, too, like the horizontal hula on his desk the night I found them. Cupcake hooked her arm through Hollis's. "I just love the Lexus," she cooed.

I loved that car, too. In fact, I'd put down the initial payment on it, which probably had something to do with my forgetfulness in dropping off the key.

"I'll get my purse," I said, heading down the hall to the kitchen, where I'd left it on the counter.

"How can you find anything in that yellow-plastic saddlebag you carry around?" Hollis called after me, an I'm-better-than-you lilt in his voice. "And why are all your clothes in the dining room?"

"Selling them," I called back, my voice echoing through the mostly empty rooms. No need to conceal the truth; the whole of Savannah would soon find out that Reagan Summerside, once-upon-a-time Beaumont, was peddling her wardrobe for cash. The Savannah kudzu vine was alive and well and knew all.

"Oh my goodness," Cupcake squealed. "I do love this pink-chiffon dress Reagan has here. Don't you love it, Hollis, honey? It's perfect for the cocktail party this evening at the Telfair Museum. I wasn't going to buy anything new since I have to duck out early for that showing on East Hall."

I came back into the dining room, and Cupcake snatched the key from my fingers and dropped it in her Gucci bag that must have cost the earth. She batted her contact-blue eyes at Hollis. "Bet I get a nice commission when I sell that big, old house for you." She added a suggestive wink, then grabbing the dress, twirled around, the soft pink-chiffon skirt flowing around her legs. "And this dress is used, so it's cheap. I'll look divine."

My skin got all tingly the way it did when I saw a wolf spider the size of a paper plate on the wall. At times like that, I'd give anything to own a shotgun. I had the same urge now. I'd shred the dress before I let Cupcake have it!

My stomach growled, reminding me that I couldn't eat shredded chiffon. I quoted a price for the dress that was double what I paid for it on sale, knowing Cupcake would agree just for the satisfaction of having what was mine. She'd already gotten my husband and my car.

"Seems a bit steep for a used dress," Hollis groused as he forked over the money.

"I only wore it once." I shoved the bills into my jeans pocket and mentally paid the electric bill and ordered a Conquistador sandwich from Zunzi's. I handed Cupcake the dress and watched her drive off with my life.

I went out to the front porch, and since I'd sold the wrought-iron furniture, I sat on the top step that could do with a fresh coat of paint. I could do with a good pity cry except two women hustled up my brick sidewalk as if on a mission. One was dressed in leopard print; the other had on neon lipstick and a black miniskirt that looked more like a low, wide belt.

"We're here for the deals," leopard print said with a big toothy smile. "Chantilly sent out a tweet." She read from her iPhone. "Mighty fine clothes at real good prices at 310 East Gaston. Louis V for dirt cheap." She looked at my house numbers. "Yep, this is the place, all right. Got any more of those Louis Vuitton purses? I got a thing for Louis."

This was a lot more action than I expected. God bless, Chantilly.

"What about a Kate Spade?" I suggested, thinking that maybe, perhaps, with a little luck and good friends, selling my clothes could develop into something more. Neon lipstick shook her head, her lower lip in a confident pout. "Kate Spade is yuppie. It's what all those bony women at the country clubs carry. It goes with their expensive new boobs and bratty kids. I'm into real class, the good stuff."

I didn't have fake boobs or kids, and I had a Kate Spade purse. But who am I to argue with neon or animal print and ready cash? "What about an Armani jacket, size 8?"

"Now you're talking, sugar." And by the afternoon, I had a few more customers and enough sales to pay a fourth of the taxes on Cherry House. Maybe the City of Savannah would be happy with a fourth of the money since the house was only a fourth restored. Borderline starvation was rotting my brain.

"Who were those people in and out of your place all afternoon?" Auntie KiKi asked as I dragged myself into her kitchen, hunting for food. She'd just put in new marble countertops and painted the walls daffodil yellow. Eyelet curtains hung at the bay window, and there were matching cushions on the six chairs around the mahogany table, which was as old as the house.

I knew there were excellent homemade chocolate chip–oatmeal cookies in the golf-ball cookie jar and snagged six, stuffing one in my mouth. "Customers," I mumbled around a mouthful of crumbs. "Real honest-to-goodness customers, with cash in hand. Chantilly's a genius."

"Do you think it'll last?"

I glanced at the clock on KiKi's Viking stove. "It lasted a few hours, and that's a lot better than what I had going on this morning with all bills and no income."

The sudden sugar rush resuscitated my powers of observation, and I realized KiKi was not wearing one of her midcalf, flowing dance skirts but a teal scoop-neck dress and Grandma's pearls that had been in our family since before the unfortunate Northern aggression. "Wow, where are you off to tonight all spiffed up?"

KiKi bit her bottom lip, smudging her lipstick. She looked down at the *Savannah Times* open on the table, the front page sporting a picture of some Atlanta TV personality covering the Homes and Gardens Tour in Savannah. I remembered KiKi was going to the opening party at the Telfair Museum, just like Hollis and Cupcake, and I wasn't. I felt like the kid in *Home Alone*, when everyone went off to have fun, and he got left behind.

"You look great, you really do. Love that dress. Terrific color—it shows off your eyes and hair." And I meant every word.

Auntie KiKi put her arm around me, giving a little squeeze. "It's just a stupid affair, Reagan, honey," she said in a light voice, the kind meant to console and make something really neat seem trivial because you weren't included. Auntie KiKi was a good auntie. "We're only going because it benefits the museum, and Putter wants to meet Raimondo Baldassare, that landscape architect."

"You're going to have Raimondo redo your gardens? You already have azaleas the size of a bus." Everyone wanted a garden by Raimondo. Those lucky enough to get him won the prizes on the Homes and Gardens Tour. The man was also deliciously gorgeous. Just having that yummy Italian in your petunias was worth the price of a garden. "I bet he's booked for a year."

"I promised Putter a putting green in the backyard for his birthday."

Everyone in Savannah called my uncle Putter. It was a fitting nickname for a certifiable golf nut who carried a putter wherever he went, including church, the Piggly Wiggly, his rounds at the hospital, and no doubt the cocktail party this evening. KiKi said it was in case a golf ball suddenly dropped to earth and he had to save the city by sinking an eagle.

Savannah was all about the Georgia Bulldogs, fried everything, extra-dry martinis, and golf. The order of importance depended on who you were and how much you'd had to drink at the time.

Feeling sorry for myself, I grabbed KiKi's hand. "Promise me you'll say you had a horrible time tonight, the tomato sandwiches were soggy, and Cupcake got drunk and passed flat out on the dance floor."

"You bet, sweet pea." Auntie KiKi kissed my forehead like she did when I was six and had the chickenpox. She pulled a Tupperware bowl of leftover meat loaf from the fridge and handed it over. "Like Cher says, 'Get yourself a deep breath and don't take any of this too seriously now, you hear.'" She paused. "I could lend you some money just for a little while till you get back on your feet."

"Thanks, but I'm still standing." *Sort of.* I tucked the meat loaf under my arm and trudged across the front yard to my house. It was easy to see where KiKi's lawn ended and mine began. She had Kentucky bluegrass, and I had Savannah dandelions.

THE NEXT MORNING I WOKE UP WITH MY HEAD BY the empty meat-loaf container. Did I really eat in bed? Then I remembered that my dining-room table was covered with clothes, and I'd sold the little green and yellow bistro table in the kitchen to AnnieFritz and Elsie Abbott, who lived on the other side of Cherry House in a small Greek Revival left to them by their cousin Willie. Three years ago, Cousin Willie dropped dead over at the Pirates' House after too many ham and redeye-gravy dinners and not enough Lipitor.

AnnieFritz and Elsie were retired schoolteachers who hired themselves out on the Q.T. as professional mourners. The only social event more important in Savannah than a big, fancy wedding was a big, fancy funeral. Every undertaker in town knew that no one got folks weeping and wailing like the Abbott sisters.

"I'm coming, I'm coming," I yelled, realizing it was the doorbell that had jarred me awake. I stumbled my way down the stairs as the chime bonged again. Maybe Chantilly sent out more tweets. I opened the front door to Raylene Carter, who bustled past me in a gorgeous ivory suit.

"What do you want for that bronze fountain you have in your backyard?" She pointed out the rear window. "Last night at the museum, I heard you were in a pinch and needing money. You bought that fountain a few years back from Raimondo Baldassare, and I need it now at my place."

Raylene's mouth pinched into a tight pout. "You look a fright, Reagan. Your mamma would be sorely upset if she saw you in this condition. She is a judge, after all. You should keep up appearances for her sake"—Raylene glanced around at the emptiness—"no matter how dire your circumstances happen to be. Now, I need the fountain right quick before they review my gardens for the tour at noon."

Looking important, she fluffed her hair. "I intend to win again this year, and I want something new and exciting so people won't go spreading those awful rumors that I don't deserve to win Best of Show like I always do." She took out her checkbook.

Up until the checkbook, I was contemplating how to toss Raylene out of my house on her Chanel-clad butt. "Seven hundred dollars." And I never blinked an eye.

Raylene opened and closed her mouth, landed-fish style, then finally managed, "Why that's just plumb ridiculous." And it was, but it was equally ridiculous that her gardens won every year on the tour. Not that her place wasn't exquisite, but so were others.

"You're taking advantage," Raylene muttered while scribbling a check. "I'm not hauling that thing in my Escalade. For this price, I expect delivery to my house, and I want it right quick. And heavenly days, fix yourself up before you come around. What will people think if they see you like this? You look like a ragpicker." She stopped at the door. "Is it any wonder Hollis went looking elsewhere?" She left quickly, and this time I was the one doing the landed-fish expression.

How could she say those things to me? So I'd hit a rough patch. Everyone hits a rough patch from time to time. Then I caught a glimpse of myself in the hall mirror, with hair sticking out in all directions and meat-loaf juice on my T-shirt. I bit back a scream.

I did the ten-minute shower, then yanked on my white skirt from Target and the blue blouse KiKi gave me for my birthday, all the while thinking of how to get the fountain to Raylene. I had sold my car just last month to cover the cost of a leaky roof, and KiKi took her mother-in-law to breakfast every week like a good daughter-in-law should. If I asked my mother to borrow her Caddy, that would open up the whole *Why are you selling your things?* discussion.

Gloria Summerside was widowed when I was two. She

was sharp, smart, and savvy and told me, "For the love of God do not marry Hollis Beaumont." She also told me not to buy the Lexus with only his name on it no matter what he said about deducting it from business expenses for tax purposes. I can still see the expression on her face when I told her I'd signed the prenup. She told me I'd clearly lost my mind, and as I look back on the whole marrying-Hollis ordeal, I realize she was absolutely right.

I was a pushover for Hollis, the older, handsome man who was really, really good in bed. Mamma was known in judicial circles as Guillotine Gloria, and no one pushed her around.

I'd paid a lot of money for that stupid Lexus, and I was going to use it! I'd put the fountain in the trunk, tie down the door, and motor my way over to Raylene's. Hollis Beaumont the third would just have to live with it, no matter how divorced we were. The lying, cheating, fornicating bastard with bleached hair owed me that much.

I grabbed my handbag and charged out the front door.

Chapter Two

"Hᴵ, IdaMae," I said as I entered Hollis's real-estate office on East Wayne. The white clapboard bungalow sported green shutters, neat gables, a brick sidewalk, and window boxes filled with wilted pansies. IdaMae had never married, and she'd been with Hollis since the day he opened the agency, twenty years ago. She was more family than secretary, and I swear the woman could make anything grow in those window boxes. This year Cupcake commandeered the job.

"Well, bless my soul. Reagan, is it really you?" IdaMae's brown eyes widened, and she put her hand to her bosom in pure delight. "How are you, honey? And how is your mamma getting on these days? I trust she's doing right well."

IdaMae rose from behind her neat desk, her yellow-and-blue cotton-print dress flowing around her like an attractive tent, topped with a white sweater. If Hollis set the AC any lower in the place, it would snow. She hugged me and kissed the air behind my left ear. "I haven't seen you in ages and ages."

It had been about a month, but between friends in Savannah, that was an age. "We need to do lunch and catch up. Next week?" IdaMae beamed her approval, then sobered when I said, "Is Hollis busy? I need to borrow the Lexus, just for a half hour or so. I want to haul something. It's important, or I wouldn't be asking. Is he in a good mood?"

IdaMae drew in a quick breath, making the flowers across her upper half sway back and forth as if caught in a spring breeze. "Oh my goodness, you know how he is about that car of his. You'd think the man gave birth to it the way he acts. Janelle drove it all day yesterday though. That girl's got him eating out of her palm—I swear she does. Anything she wants, she gets . . . usually."

IdaMae leaned close enough that I could smell Orange Blossom, the fragrance of choice of a true Southern belle, even if the belle was nearly fifty and her family had fallen on hard times and been forced to surrender their membership to the Oglethorpe Club. "Word has it Hollis and Janelle had a spat at that cocktail party last night. She made a scene right there in front of everyone and then drove off in her car, leaving Hollis standing by himself in the parking lot and mad as a hornet. I'm not one for sorting out dirty laundry in public, mind you, but I sure wish I could have seen that with my own two eyes."

"And you should have been there, IdaMae." Hollis and I had taken her to the Homes and Gardens Telfair cocktail party for years, just as we had her over for Christmas dinner and celebrated her birthday at the Pink House, which just happened to be her favorite restaurant. Then Cupcake came into the picture, and life as we knew it ceased to exist.

"When I asked where Janelle was this morning, Hollis said he hoped to never lay eyes on the woman again. Then he stormed into his office and slammed the door hard enough to rattle the windows; can you imagine? I made arrangements to have the Lexus detailed this afternoon as a little surprise and cheer him up a bit. Right now, he's meeting with Reverend Franklin." IdaMae nodded to the front conference room. "I think the reverend's soliciting donations for his family-values campaign. He dropped off some papers yesterday. He's such a fine man. He was good to my mamma when she was sick over at the nursing home. Came to see her every week."

"Family values? Hollis?" I rolled my eyes so far back in my head that I saw where my ears connected.

"Franklin's a friend of the Beaumonts, and you know that his wife is Hollis's second cousin. Family counts for plenty, and nowadays money's money. I don't think the reverend and Janelle much like each other, though. When he called to see if Hollis was going to be in this morning, he asked if Janelle would be on the premises. I told him she never comes in before eleven."

A sly smile made its way across IdaMae's face. "You know, I'll just go see if the Lexus key is in Hollis's jacket. You could use the car and get it back here right quick. It's parked out back, and he wouldn't even know it was gone now, would he? We'll make this work for you, honey. That's what friends are for." She went after the key.

I didn't need Hollis upset that I was using his car as a delivery van. I wanted to keep him in Zen mode till he signed over Cherry House. Smiling, IdaMae came back and dropped the key in my hand. "Be careful now, you hear?"

AS I DROVE DOWN HABERSHAM THE SMELL OF FINE leather and the feel of an electronically cooled seat chilling my derriere made me realize just how much I'd missed this car. Right now I missed any car. I pulled up next to the gnarled cherry tree in full bloom that gave the house its name. The aroma was incredible, the tree a bouquet of pink and white, and half the reason I persuaded Hollis to buy the house years ago.

The other half was that I'd loved this house since I was a kid, riding my bike by it when visiting Auntie KiKi. I watched it deteriorate bit by bit, and I knew I could save it. The fact that I'd never hammered or screwed or sawed a thing in my life didn't deter my enthusiasm. It should have.

Auntie KiKi scurried out the front door waving her hands in the air. "Where in the world have you been?" she panted, leaning in through the open car window, her cheeks flushed. "When I got home from breakfast, there were three people waiting on your porch ready to shop, of all things! They said they got one of those tweets." She *tsk*ed, the universal sound of exasperated Southern women everywhere. "Whatever happened to the days when you got a nice phone call from a friend telling you what was what?" she lamented. "You have customers in your dining room, and I have a waltz lesson with Bernard in ten minutes." She heaved a weary sigh.

Bernard Thayer was seventy, had no rhythm and less coordination, had been Mr. Weather on Savannah TV for thirty years, and was determined to wind up on *Dancing with the Stars*. KiKi thrust a wad of bills at me. "I went and got stuff from my own closet to sell to spruce up your inventory. My black-and-white coat that's gotten too small somehow went for thirty bucks." She blinked. "What in the world are you doing with the Lexus?"

"I sold that fountain in the backyard to Raylene Carter for a small fortune. Now I have to deliver it as well as get the car back before Hollis knows I took it. I sort of didn't tell him."

"Oh, honey, grand theft auto—your mamma will be so proud."

I ignored the possibility and popped the trunk. "Take a look-see at how much room we have. Hollis stores his real-estate junk in there."

"We?"

I grabbed Old Yeller and rummaged for keys to the shed as I headed for the backyard. "I've got a cart, and we can haul the fountain and—"

"Sweet Jesus in heaven! Uh, Reagan, honey," KiKi called, her finger crooked at me in a come-here gesture. "We have junk, a great big pile of it."

"We'll dump it on the lawn," I said hurrying back to the car to help unload. "If I have to hire movers, I won't make any money at all, and we're running short on time and . . . Holy mother of God!" My gaze landed on Cupcake, face up, eyes wide open, and dead as Lincoln right there in Hollis's trunk.

KiKi and I stared, neither of us breathing. KiKi finally whispered, "She doesn't look nearly as good in the pink chiffon as you do."

"Maybe because she has blood in her hair and is rolled up in plastic like a hot dog in a bun." I made the sign of the cross for disrespecting the dead.

"There is that." KiKi sounded faint and slowly slumped to the curb. We sat together holding hands, trunk still wide open like a casket at a viewing. "You wouldn't happen to have a martini in that purse of yours, would you?"

A woman in a poison-green tank top, white jeans, and stilettos hustled out of my house, her tiny heels clacking on the brick walkway. "Is that more clothes in the trunk? I bet it is," she giggled. "Let me at it."

"Don't look in there," I said in a rush, putting up my hand to stop her.

She sidestepped around. "No way! I get first dibs and . . . Lord have mercy!"

Savannah tends to get real religious during times of great anxiety. Stiletto Girl slapped her hand over her mouth, her eyes the size of duck eggs. She ran back inside as fast as her teetering heels would allow. There were a few screams from my dining room and sirens approaching.

"How could Cupcake be dead?" I wondered aloud, trying to make sense of all this. "A few times I've wished her demise, but this is for real. What is she doing in Hollis's trunk?"

"Not much, honey," KiKi said in a far-off voice. "Not much at all."

Two cruisers slid to a stop, and my dandelion front yard was overrun with blue uniforms, a lot of nosy neighbors, and gaping customers. A woman about five feet tall and just as wide, dressed in polyester navy pants and a white wash-and-wear blouse, introduced herself as the lead detective and told me and KiKi to move, as the police needed access to the car.

Still holding on to each other and averting our eyes from the Lexus, we staggered our way to the porch. The detective asked if I knew the woman in the trunk. When I said her name was Cupcake, the detective gave me an exasperated look and took a bottle of water from her purse, which was even larger than mine.

She handed me the water, then walked over to AnnieFritz and Elsie Abbott, who were standing by the cherry tree. They must have had better answers because they didn't get nasty looks or water, and the detective was scribbling like mad in her little brown book. My guess was the sisters called the cops. Nothing happened in Savannah that they didn't know about in under ten minutes flat.

Auntie KiKi sipped the water. "Hollis and Cupcake had a humdinger of a fight at the museum last night."

I glanced at the car's license plate, with "HB3" on it, for Hollis Beaumont the third. "I heard. You don't really think that Hollis would actually—"

"Of course not," KiKi added in a rush. "I was just thinking out loud is all." She took another swallow of water. "I mean, the man's full of himself and an ornery jackass, but he's not a you-know-what." She couldn't say the *m*-word any more than I could. "You think they'll arrest Hollis?"

My brain hadn't jumped that far ahead. My thoughts were limping around in circles, wondering how this day got so bad so fast. "Maybe I should tell Hollis what's going on. It's the least I can do after borrowing his car and having all this happen. Think the police will mind if I leave?"

KiKi slumped against the front of the house, and I eased

her down to the porch floor. She looked up at me, her eyes sort of rolling around in their sockets. "You're driving a car with a dead person in it. If the cops want you, honey, they'll find you."

"Are you okay?"

"I think I'll cancel the waltz lesson."

KiKi downed more water, and I backed off the porch, then ran for the real-estate office. Pumping my arms, I tried to look like a jogger and not someone in a state of pure panic, though I suspected the white skirt and flip-flops sort of blew my cover. I felt as if everything was happening in slow motion, and I couldn't get enough air into my lungs.

I stumbled through the office door of the real-estate office, and IdaMae glanced up from her computer. "Oh dear me, you look plumb awful. Did something happen to the car?"

I crumpled into a chair and put my head between my legs so I wouldn't pass out. Why couldn't I be more of a kick-butt kind of woman, like Lara Croft or Xena or even Kim Kardashian? Kim wouldn't have to put her head between her legs so she wouldn't pass out. "Hollis!" My shout was more of a squeal.

"Where's the Lexus?" IdaMae asked, a bit frantic.

"It's at my place." I couldn't do anything except remember to breathe and stare at the green carpet with little white flecks in it. Good thing I hadn't had breakfast or there would be more on the carpet than flecks.

"What's going on?" Hollis's footsteps came my way. I could see the tips of his Top-Siders out of the corner of my eye.

I rolled my head to look at him. "It's about your car. Janelle's in it."

He held out his hands in a so-what fashion and gave me a so-what look to go with it. If Hollis was the killer, he wouldn't be standing there all ticked off that I interrupted his meeting; he'd be freaking out and heading for the border when he heard I had the Lexus. "She's dead, Hollis."

"She doesn't think much of you either, Reagan."

The front opened, and two police officers and Detective Something-or-Other entered. "I'm Detective Aldeen Ross," she said, and flashed her badge.

"Sweet Jesus," Hollis whispered in a strangled voice, his face white. He plopped down in IdaMae's vacated chair. "Janelle really is . . . dead?"

Reverend Franklin came to the doorway. "Janelle? Dear God. What happened?" He put his arms around a sobbing IdaMae, who looked worse than any of us.

"There's more," I added in a rush. "I borrowed the Lexus and found Janelle's body in the trunk."

Detective Ross gave me a nasty look for giving Hollis a heads-up. "We need to talk to both of you at the police station," she said.

"Me?" My head snapped around so fast I pulled a muscle in my neck. "Why me?"

IdaMae gasped between sobs. "Now just a minute here. These two very fine people would never take part in a murder, of all things. I can vouch for them. They happen to be dear friends. Family."

IdaMae's vouching apparently didn't carry much weight because Ross pointed a stiff finger toward the door. Rubbing my neck, I followed Hollis to the cruiser, chain-gang style. We sat side by side in silence, Hollis sweating like a mule in the field, his eyes straight ahead. That he wasn't pitching a holy fit I'd taken the Lexus proved just how scared he truly was.

At the Bull Street Police Station, Hollis got ushered across the hall, and I wound up in a putrid blue room with rusted bars on the windows and metal chairs and a sticky table. I didn't want to know what the sticky was. Another detective, with a shaved head and full mustache, asked me questions, and after two hours, he said I could go.

I know zip about police procedure except for all the misinformation on TV shows, but I didn't think I was much of a suspect. Putting the victim on full display in front of my own house with the trunk wide open for all the world to see didn't smack of master criminal. The bald cop knew Raylene, so he believed the fountain story. We both agreed it would be a crying shame if the old battle-ax won Best of Show again this year.

By the time I left the station, I had a brain-melting headache. No food, finding a dead body, and being out seven hundred desperately needed dollars might have had something to do with it. That Hollis's devil-incarnate lawyer, Walker Boone, was waiting on the sidewalk didn't make me feel one lick better.

Boone was tall, thirty-three, with black hair and dangerous black eyes. Word had it he was once a member of the Seventeenth Street gang over on the West Side and had the "17" tattooed on his arm to prove it. Hollis got Boone a sweet deal on a Federal-style historic home right on Madison Square, and Boone got Hollis a sweet deal in our divorce. I hoped they both rotted in hell for all eternity. Today Boone wore faded jeans and a blue sport shirt, and women were staring and salivating.

"What?" I asked as he approached.

"Why did you take the Lexus?"

"I needed to move a fountain that I recently sold because my fine Southern ex-husband and his fine attorney left me penniless."

"You were the one dumb enough to sign a prenup," Boone said in a flat lawyerly voice while writing something on a legal pad. If I strangled him dead in front of the police station, I probably wouldn't get away with it, but it was darn tempting all the same. Hollis came out of the station and walked over to us, looking scared spitless.

"So they didn't book you?" I asked. Hollis would not fare well in jail. He was rich, a mamma's boy, and liked expensive things. I had a bad feeling he'd be the expensive thing everyone wanted in jail.

"They'll book him soon enough." Boone wrote something else on his pad.

"Aren't you a little ray of sunshine today," I couldn't help but say.

Boone ignored me. He had done a lot of that during the divorce proceedings as well. "Hollis is the main suspect, and there's solid evidence stacked against him. The police are getting more to make sure they can hold him."

Hollis shoved his hands deep in his pockets. "I didn't kill Janelle. I might have felt like it, but—"

"Not here," Boone interrupted with enough steel in his voice to make the hair on my arms stand straight up. I'd never heard the steel before, even during all the divorce arguing. I suddenly believed the Seventeenth Street gang rumor.

"Go home," Boone ordered Hollis. "Take a shower, and be at my office in an hour, and don't talk to anyone."

Boone left in a rush, and I said to Hollis, "I know you didn't do this. Boone will get you off." Hollis's shoulders slumped, and I patted him on the back in an it'll-be-okay kind of way.

"Look," he said, making my stomach clench into a hard knot. Nothing good ever started with *look*. "I know I said I'd give you Cherry House, but I can't do that now. I'll have to sell it to pay Boone. This is going to be expensive, Reagan, really expensive."

I yanked my hand away. "You . . . You bought Janelle an engagement ring—big, huge, and sparkly. Sell it." When I married Hollis, I got a ruby heirloom that I gave back to his mother after the divorce because she wanted to keep it in the family. I'm sure if I looked in the mirror I had "stupid" written on my forehead somewhere.

"Janelle had a pricey manicure, Hollis. She had a Gucci handbag, of all things. Do you have any idea how much they cost? You have enough money to buy my dress for her, and you live in a ritzy town house. Sell the place. Get your money that way."

"The town house is mortgaged to the hilt, and the rest is all on credit. You know what the real-estate market's been like. I'm hanging on by a thread here till things turn around."

"Your parents? What about hitting them up for a loan?" Desperation raised my voice a few octaves.

"They lost a ton in the market, and since Dad's heart attack, he hasn't been working—"

"You promised, Hollis." My voice was shrill and uncontrolled now. Heads turned in my direction.

"Hey, I didn't plan on getting charged for a murder I didn't commit. We got Cherry House for next to nothing because the Victorian District was just taking off when we bought in, and the house was a total disaster. There's nice equity there, Reagan."

"My hard-work equity, and I used my inheritance from Grandma Harris as part of the down payment." I punched his arm and hoped it hurt. "You got the Lexus, the business, the Cupcake. I won't sell. I refuse. I won't sign anything."

Hollis's eyes cleared, and he tipped his chin in that infuriating know-it-all Beaumont way. "You'll sell. You're the good girl; you're not Janelle."

His voice hardened when he said Janelle's name. Something sparked in his eyes, and it wasn't sadness. For sure it hadn't been there yesterday when I saw the two of them in my hallway doing the lovebird routine. "If you turn your back on me, you'll be the vindictive witch, and that's not you at all."

"I'm learning real fast."

"You're your mother's daughter, Reagan. She does things by the book, and the apple doesn't fall far from the tree. Letting me go to jail for something I didn't do isn't right, and you know it. Cherry House is all that's between me and jail," he ground out.

"But . . . But . . ."

But Hollis walked off because he didn't give a rat's ass what I had to say. The cold, hard truth was that he could go to prison for his whole life . . . or worse, and in the great state of Georgia there was indeed worse.

Cold sweat slithered down my back at the thought.

Hollis wanted to sell the house I'd renovated to save his miserable, worthless, arrogant hide. He and Walker Boone were back in my life, and the two of them were screwing me all over again.

Chapter Three

April in Savannah is my favorite time of year. The twenty-three parklike squares with humongous pink, purple, and white azalea bushes and giant magnolias everywhere turn the city into one big Impressionist painting. Palmetto bugs are still at a minimum, temperatures linger below steam-bath levels, and the live oaks draped in Spanish moss haven't wilted from the blasts of summer sun.

Spring in Savannah is as close to paradise as one gets on this here earth, but not this year. Cupcake was dead, and she was messing up my life even from the grave.

"How are things at the police station these days?" Auntie KiKi asked as I plodded up to the front porch of my house after taking the bus home. KiKi sat alone on the top porch step. No cops, no cruisers, no neighbors; Lord be praised for that. The downside was that any chance of customers coming to shop vanished, too. Not that it mattered much with Hollis threatening to reclaim my house. "The gossips are having a field day," KiKi went on. "They're mighty appreciative. It's been a quiet couple of weeks out there."

"Always glad to do my part." With a messy divorce and now Cupcake in the trunk, I'd done more than my part. KiKi held up two martini glasses, a silver shaker at her side. She sipped from one glass and handed another, with three olives skewered on a toothpick, to me. It was a three-olive kind of day. I took a sip, letting the cool liquid slide down my throat. "The police aren't thrilled about the body in Hollis's car, so he's going to sell Cherry House right out from under me to pay Boone to get him off."

"The bastard." KiKi hiccupped. "Like Cher says, 'Don't take your toys inside just because it's raining.'"

"I don't get it." I sat and took another sip of martini. On an empty stomach, this would do me in, and right now that was a good thing. Numb was welcome. "I have no idea what it means."

KiKi hiccupped. "You won't care either once you finish off that drink." She bit the olives from her toothpick one by one and munched.

"Where's the Lexus and the . . . passenger?" I asked.

"Coroner came out himself and took care of things," KiKi said around a mouthful, a bit of olive juice dribbling down her chin. Auntie KiKi was feeling no pain; Auntie KiKi wasn't feeling much of anything. "He had a body bag and one of those gurneys."

Auntie got a little pale at the body-bag reference. She refilled her glass and downed half of it. A little alcohol-induced color returned to her cheeks. "James Hewlett plays golf with Putter. James is the coroner here in Savannah; did you know that? He usually sends some underling to mop up . . . That's what he called it, mop up. He came himself today."

She knocked back the rest of the drink and licked her lips to catch every drop. "He recognized the address and made me the martinis before he left." She held up the shaker, Savannah's answer to Prozac. "They towed the Lexus off on one of those flatbed trucks for processing. I have no idea what processing is, and I don't want to ever find out. James said Cupcake appeared to have suffered blunt-force trauma to the head, though he couldn't be sure because of the plastic wrap. I'm never watching another *CSI* TV show as long as I live, and I'm giving up plastic wrap."

"Walker Boone says they'll charge Hollis for sure; it's just a matter of time." I took a swallow of booze, and East Gaston started to spin. "What do you think Hollis and Cupcake fought over last night? Hollis didn't seem all that broken up that Cupcake was . . . gone. He wasn't dancing in the streets, but neither was he tearing up, sniffing, or blowing his nose like when his uncle Cletus died."

"Uncle Cletus left him his gun collection and his antique slat-top secretary. Cupcake left him a boatload of trouble," KiKi slurred. "It's possible he finally found out she had something going on with Urston Russell."

I fought the beginning buzz in my brain and put down the mostly unfinished glass. "Urston? The guy who judges the Homes and Gardens Tour? Cupcake doesn't know a petunia from a pansy. You should see the window boxes at the real-estate office. Why would Cupcake have anything to do with Urston Russell?"

KiKi gave a dopey smile, her eyes unfocused. "Cupcake volunteered to head up promotions for the tour this year.

Guess she and Urston got involved. Last night I saw them together, and he was giving her money."

KiKi brought the glass to her lips, and I snatched it from her fingers. "How much money?"

"They didn't invite me to count it." Glaring, KiKi grabbed back the glass. "I was coming out of the little girls' room when I felt a draft all the way up my backside. My dress was stuck in my girdle. Don't you hate when that happens? I ducked into a back hallway to fix myself, and lo and behold, there was Urston handing off a wad of bills to Cupcake. At first I thought he was paying for you-know-what, but he didn't look like a man getting you-know-what 'cause he was whispering angry stuff and looked kind of pissed. Not 'xactly pillow talk."

"The man's sixty-three with a paunch. He wears a red bow tie and passes wind in public. Good grief." I waved my hand in front of my nose at the memory. "Why didn't you tell me this before?"

KiKi plunked the martini glass down on the porch with a solid thud, her eyes little slits, her lips tight together. "If you recall, it's been a whopper of a morning—moving a fountain, finding a dead body—and this alcohol is for medicinal reasons. I forgot about Urston till you mentioned the argument with Hollis. Putter said I should butt out. He also said Urston's got a love affair with the ponies."

"Cupcake was a lot of things, but I doubt she was a bookie." A ray of hope warmed me all over. "But I do believe she was up to something, and so was Urston. Oh, this is good, really good. I should tell Boone. It gives him another suspect to focus on and takes the heat off Hollis."

I stood, then sat right back down, suddenly feeling

depressed. "Except the minute I walk into Boone's office the clock starts ticking, and I start paying. Bet he bills by the hour, and I have five minutes of information to hand over. The rat-bastard should be paying me if I'm giving him clues."

"I don't think that's how the rat-bastard works." KiKi's eyes closed, and she leaned back against the porch railing. She kicked off her left dance shoe, then the right one, and stretched out her legs. She tipped her face to the sun. "Don't you love this time of year?" If she were a cat she'd have purred. Bless the healing powers of a good martini.

"Maybe I should find out what Urston and Cupcake were up to. The more information I get, the less time Boone has to spend on the case, and the lower my bill. If I find out who really killed Cupcake before Hollis goes to trial, I can save a bundle. It's court time that costs, and with your connections to the local gossips and all the dirt the Abbott sisters pick up at the wakes, I bet I can find out a bunch of stuff, maybe even who the killer is, and I work for free and—"

KiKi bolted straight up as if stuck by lightning. She grabbed my shoulders and held tight, looking me dead in the eyes. "Are you out of your ever-loving mind?" She shook me, and I bit my tongue. "Someone's murdering people and stuffing them in trunks. Then there's the problem of you snooping around in a city where firepower outnumbers citizens, and the citizens don't care much for snooping. We have no idea why Cupcake wound up where she did. Whoever happens to be responsible has done the deed once, so a second time around is a piece of cake. Just take the Urston information to Boone, okay?"

KiKi flopped back against the railing. "Lordy, that plumb wore me out. I need a nap."

"Do you realize that after five years of trial and error and reading every blessed how-to book in the freaking library, I now know how to rewire a house; install faucets, sinks, and bathtubs; and tear off ten layers of wallpaper in one fell swoop?" I pointed to the flaking white paint on the front door, which still had its original glass and brass hardware. "I love that front door. I love this house. I'm selling all sorts of my stuff and everyone else's to keep it. What if you had to give up Rose Gate, huh? How would you feel about that?" I nodded to her perfect house, which was painted blue and green and had a corbelled chimney, an oversized parlor that served as a dance studio, and an ironwork fence with a rose-patterned gate.

Auntie KiKi sobered and made the sign of the cross to cancel the blasphemy of losing Rose Gate. "What if you wind up on a slab at the morgue with coroner Hewlett peering over your naked dead body?"

"No one expects me to be looking for Cupcake's murderer. Everyone thinks I'm tickled to my toes that Cupcake is dead and gone. There's no love lost between Hollis and me, so why would I want to see him go free? I'll fly under the radar."

"You never fly under the radar. You're a king-size blip on everyone's screen." Auntie KiKi counted off on her fingers. "Your mother's a judge, you married the town playboy, who everyone knew was a playboy but you, and you drive cars with dead people in them. Let Boone take care of this. He has connections. No one messes with that man. He has the tattoo to prove it."

"Have you ever seen it?"

"Well"—Auntie KiKi's lips formed a sly smile—"Angie

Gilbert's a nurse over at Doc Wilson's, and she gave Boone a flu shot once. There it was, that '17' on his shoulder, big as you please. She nearly peed her pants. He is one fine-looking boy."

"He's Darth Vader minus the voice and cape." I stood and pulled Auntie KiKi to her feet. I held on to her till she steadied. "Go home, eat something."

"And what are you going to do? Get yourself into trouble, no doubt."

"I thought I'd pay IdaMae a visit. She was mighty upset this morning when Hollis and I got hauled off to the police station. The poor woman was beside herself. She deserves better. I'm going to get her a sandwich and cheer her up. Food cheers everyone up."

"And then you're going to ransack Cupcake's desk."

"I was thinking more like her computer. Come distract IdaMae for me."

KiKi held up her hands as if warding off evil spirits. "I'm not being party to this. Your mamma would skin me alive."

"I'll dance with Bernard, be his partner for a whole month, and you won't have to. Think of your poor abused feet." The reason I could do this is that the summer I turned thirteen I was antsy, chubby, and pimply, and KiKi taught me to dance. You name it, I learned it—everything from the fox-trot and salsa to the electric slide and hip-hop. By the time I went back to school in September, I'd lost fifteen pounds, found the magic of Clearasil, and was a hit at school parties. Dancing isn't just for the stars.

"Two months." KiKi picked up her shoes instead of putting them on. Guess she knew from experience that heels, martinis, and steps weren't a great mix. "We'll get

Conquistadors from Zunzi's. What do you think is in that special sauce? I want to take a bath in that sauce."

Auntie KiKi gave me a long, hard look. "And if you find out anything more about Cupcake, even one little thing, you'll take it, along with what we know about Urston, straight to Boone as fast as you can. People will put two and two together soon enough and know you're snooping. That includes the killer."

"I'll drive."

"You gotta promise me, okay?"

TWENTY MINUTES LATER, AUNTIE KIKI, IDAMAE, and I sat around the conference table at the real-estate office, wolfing down sandwiches and garlic bread. Extra stress justifies extra carbs.

"I can't believe Janelle's gone," IdaMae said over slices of chicken sticking out between chunks of French bread with sauce dripping off the end. Is there anything better than dripping sauce?

I took a bite of my sandwich and for a moment thought I saw Jesus. "What do you think happened?" I asked around a mouthful.

IdaMae's eyes were blank, nothing registering. Her usually neat bob looked as if it had been combed with a weed-whacker. "What do you mean?"

I tried to make it sound more like three women chatting over good food and less like an interrogation by Detective Ross. "Why would someone want Janelle . . . dead? I mean, we know Hollis isn't responsible, so who is? Maybe we can help Hollis stay out of jail."

"Do you think we can do that? When the police arrived this morning, I thought for sure they'd arrest Hollis." Ida-Mae's eyes got all watery, her shoulders slumped. "I went to the library last night when I should have come back here to catch up on some filing. I could have been Hollis's alibi." She put her sandwich down, then buried her face in her hands. I put my arm around her and then gave her back the sandwich. She started eating again, methodically biting and chewing as if on autopilot, a terrible waste of a Conquistador; every bite should be savored.

Questioning IdaMae was getting me nowhere. I needed a look at Cupcake's laptop, which sat closed up like a clam on top of her desk. In no time, the police or Boone would nab it, and my chance to check it for information would be gone.

"Why don't you go home," I said to IdaMae after we'd polished off the last of the bread. "It's been a long day."

"I have things to take care of. Hollis called me from the lawyer's office and said he'd stop by in a bit. I need to be here for him. It's the least I can do."

I could level with IdaMae about snooping around for Hollis's sake, but then word would get out fast, and everyone would have their guard up. IdaMae may be a Southern belle, but she was also a Southern blabbermouth. "You need fresh air. You'll feel better. I'll watch the office." I gave KiKi a pleading look that said *Do something*.

She took IdaMae's arm and they stood. "Just a turn around the block, honey, I insist. It's for your own good." Not giving her any choice, Auntie KiKi escorted IdaMae out the front door, just like she escorted reluctant teenage boys around the dance floor. They didn't have a choice either.

I counted to twenty to make sure the duo was really gone,

then took my purse to Cupcake's desk and fished out a pen and a receipt from McDonald's so I could write notes on the back. I flipped open the laptop. Nothing but files on homes sold, homes for sale, loan applications, and a lot of other real-estate stuff.

I faced two months of Bernard and smashed toes for this? The computer wasn't even password protected. I clicked on the file marked "Homes and Gardens Tour" and pulled up schedules for radio and TV spots, interviews with home owners, and local-celebrity interviews like Raimondo Baldassare and Urston Russell. I scribbled down the schedule, because it had Urston's name, and shut the computer.

I pulled open the long, thin drawer across the front of Cupcake's desk to find pens, business cards, promotional magnets advertising Janelle Claiborne, and a bottle of Essie's Adore-a-Ball Pink nail polish. Cupcake had her faults, but she had excellent taste in polish. The side drawer held expensive hand lotion from that chichi boutique on Broughton Street. There were more real-estate brochures and a flyer for a "Family Values Rally," with Reverend Franklin and his wife and five kids on the front.

The back of the flyer listed rally dates and locations, with every other one circled in red marker. Cupcake at a family-values rally was hard to imagine; going to three of them boggled my mind. According to IdaMae, Franklin didn't like Cupcake, and I assumed the feeling was mutual. So why the flyer?

Footsteps sounded on the front stoop. I quickly shut the drawer and dropped the flyer, pen, and receipt in Old Yeller. Slinging my purse over my shoulder, I jumped out of Cupcake's chair, looking all sweet and innocent as Hollis shuffled in. His jacket was wrinkled; his shirt, worse. He looked like something a dog dragged out of the river.

"What are you doing here?" he asked.

"I brought IdaMae lunch, and she's out taking a walk with Auntie KiKi to get some air while I clean up and mind the phones. What did Boone have to say?"

"He told me to get out my checkbook and pray a lot."

I gave in to my curiosity. "What did you and Janelle argue about last night?"

Hollis looked at me for a long moment, then let out a deep breath. "I'm an idiot, a big fool. Janelle used me, and I bought it, the whole shebang."

Hollis ran his hand through his hair and sank into a chair. He had never suffered from low self-esteem. He never called himself an idiot or a fool. Hollis thought he was adorable; just ask him.

"What did Janelle do?"

He shrugged. "It's not important now. She's dead, and my life goes back to normal."

"Uh, Hollis, normal is not you in the slammer. We have a long way to go before we hit normal around here."

"I don't know who killed Janelle. Her death had nothing to do with me or our argument last night. She wasn't the woman I thought she was, that's for sure."

The door opened, and this time Detective Ross and two uniformed policemen came in. My heart stopped, and Hollis was no longer breathing.

Ross said, "Hollis Beaumont, you are under arrest for the murder of Janelle Claiborne. You have the right to remain silent." She droned on with the rest of the litany of rights as the uniformed cops hauled Hollis to his feet.

"What can I do?" I asked Hollis. Going though a divorce was bad, but getting hauled off to the slammer was terrifying.

Hollis's eyes weren't focusing, his brain not functioning. "Water my plants? Call Boone? Give my mamma a kiss?"

I could handle Boone and plants, but kissing Penny Beaumont was not happening. He dropped his keys in my purse as IdaMae powered through the doorway, a woman on a mission.

She elbowed her way past the cops and threw her arms around Hollis. "What are they doing to you?" she wailed.

Detective Ross was at the part "can and will be held against you" when the uniforms handcuffed Hollis. IdaMae collapsed into a chair mumbling, "This is all so wrong. Why wasn't I here? How can this be?"

"What evidence do you have that I killed Janelle?" Hollis asked Ross, the reality of the situation settling in.

Ross flipped open her little brown book. "Body was in your car and a neighbor saw the Lexus over on East Hall last night about the time of the murder. 'HB3' is a pretty distinctive license plate, Mr. Beaumont."

Hollis looked dumbfounded. "I wasn't on East Hall. Janelle showed a house there. I was here at the office doing paperwork. If I was going to murder my own fiancée, why would I use my own car that's easily recognized?"

"You argued with Ms. Claiborne at the Telfair Museum," Ross continued. "Anger makes people do rash things. We found Ms. Claiborne's car parked on Hall. Neighbors said your car pulled around in back of the 'For Sale' house around nine o'clock, then left ten minutes or so later. Ms. Claiborne was wrapped in plastic that matches the cut end of the plastic protecting the carpet in the house. Get yourself a good lawyer, Mr. Beaumont."

The cops led Hollis out the door, and I called Boone on the office phone. I knew his number by heart from the divorce, 1-800-DIRTBAG. I left a message on his voice mail. I wondered if he knew my number by heart, but that was impossible because Boone didn't have a heart. And there was the little problem of the fact that I no longer had a phone.

Auntie KiKi got IdaMae a glass of water, and we bundled her into KiKi's Beemer and took her home. We got her tea and brandy that was more brandy than tea, reassured her that everything would be okay, then left.

"Well, Hollis has certainly gotten his do-da in a wringer this time," Auntie KiKi said as we stopped at a traffic light on Abercorn. "Did you find anything at the office?"

"I'm not sure what I'm looking for. How would you like to go to a family-values rally tonight?"

"I think our family values are doing okay. How about a double dip of Old Black Magic at Leopold's instead?" KiKi countered. "All that singing and alleluias gives me heartburn, and I'd rather give my heart a workout over ice cream with bits of brownie and chunks of chocolate."

I pulled the family-values flyer from my purse. "I got this from Cupcake's desk. The only thing she valued was money and more money and definitely not family. IdaMae said Cupcake and Franklin weren't exactly bosom buddies, so why the flyer?" I flipped it over. "She has dates circled on the back, and tonight is one of them. The rally is up at Johnson Square. I hate taking the bus at night, and we really should check in on IdaMae later."

"We? What happened to turning all this over to Walker Boone? I thought that was the plan." The light turned green and KiKi pulled forward with the rest of the afternoon traffic.

"I know you don't want to hear this, but I'm not handing anything over to that overpriced ambulance chaser. I have a better chance of finding the killer than he does, and when I do, he and Hollis will never darken my Victorian doorway again."

"You fix plumbing, rotting floors, and rafters, and you sell clothes. The only thing you've ever uncovered is termites. You can't be putting yourself in danger like this. It's just not right. What if something happens?"

"It's a family rally, nothing dangerous, but I'm not sure what I'm looking for." I bit down on my bottom lip. "You know more people and their business than I do. Maybe you'll see something or someone. Come with me."

"*American Idol* is on. You know I love *American Idol*."

"I'll do another month with Bernard."

"I'll be ready at six."

Chapter Four

"THAT is absolutely the worst parking job I've ever seen in my life," I said to Auntie KiKi. I frowned at the Beemer sitting kittywhumpus at the curb. "You're going to get a ticket."

"I have a martini headache. Any Savannah cop would understand about a martini headache and bad parking." KiKi rubbed her forehead, then tucked her purse under her arm. We started down Whitaker. "How did I let you talk me into this?" KiKi asked me. "I should be curled up in front of my TV with Putter snoring at my side and forgetting this day ever happened."

"It happened, and tomorrow when Bernard is mashing my toes instead of yours, you'll be mighty thankful."

A warm glow from wrought-iron lamplights peeked though the Spanish moss and overhanging live oaks. Early evening traffic ran heavy with tourists going the wrong way on the one-way streets and looking for restaurants recommended on Yelp. Dodging a horse-drawn carriage, KiKi and I crossed to Johnson Square, the first square laid out by founding father James Oglethorpe and his merry men. There were twenty-three squares left, progress seeing fit to turn two of the original ones into parking garages before the good citizens of Savannah chained themselves to trees and threatened anarchy.

"Big crowd," KiKi said, our steps slowing as we got close to the makeshift stage by the sundial that didn't work for beans since it was under the trees. "The press is even here; must be a slow night for Savannah mayhem."

Looking like one of those preachers on Sunday-morning TV, Franklin stood tall at a podium, family at his side, his voice tinny over the cheap microphone. KiKi gazed longingly at a park bench. "Think anyone will notice if I laid down here and went to sleep for a bit? Why did we come here?"

"The question is why would Cupcake come here?"

"Well, bless her heart." KiKi's voice dropped to a whisper, her eyes fixed on the stage. "Virgil's wife is downright homely and then some. I mean like bow-wow. Next time I get my promo pictures done for *Dancing with KiKi*, I want the guy who took her photo for the front of that there flyer you showed me. Being a reverend's wife must be mighty hard on a woman."

I gave KiKi the *Shush; mind your manners* look, but I had to admit she was right as rain, and, unfortunately, all five kids favored Mrs. Birdie Franklin more than the reverend. "Birdie is Hollis's second cousin. I see her once in a while, and every time she looks more . . ."

"Homely," KiKi finished.

"I was going for tired, but homely fits."

Franklin's sermonizing wound down to a mixture of "alleluia"s and "amen"s, and the choir started up with "Amazing Grace." People shook Franklin's hand and dropped money into a box at his side. I pulled a few bills from Old Yeller that I'd earmarked for luxuries like toilet paper and shampoo.

"You're donating to the cause?" KiKi eyed the ten dollars in my hand.

"I want to ask him about Cupcake, and this gives me an excuse to get close and not look conspicuous."

"You don't think *'Bless you, Reverend Franklin, and did you happen to whack Janelle Claiborne last night?'* is a mite conspicuous?"

"I'll think of something." I made my way to the stage, and when I got to Franklin, I handed over the money. He smiled but it morphed into a frown when I added, "Are you doing the funeral service for Janelle Claiborne?"

His lips thinned to a straight line and his eyes went cold, his voice the same. The other side of family values? "It's my understanding that Janelle Claiborne is to be transported back to Atlanta and buried there. That's what her mamma wanted. That's where she's from, you know."

I did know, but before I could ask why he went to see Hollis and why he didn't care for Cupcake, a cute young woman nearly as tall as Franklin came up beside him. She had long auburn hair pulled back in a gold clip. "That Janelle person should have stayed in Atlanta for all our sakes," she said in an angry voice.

"Because she surely would have been safer there," Franklin added in a rush, and then gave the girl a warning glance.

Not that anyone would have noticed the glance unless looking for something. I was looking for anything. "We are all mighty upset over this tragedy here in our fair city. Our hearts go out to Janelle Claiborne's family and friends." Franklin sounded like a rehearsed news bite from a government office. He moved to the next person in line, cutting me off completely and giving me nowhere near ten bucks' worth of information.

I found KiKi next to a street vendor, the side of his van propped open to display chips, sodas, and meat of questionable origin. KiKi eyed a hot dog getting decked out for consumption by a man in a straw hat wearing a "WWJD" T-shirt. What Jesus would probably do is not eat here. "Find anything out?" KiKi asked.

"That if food causes nightmares, you're doomed," I whispered then added in a normal voice, "Did you order one for me?"

"You criticized my parking. I should let you starve."

"Do you know who the gal is beside Franklin? I don't think she cared much for Cupcake."

"That there is Sissy Collins," the vendor volunteered as he added a squirt of mustard to KiKi's hot dog creation, then mine, and sprinkled on onions. Street meat, come to mamma! "She's the church deacon, and I thought she had a real liking for cupcakes, especially chocolate ones. She ate two at our last covered dish. My wife and I go to the reverend's church, you see." The vendor gave me a look that suggested if I kept holy the Sabbath I'd know about these things.

Auntie KiKi and I took our dogs and found an empty bench by the monument to Nathanael Greene. That Mr.

Greene had his very own square over on Houston but his monument here in Johnson Square was just one of the little mysteries of life in Savannah. We watched families make their way to the stage while we scarfed hot dogs and licked bits of relish from our fingers. "You're awfully quiet," I said to KiKi, who was never quiet.

"Just look up on that stage and tell me what you see."

"My ten bucks gone forever, and I want it back."

"It's just like Cher says, 'Women are the real architects of our society.' We have the cute little deacon, the handsome minister, and mamma bear and her cubs gone home. It's the minister and the deacon who don't like Cupcake, not the minister and the wife, or the minister and the organ player, or the Sunday school teacher or the church usher."

I had a bad feeling where this was going and made the sign of the cross so God wouldn't strike us dead for thinking bad things about a minister. Women of the South died peacefully in their sleep in their best jammies, not in a park chowing down on a hot dog and pointing accusatory fingers at men of the cloth.

"Franklin's a man, and I've been watching couples dance around my parlor for thirty-five years now. Some want to look good at the country-club dance and that's it; others go home and do the rumba, if you get my drift. Those two up there on that stage are all about the rumba."

I watched the body language as we polished off our dogs. Those two were too close, too touchy, too many glances. "Do you think anyone else suspects?"

"No one else is looking."

"We need to go home." I pulled KiKi to her feet. "We're both going to fall asleep on this bench and get arrested for vagrancy." We started for the car. "Tomorrow will be better. Lordy, it's got to be better."

"For me, maybe it will be," KiKi said with a devilish glint in her eyes. "I'm not the one dancing with Bernard Thayer at nine o'clock in the morning."

AT EIGHT O'CLOCK I DRAGGED MYSELF OUT OF BED, and it wasn't because my alarm went off but because there was pounding on my front door. This was how yesterday started off. I felt like Bill Murray in that movie *Groundhog Day*, where he kept living the same day over and over. I couldn't do yesterday over and over; I didn't have the intestinal fortitude for more yesterdays. But when I opened the door, it wasn't Bill Murray or Raylene on the other side but, "Mamma?"

"Mercy, Reagan, honey, what is going on with you? It's all over town." Mamma stepped inside and closed the door. How could anyone look so together at eight in the morning? She had on her best black suit, and her short bob had every salt and pepper hair in place. Of course, Judge Gloria Summerside would have it no other way.

"I had calls every fifteen minutes yesterday," she went on. "Everyone wanted to tell me about you finding Janelle dead in Hollis's car and Hollis being arrested and you taken in for questioning. I was in court and couldn't get here, and last night when I came over you were gone, and your cell phone's been disconnected, and I think something's living under your front porch."

She took a quick look around at the dining-room table piled with clothes and the other, empty rooms. She brushed a strand of hair from my forehead and kissed the vacated spot. "Are you all right?"

That was a loaded question if I'd ever heard one. If there's one thing I've learned from being the daughter of a lawyer who excelled her way up to judge, it's that the best defense is to answer a question with a question. "Do you think Reverend Franklin is having an affair with his deacon?"

Mamma gave me the *Nice try* look that mothers and judges do so well. "I have no idea about the reverend, but I do know it doesn't look good for Hollis."

"He's got Walker Boone as his attorney, and Hollis is selling Cherry House to pay him."

"Boone? Again? Those two are a worrisome duo, especially when it comes to you. I'm sorry, Reagan, I truly am." Mamma studied me for a minute, like she had the time I used her credit card to buy tickets to Prince. I was going to pay her back with my babysitting money, I swear. "Why did you want to know about Reverend Franklin?"

"Idle curiosity."

Mamma checked her watch. "I have to be in court." She took both of my hands in hers and looked me dead in the eyes. She hadn't done that since she made me promise not to vote for Kerry back in '04. "I know you love this house, but swear to me you won't get involved trying to find out who killed Janelle."

"Now what would ever make you think I'd do a thing like that?" I did my best to sound thoroughly aghast, hoping to sound convincing.

Mamma held a little tighter. "Because that's what I would do." Before I could respond, Mamma was out the door and driving away in her black Caddy. I watched the car fade down Gaston, then turn onto Drayton. Who would have thought that the most conservative judge in Savannah would even consider going after a murderer? Even though I did vote for Kerry, Mamma and I weren't really all that different . . . sometimes.

"Unless you intend to give Bernard his dance lesson in hot-pink pj's, you better change," Auntie KiKi said as she trudged up onto the porch. She leaned heavily against my front door. "If I was any more worn out, I'd be lying in a coffin out there in Bonaventure Cemetery. Was that Gloria's car I saw parked out front?"

"Mamma can be pretty cool."

KiKi gave me a little wink. "She has her moments, but the woman can't dance for diddly. Now get a move on."

I was tired, too, and the thought of driving Bernard around the dance floor made my toes curl—for good reason. "I might have customers," I offered as a last-ditch excuse not to take on Bernard. "I need to make money. I need to open my store."

"Honey, there was a body right outside your house yesterday. I don't think anyone will be showing up at a murder scene to buy clothes. Your store doesn't even have a name. What kind of store doesn't have a name? And you promised about Bernard, and I'm holding you to it."

"Hi there," a woman called from the open window of her car as she slowed to the curb in front of the house. "Is this here that prissy consignment shop I heard about on the news?" She pointed down at the street. "Was the car with that body in it right there? Lordy, that must have been something, finding a body in a trunk like that. I like your pj's. Do you have any more in that store of yours?" The woman parked her Prius and killed the engine. She made her way up the path and gave me the once-over. "Well now, you looked kind of foxy on the TV yesterday. What happened?" She pushed past me and went inside, searching through the clothes on the table and a few I had hanging from the antique brass chandelier in the middle of the room.

KiKi shrugged. "You could do with a little concealer, and you need to be getting more clothes in here to sell; we're almost out. I brought my Nordstrom's catalog over so you can get familiar with what's new and what's expensive and what prices to put on things." She sat on the steps and flipped the magazine pages. "I'll mind the store, and you get yourself dressed. Remember to be nice to Bernard. He pays double."

An hour later, I hobbled back to my house and plopped down on the steps beside the bill pile and KiKi. "Look at this," KiKi said, waving her hand over the shoppers in the dining room. "Murder truly is good for business. I never knew people could be so ghoulish. Everyone wants to know every gory little detail about Cupcake and the body. I sup-pose it's like Cher said: 'There is no such thing as bad publicity.'"

"Cher said that?"

"She would have if she'd thought of it first. We've been busy as ants at a picnic. I'm thinking it's all because of the body in the Lexus, but now we are getting clothes to sell. I also took in some costume jewelry that looked kind of nice, and maybe we should start to do furniture. While you were gone, I went and named your store the Prissy Fox. I got it from our customer this morning before you went dancing with Bernard. How is he?"

"How is *he*?" I growled, then peeled off my left shoe and

held out my red big toe. "*He's* just fine and dandy, thank you very much."

There was a knock at the door, and KiKi stood. "We need one of those 'Open' signs so people can come right on inside like a real store."

A real store, I thought to myself. I had a long way to go before that happened, but at least people were here looking around. KiKi admitted a woman in her midforties with styled blonde hair and a tan knit suit. She gazed past KiKi, spied me on the steps, and hurried over, holding out her hand. I shook it as she gushed, "I saw you on the news yesterday. I'm Dinah Corwin. I wanted to meet you, since we have so much in common, and that common thing is now dead and gone, Lord be praised."

I didn't think it was good karma to be praising the demise of another human being, but I wasn't wearing sackcloth and ashes about this particular event either. "Cupca . . . Janelle wasn't one of your favorite people?"

"Oh, honey." Dinah laughed and put her hand to her chest to contain the jubilation. "I'm with WAGA Atlanta. I do the *Georgia Southern Style* segment of the news every Monday, Wednesday, and Friday. I'm here to cover the Homes and Gardens Tour you-all are having this week. I saw on the news about Janelle. Today is a fine day indeed."

Dinah did a little happy Snoopy dance right there in my hall. "I was celebrating with a nice pinot at the Marshall House, where I'm staying. That hunky bartender with the dreamy bedroom eyes gave me the dirt on Janelle breaking up your marriage, too. Said your husband ditched you just like my husband did to me back in Atlanta when Janelle came along. Of course, she never married the old fool, just bled him dry. He bought me a cute little blue Gucci handbag with a braided handle for our anniversary, then swiped it right out of my closet and gave it to that little round-heeled Sue. A month later, she left him and moved here to Savannah. Lucky you. I, on the other hand, got myself a new beau in Atlanta. Henry. We've been going together for six months now. I suppose all's well that ends well."

I blinked a few times trying to take this all in. "Your husband? Janelle?"

"But now she's dead as a doornail, and I have Henry. With all my celebrating last night, I spilled a glass of wine on my black dress and lost one of my favorite earrings to boot. I'm hoping you can fix me right up in an outfit I'll look good in. I wanted to throw some business your way if I could since we're sort of connected 'cause we married low-down conniving cheaters who did us wrong. I have a ton of interviews scheduled, you see. Tonight I'm at"—Dinah took her iPhone from her purse and touched the screen—"Raylene Carter's house. Seems her garden is the front runner for Best of Show fourth time in a row. From what I understand there'll be garden parties all week long but tomorrow night, I'm having a little wake of my very own over at the Marshall House to observe this momentous occasion of Janelle dead and gone. Spread the word, honey. Drinks are on me. I shouldn't be so vocal about this, but I simply can't contain myself."

Obviously! I slipped on my shoes, my big toe screaming *no, no, no* in protest then hobbled over to Dinah. I showed her some new black dresses I'd taken in on consignment then retrieved a box of earrings. A half hour later, I finally found ones similar enough to make her happy. If every sale was going to be this hard, my shop was doomed from the start.

After Dinah left, KiKi whispered to me, "Mercy me, Cupcake had a checkered past?"

"Better than that, Cupcake had enemies. Franklin, Sissy, Urston, and now Dinah Corwin. It's getting to be a regular laundry list of people who wanted her out of the way. I wonder if Hollis . . ."

"Honey, Hollis knew Cupcake was young, stacked like a brick outhouse, and that his marital status at the time was not an issue. In the world of Hollis Beaumont the third, what else is there to care about?"

"Being in the slammer. I'll keep the Prissy Fox open till noon. I need the business. Maybe a few more curious customers will drift in, and are we really going to name this place the Prissy Fox?"

"Better than Ye Old Secondhand Store."

"You convinced me. I'll close up for lunch, then go visit Hollis."

"And then you're going to visit Walker Boone, right? You have a lot of information now and real suspects besides Hollis. Let him handle things, honey."

I crossed my fingers behind my back. "You bet."

You bet wasn't exactly a full-fledged lie to my dear auntie, who would worry herself to a frazzle if she thought I was in danger. Worse still, she'd tell Mamma, and then they'd both worry. In my opinion, it was the duty of a caring daughter and niece to prevent her mother and auntie from any sort of frazzle on her part.

HOLLIS LOOKED BAD. THEN AGAIN, JAIL WASN'T exactly a Sedona spa. I sat at a long metal table separated into cubes. A piece of glass perforated with holes to let voices though and nothing else divided me from Hollis. I handed a police officer the cheesecake I'd picked up for Hollis from Sugar Daddy's. Guess the cops were going to stab around in the goo to make sure I didn't sneak in a hacksaw.

"You look good," I lied.

"Boone better get this straightened out and fast. That's why I'm paying him."

Actually *I* was the one paying Boone, but this didn't seem the best time to quibble. "Why weren't you bawling your eyes out when you found out Janelle was . . . dead?"

"You came here to ask me that?"

"I brought cheesecake." Hollis loved cheesecake. If anything would get him to open up and tell me what was going on, it was cheesecake. "Did you know Janelle was fooling around before? That she broke up a marriage in Atlanta? Why do Reverend Franklin and his cute little deacon have Janelle on their do-not-like list?"

The first two questions passed over Hollis without so much as a raised brow, but the Franklin-Sissy issue warranted a clenched jaw and flared nostrils. Pay dirt!

"Leave it alone, Reagan. I'm not telling you anything, no matter what kind of cheesecake you brought." His eyes narrowed. "What kind did you bring?"

"Raspberry amaretto swirl."

"Glory be." He licked his lips, his eyes glazing over. "Franklin has nothing to do with Janelle's death, so forget it."

"Janelle wasn't the cute little pixie doll you thought. She was up to something, and it wasn't just selling houses."

"Let Boone handle this. You're just going to screw things up, like you always do."

Now I understood the reason for the glass partition; it was to keep me from strangling Hollis with my bare hands. "You're the one who screwed up my life in so many ways. If I didn't have just fifteen minutes with you, I'd gladly list them. Tell me about Janelle and Franklin; you owe me that much. I brought you cake!"

"Franklin has kids, and you know his wife is my cousin. We're family, and I don't want to see Birdie hurt. Drop it." Hollis ran his hand over his face, looking exhausted.

So, what would hurt Franklin's wife? Duh! Another woman! I knew all about that kind of hurt. Auntie KiKi was dead-on about Sissy and Franklin. Auntie KiKi had great rumba radar. "Franklin's having an affair with his little deacon."

"Leave it be," Hollis repeated, this time adding some stern to his voice. Translation: *there was more than just an affair to deal with.*

"I bet Janelle knew about the affair, and that's why Franklin and Sissy didn't like her. So why did he look so awful yesterday at your office when he heard Janelle was dead? He should have been jumping up and down and doing cartwheels across the room. His secret was safe." I sucked in a quick breath. "Unless he wasn't safe. Bless my soul, Janelle had pictures, or love letters, or something. Intrigue."

Hollis had that same *Oh sweet Jesus* look in his eyes he did when I caught him and Cupcake on top of his desk at the office two years ago. It was the look that said *Busted!*

"What tied Janelle to Franklin and Sissy was that she

was blackmailing them, and Franklin doesn't know where the blackmail goodies are."

"Franklin's a minister and doesn't have two dimes to rub together for blackmail. You're way off base."

I felt more like I was rounding first and heading for second. "His wife is a Beaumont, and she *does* have money. Of course, Franklin getting it to pay off Janelle to keep her quiet might be a little tricky since then he'd have to tell dear Birdie why he needed it."

Hollis whispered though clenched teeth. "The day before the murder, Franklin came to me about Janelle and asked me to get her to back off and leave him alone. Before that, I swear I had no idea what Janelle was up to. I tried to tell her to stop, but she just laughed in my face. Said Savannah was easy pickings with all the secrets. She said that's why she hooked up with me. She got to know everyone's business."

"That's what the argument at the Telfair was about, and why you weren't all that overwrought at Janelle's death." Hollis gave me a shoulder shrug that said I was right. "What about bail and getting you out of here?"

"First-degree-murder charges and all the evidence against me makes bail a freaking fortune."

A red light came on in the front of the room, where the cops were holding my cheesecake hostage. A loudspeaker blared that visiting time was over.

"Stay out of this, Reagan. I mean it. You're going to make things even worse than they already are. Boone will take care of everything. He's smart; he'll find the killer."

And he probably would, I thought to myself as I left Hollis and followed the yellow line on the floor with the other visitors to the exit. But in the process, I'd lose my house for sure. I had my laundry list of suspects who could have knocked off Janelle, but Boone knew stuff too, stuff I could really use. The big question was how to get him to tell me.

During the divorce, I was mad as a rat in a trap, and it showed. In those days, visions of Walker Boone's head on a stake outside the courthouse gave me great comfort, and he was aware of that since I might have mentioned it a time or two. Now I was smarter, calmer. For sure I was over Hollis, and I could play Walker Boone to get what I wanted, right?

I was Hollis's ex and the one who found the body, so asking Boone a few questions was logical enough without making him suspect I was trying to find the killer. And since I spotted Boone walking across the parking lot at that very moment, now was as good a time as any to wheedle information. I slapped on my best Little Miss Innocent smile and set my brain to wheedling mode.

Chapter Five

WALKER Boone strode across the police parking lot as if he owned the place. He stopped twice to talk to police officers. Boone was a tough guy to figure, with gang connections, cop connections, and bedroom connections. That last connection was the constant talk of Savannah.

No doubt Boone got information from all these sources, but I had Auntie KiKi, the dancing gossip queen, and Elsie and AnnieFritz, local funeral busybodies. My informants weren't nearly as colorful as Boone's, but I figured they were just as good.

"Here to see Hollis?" Boone asked as he walked up next to me. "Who would have thought?"

He had on jeans and a white button-down shirt, rolled at the sleeves, and he looked like Robert Downey Jr. on a good day. Not that I cared. I still wanted his head on that stake.

"I know Hollis is innocent, and it would be a pity for him to go to jail."

"A year ago you wanted him neutered."

"Still not a bad idea, but I'm over Hollis and want justice done. I brought him cheesecake."

"From Sugar Daddy's?"

"Is there anyplace else?"

Boone folded his arms across his chest, which was sculpted by frequent trips to the gym or duking it out at the bars on the West Side. "So did Hollis tell you what you wanted to know about Franklin?"

I did the arched eyebrow to enhance my innocent act. "The reverend?"

"Unless you know another Franklin?" Boone gave me the smile that said he knew something I didn't. I'd seen a lot of that smile in the last two years. "You and Miss KiKi were at the family-values rally last night, and unless the two of you developed a religious streak, I suspect you know about Janelle and her extracurricular activities."

"Activities?" I repeated, putting the emphasis on the final *s*.

"Answering questions with questions; your mamma taught you well." Boone's expression turned serious, his eyes dark and ominous, like yesterday, when he told Hollis to keep his mouth shut. "I don't know who the killer is, but he'll kill again to cover his tracks, Reagan. If you're in his way, it won't be pretty."

I willed myself not to run off like some scared little rabbit. I had a house to protect. And I had a business to run, maybe. "And just how much do I owe you for this extraordinary piece of information? Three hundred dollars? Four hundred?"

"Meaning . . . ?"

"Meaning Hollis is selling Cherry House to pay you, and I'm keeping track of the bill. How much do I owe you so far?"

"Cherry House?"

"My Victorian, in various stages of repair." Or disrepair, depending on how you looked at it.

"I didn't know about the house."

"Well, you do now, and if I get in your way while trying to figure out who really did kill Janelle, you'll have to just live with it."

"The critical word is *live*. Go home and wallpaper something."

"You go home and wallpaper something. You and Hollis got everything in the divorce, but things are different this time around. You're not holding all the cards." I headed for the bus stop, my stomach in knots. I had found out nothing from Boone and hadn't the foggiest notion what in blazes he was up to. So much for me playing Walker Boone. Then again, he hadn't played me either.

I needed a sandwich. Something yummy and comforting without the benefit of veggies and low-cal dressing. I always felt better with a sandwich in hand; didn't everyone? I walked the three blocks to Parkers, the only gourmet gas station in Savannah—probably in all of the South for that matter. Back in the day, when I had a car, I could get a tank of Chevron and a meat-loaf sandwich with provolone cheese so tasty I'd seen grown men cry at the first bite. I couldn't really afford a sandwich after splurging on Hollis's cheesecake, but I needed comfort food after dealing with Boone. During the divorce I'd put on five pounds using that particular piece of logic.

I took my sandwich to go, caught the bus, and got off by Hollis's office. Maybe IdaMae knew where Cupcake might have kept important things like a will, an insurance policy, a picture of Franklin and Sissy playing tonsil hockey.

"Goodness me," IdaMae said as I came through the door, nearly colliding with her. "Reagan, honey, I wasn't expecting you. What a pleasant surprise."

"Are you off to lunch?" I asked, spotting IdaMae's pocketbook in her hand. I held up my Parkers bag and made it do a little dance in the air. "I brought lunch to you. We can share."

"Oh, I'd just love that. I truly would." She studied the bag. "It's meat loaf, isn't it? Nobody does a meat-loaf sandwich like Parkers. But I'm off to show a house up on East Huntington to potential buyers."

"You're showing a house?"

"I didn't know what else to do. This nice man said he and his wife wanted to see the place. I need to keep the office going for Hollis, and I've been the secretary here long enough to know the ropes. I got my real-estate license some years back so I could keep up with all that happens around here. Do you think I can do this?" IdaMae stood straight and tall, showing off her blue suit. "How do I look?"

"Very professional, and I think you'll be great at showing houses. I know I'd buy a house from you."

She blushed and checked her watch. "Oh dear, I'm gong to be late." She giggled like a schoolgirl. "Wish me luck, honey. I'm so excited."

"Do you have any idea where Janelle might have kept her personal papers? Maybe she had an insurance policy, and if it was big, the beneficiary had motive to kill her."

IdaMae flipped off the office lights and reached for the doorknob. "I think Hollis was her insurance policy. I overheard her talking to her mamma once on the phone, and she said being with Hollis would make her rich. Maybe she knew something about the revival of the real-estate market that we didn't. Hollis has every penny sunk into keeping the office open. A few times he had to cover my paycheck from his own personal account. These have been some tough times around here, I can tell you that."

She air-kissed my cheek. "I plan on visiting Hollis tomorrow. Would you like me to go and water those plants at his place? He said he tried to call you, but your phone is disconnected."

"If you keep the agency going, the least I can do is take care of things at the town house." It would give me a chance to see if Cupcake stashed what she had on Franklin there. Not that I held out much hope on that score. With Hollis living there too, it didn't seem likely I'd find much incriminating information lying around.

"Did Dinah Corwin come to your place?" IdaMae asked as we stepped out onto the stoop. Little white petals from the crabapple tree at the corner fluttered over us like soft, fragrant snow. This was as close to snow as Savannah got, and that was just fine by me.

IdaMae locked the door then added, "She came here looking for you, and when she said she needed a nice little black dress, I mentioned your shop. I heard all about your new place over at the Piggly Wiggly when I was waiting in the checkout line. Sounds like a fine idea, and the word is spreading. I think seeing it on TV when you went and found Janelle in the Lexus had something to do with it."

Well, I'll be. Cupcake finally did something good for me, I thought as IdaMae added, "Did Dinah Corwin invite you to her wake for Janelle? I never heard of such a thing in all my life. Janelle was nothing but a two-bit floozy, taking Hollis from you the way she did. I can't say I'm all that sorry she's out of the picture." IdaMae bit her bottom lip. "I just hope Walker Boone can catch the real killer."

I wished IdaMae luck with her showing, then walked the three blocks to my place. It was a perfect spring day, with the whole city smelling like warm earth and sunshine. I took the steps up the front porch just as Chantilly pulled her UPS truck to the curb. "How's business?" she called from the door, wide open for quick grab-and-go package delivery.

I gave her a thumbs-up sign and retraced my steps down the walkway. I leaned into the cab. "I need clothes to sell," I said to her. "I'm nearly out of merchandise."

Chantilly turned in her seat. She had on her brown shorts uniform in honor of the warm day, and I noticed a small rose tattoo on the inside of her leg. A UPS driver with pizzazz. She eyed my Parkers bag. "You wouldn't happen to have a meat-loaf sandwich in there, would you? I could put out the word and get you some mighty fine clothes here real quick for a meat-loaf sandwich from Parkers."

I was so hungry that my stomach thought my throat was cut. I forced myself to hand up the bag. "Extra provolone."

"Is there any other way?" She peered into the bag, and I caught a whiff of warm beef and seasonings smothered in cheese. A hint of drool formed at the corner of Chantilly's lips.

"When you put out the word, say it's a consignment shop— I don't have money to buy things outright. What do you think about a seventy-five, twenty-five split, with consigners getting the seventy-five?"

Chantilly slid out the sandwich, unwrapped it, and took a bite, a chunk of provolone dropping on her leg. I swear it took every bit of self-control I had not to swipe up the cheese and eat it.

Chantilly said around a mouthful, "That's bad business, girlfriend. You need a fifty-fifty split. It's their clothes but your shop, and you're doing the work. You'll have to come up with some kind of bookkeeping system and give people account numbers to keep track of what sells and how much you own them."

"How do you know all this?"

She licked a glob of mayo from her finger, then pointed to the back of her truck. "It's like the packages here. We keep track of where they go and who sends them by using numbers and accounts. We stick the information to the package and match it to delivery information we keep on file. We're all computerized, but you can do the same thing with a notebook. You'll have to devise a tagging system to tell what clothes belong to what customer, then mark the account when there's a sale."

She glanced at her watch. "Lunchtime's over." She balanced the sandwich on her knee and put the truck in gear. She gave a little sandwich salute, then took off with my lunch.

When hungry and broke, there was only one place to go, the free-food store. Translation: KiKi's kitchen. I crossed the lawn and took the stone path that led through the rose wrought-iron gate to the backyard. Uncle Putter was bent over a golf ball, club in hand, meditating or whatever it was golfers did when trying to get a golf ball to accomplish a specific task. I tiptoed by so as not to interrupt the spiritual moment and slipped in through the back door. I gazed upon Mecca, otherwise known as a well-stocked fridge. When I opened the door, I'm sure I heard angels sing.

"Let me make you a sandwich," KiKi said as she came into the kitchen.

"Thanks," I mumbled around a fried-chicken drumstick clamped between my teeth. I sat down at the kitchen table. "Chantilly's sending out the word to get us more clothes for the shop."

"Us?" KiKi let out a deep sigh and piled ham, turkey, tomato, and sliced avocado on whole wheat bread. "Some people at my age retire, you know. I should start thinking about retiring. I'd look great in one of those golf carts tooling around a retirement village down in Florida."

"You'd never leave Savannah, and if I can't retire, you can't retire."

"I'm sure there's a thread of logic there somewhere."

Not necessarily, but I couldn't have my auntie heading off to parts unknown. "I went to see Hollis, and he's ornery as a caged cat." I bit into the sandwich, and my eyes crossed in ecstasy. "There's a special place in heaven for you."

"That's because I resold your fountain. Raylene's having a cocktail party tonight and needs to impress. She sent the Italian stallion, Raimondo Baldassare, to get it. Nearly had a heart attack when I answered the door and there he was in all his handsomeness. Lord have mercy, the man is a hunk. Anyway, I couldn't find the pump part of the fountain and told him you'd drop it off for Raylene later. You know, Putter and I could do with a vacation in Italy. Can you imagine a whole country of Raimondos?" She fanned herself with a napkin.

I nearly wept, but it wasn't over the prospect of Italian men. "Money? I'll have real money in bulk from selling the fountain? I can stock my own fridge."

KiKi kissed me on the head. "Now, where would the fun be in that, sweet pea?" She took a seat across from me at the round mahogany table. Rumor had it that both Lee and Grant had eaten at this particular table. I had my doubts whether that was true, but it made one heck of a story to pass on in the family. KiKi said, "Putter and I are going to Raylene's bash tonight, and I was thinking that if you dropped off the pump late, you could sort of stick around and keep me company. There's going to be a lot of uppity people there, and I'll need a friendly face. I can take just so much uppity in one night. Everyone's going to be talking about Cupcake. We don't want to miss that."

"I don't know. Raylene will have a hissy if I hang around. She'll ask me to leave, and it will be downright embarrassing. She's part of the Beaumonts' social circle more than mine, so my former in-laws will be there, and I don't need more Hollis in my life right now. And I do have a haunted-Savannah walking tour tonight for the Cincinnati Woman's Sewing Circle visiting here."

"The ghost tours never start till later when all the Savannah ghosts are up and about, and the Beaumonts won't show up with Hollis in the slammer, tarnishing the family name and all. Raylene wouldn't dare ask you to leave with everyone at the party. She'll be on her best behavior and welcome you as a dear friend. I bet she'll have The Lady and Sons do the catering, and that means Paula Deen's deviled eggs. Can you really pass up Paula's deviled eggs?"

Paula Deen was one of those true Southerners who put Savannah as well as herself on the map with the cooking secret of a stick of butter and a cup of cream in every pot. I downed the last bite of sandwich, thanked Auntie KiKi for feeding the hungry, and said I'd be at Raylene's around six.

Uncle Putter was meditating over another golf shot, or maybe it was the same one. Hard to tell, and I knew better than to interrupt by asking something so mundane as "How are you?"

I rounded the corner and headed for my house but stopped dead at the property line, one foot on lush green, the other on lush weeds. *Well, bless her heart!* When Chantilly sends out *the word,* people listen. My porch had three ladies carrying hangers of clothes, and it all looked like really nice stuff. If I wanted to keep the Prissy Fox prissy and only take good-quality items, I had to figure out a nice way to tell someone their clothes weren't good enough. Men in Savannah weren't the only ones who packed heat these days, and "Your dress is downright ugly" and "I don't want it anywhere near my establishment" sounded a mite confrontational.

By five I was tired to the bone with trying to come up with a system to keep consigners straight and mark what clothes belonged to whom. For now, I pinned account numbers along with the price to the clothes, then marked down the name, account numbers, and prices when the items sold. I needed one of those barb-gun things that attached price tags to the clothes instead of pins, and I really needed a crash course in Bookkeeping 101.

I closed the Fox at five, grabbed a shower, and got a blue

dress from the stash in the shop. Another good thing about running a consignment shop was an extensive wardrobe at your fingertips. Buy it, wear it, have it dry-cleaned, and resell. I couldn't afford to do that often, but Raylene's party meant I had to look good. Hadn't I seen the cutest pair of taupe strappy sandals that had just come in? The heel was higher than what I usually wore, but considering I usually wore flip-flops, anything was higher.

With Urston on my *maybe* list of murderers, this could be a very interesting night. Maybe I'd find out what exactly he and Cupcake were up to and why he was giving her money.

Chapter Six

"About time you got yourself here," Raylene huffed when she answered the door of leaded-glass panes and gleaming brass hardware. "I have guests arriving any minute now, and I want that fountain up and running right quick or I'm stopping payment on my check." She made a sour face, then stepped aside to let me enter. "Do you always carry that ugly yellow purse everywhere you go? A little evening purse wouldn't hurt, you know. Something with class."

Raylene had married Junior Carter, of Carter Bank and Trust fame, and went from nobody to somebody in six months flat. That Junior Jr. was born two months *premature,* weighing nine pounds, six ounces, may have had something to do with the speedy wedding. Raylene, Junior, and Junior Jr., aka JJ, now lived in the historic Lester Reed House, a huge white antebellum Greek Revival with seven fireplaces, a side veranda, and the ghost of Lester Reed's cat, or so we tour guides embellished.

Raylene pointed to the back. "Raimondo is putting the final touches on the gardens, and for pity's sake. don't step on anything and kill it dead, but get that fountain running. That newswoman here from Atlanta is taking pictures of the gardens tonight and doing interviews." Raylene stood tall, looking very impressed with herself. "She's interviewing me and Junior in the library, so don't you be wandering in there and disturbing her while she's setting up."

Raylene scurried off, and I followed the hallway past lovely rooms filled with beautiful antiques and rich fabrics in shades of gold, yellows, and blues. Raylene may be a snob of the first order, but she had an incredible house. Pushing through the double French doors that led outside, I spied Raimondo bent over an azalea bush. He expertly cut off blooms that had dared to die in Raylene's yard and stuffed withered petals and stems in his pocket so as not to leave plant shrapnel.

"Mr. Baldassare?" I came up behind him, enjoying the view—and not of the flowers. Raimondo was tall, dark, and gorgeous, with an excellent butt.

He stood and turned, then flashed a dazzling smile, his teeth white and perfect against his Italian skin. "Ciao e saluti."

I had no idea what that meant, but it sounded sexy as all get-out and turned my legs to Jell-O. I put out my hand to shake his. He held out a withered dogwood bloom. He laughed and slid it into his pocket, but when he pulled his hand out a dead daffodil petal and tulip leaf came with it. "I am like a kangaroo with many pouches." He laughed, his dark eyes twinkling as he shook my hand. He picked up the leaves and petals, and I took the fountain pump from my purse.

"Sorry I wasn't around when you stopped by my house," I said to Raimondo. "I'll get the fountain up and going in no time."

My fountain was made up of metal and stone lily pads, with water flowing from one to the other, surrounded by birds and animals. Raimondo had it tucked into a corner of the garden surrounded by tulips, daffodils, and green moss. As much as I hated to admit it, the fountain looked a lot better in Raylene's garden than it ever did at my place. That she had a top-notch Italian gardener on retainer and an end-less supply of money may have had a little to do with it.

"It only takes a few minutes to get the hoses connected," I explained. "Then I'll need to fill the basin."

"I will do that for you." Raimondo's smile widened a bit, and he added, "The blue color of your dress is beautiful with your eyes. You have lovely eyes."

I suddenly felt light-headed and with an honest-to-good-ness urge to swoon. Until this moment, I had no idea what a swoon was. I think I thanked Raimondo, than floated over to the fountain and started sticking tubes and plugs together, the chore taking twice as long as it should have since floating got in the way of concentration.

A string quartet started up from the veranda, and *ooh*ing and *aah*ing guests spilled out into the torch-lit garden. I stepped back to check that the fountain trickled from lily pad to lily pad without sloshing over the edges and bumped right into Walker Boone. Tonight he had on a navy sport coat and khaki pants. Considering he spent his pubescent years between street fights and drive-by shootings, he cleaned up pretty good.

He snagged a glass of champagne from a waiter wandering though the crush and handed it to me. Very un-Boonelike, and I wish he'd snagged a deviled egg instead. "What do you want?"

His brows drew together questioningly, but it was strictly for show. He knew I was onto him.

I said, "So, what—you give me something and now you want something in return."

"Actually the drinks are free."

"You still want something."

A waiter served Boone a beer in a bottle with some snooty label, but a beer is a beer, and it suited Boone better than champagne ever would. "Are you staying away from church rallies?" He held up his hand to stop my protests. I guess the *Drop dead* expression on my face hinted as to what I was thinking. "I know you don't take orders from me, but this time do it. There are more people involved with Hollis' case than you think, and they all have a lot to lose. Let me handle things, and forget about your house. There are other houses."

"Not ones I've rebuilt from the ground up." Or maybe it was the top down. It was hard to remember with all that rebuilding going on, but this latest information from Boone about more people being involved was very interesting. I'm sure his intention in telling me this was to get me to back off, but it had just the opposite effect. *What people? What were they losing?*

"You're out of your league, Reagan."

"Or maybe I'm getting too close to finding out what's

really going on, and you're worried you'll look bad if I get to the truth before the big, bad lawyer."

Boone took a swig of his beer and rocked back on his heels. "That's not going to happen."

"Or you're afraid it will." I made little chicken sounds. I was poking the bear, and it felt good. "This time there's no prenup or legal mumbo jumbo getting in the way of my doing what I want."

"This isn't something you and your auntie talk about over sticky buns and pecan coffee for kicks. This is serious."

Two years ago, Boone could intimidate the snot out of me, but not now, not this time. "How much do I owe you so far? It better not be much because you haven't done much. Hollis is still in jail."

I handed my glass to a waiter, hiked Old Yeller up on my shoulder, and turned to leave, but the heel of my cute little strappy sandal got stuck in the grass. I wobbled, trying to steady myself, promising God I'd go to church for a month if he'd spare me from falling flat on my face at Raylene's party and—most of all—right in front of Walker Boone, who I had just made chicken sounds to. Like Cher says, "The worst thing in the world is to be uncool." Uncool was happening real fast.

Boone snagged my elbow, holding me upright. God did indeed work in mysterious ways. "You can't even walk across the garden without causing a scene. The killer will see you coming a mile away," he whispered as he drew close.

I wiggled my arm from his hand and took off in search of a deviled egg. To eat it or throw it at Boone, I wasn't quite sure yet.

"Honey, what's got you all in a dither?" Auntie KiKi said, sidling up next to me.

I glared at Walker Boone's back as he chatted with Urston Russell. Urston had his red notebook tucked under his arm. He and his committee must have just come from judging someone else's garden. Word had it Urston would go off by himself after a judging and make notes. He never let that red notebook out of his sight, and everyone knew that at home he kept it under lock and key. KiKi's gaze followed mine, and she let out a dreamy sigh. I was willing to bet the bank she wasn't sighing over Urston. She said, "Whatever that man did to you this time, he did it while looking right nice. Walker Boone sure does fill out a jacket to perfection."

KiKi cut her gaze back to me. "I came over here to let you know your fountain isn't working right, and water's spilling over the sides and making a soggy mess in the grass. You know how Raylene is about messes. Given half a chance, she'll use it as an excuse to stop payment on your check."

I glanced at the fountain, which was making uneven splashes instead of tranquil drip-drops. "I'll take care of it. I'm counting on that check to pay bills. I think we should go to the wake Dinah Corwin's hosting tomorrow night." What better place to find out who else was involved with Cupcake?

KiKi took a glass of champagne from another waiter passing by and downed it in one gulp. "I knew when I saw you and Mr. Hunk together there'd be fireworks. You got something cooking in that brain of yours, I can tell."

If I told KiKi the truth about going it alone on finding the killer, she'd wring her hands, say novenas, and add me to the prayer list at church. "No fireworks," I assured KiKi with a big smile. "As a matter of fact, I'm going to stop by

Boone's office tomorrow for a chat. I might find something out at the wake that could help him out."

I could go to Boone's office, so this wasn't a lie at all. His secretary and I had become good friends during the divorce. I could sneak up the back stairs that had been closed off when the offices were remodeled, chat with Dinky, the secretary, over lattes, and not have to see Boone. She might even know some dirt about Cupcake. "We'll get free martinis from Dinah," I said to KiKi. "We'll see who else at the Marshall House is celebrating Cupcake's demise."

"And you'll tell Boone all about it?"

I'd tell him to take a long walk off a short pier, but instead I said to KiKi, "I promise to go to his office."

KiKi batted her green-shadowed eyes. "Well, now that I think about it, Marshall House does do a right-fine martini, with those big olives stuffed with blue cheese. I'll bring Putter. You wouldn't believe the gossip that takes place over those little white balls. It makes the gals at the beauty salons look like a bunch of amateurs. We have to do an obligatory appearance at the Paxtons' anniversary party first, but we'll be there."

I left KiKi and skirted around an array of purple and white creeping phlox, the grass verdant and green. I stooped down behind the soggy fountain, which was listing to one side and making—God forbid—a puddle. I wedged myself between the fountain and the bamboo fence, which was covered with yellow trumpets of Carolina jessamine that separated Raylene's garden from the yard next door. Rummaging around in my purse that was just about the same color as the trumpets, I came up with a lipstick, a spiky brush that did horrible things to my hair, a mascara I hated because it left clumps, and two rolls of half-eaten cherry Life Savers. I'd contemplated cleaning out my purse, but, thankfully, I hadn't gotten around to it. Now I could jam all that unwanted stuff under the back edge of the fountain and level it out.

I plastered my bag against the fountain as a cushion to push it forward, the water making it heavy. I slid the mascara tube under the one end, followed by the lipstick, then heard Raylene's voice low and threatening coming from the other side of the trumpet-covered fence. A lot of what she said got lost in the splashing of the water, but it was Raylene's holier-than-thou voice in a tirade saying, "The little slut is dead, so what's stopping you?"

As far as I knew, there was only one recently dead little slut around here. So Raylene Carter was a member of the we-hate-Cupcake fan club. Someone replied to what she said, but it was more of a whisper, and Raylene added, "I paid a pretty penny to take care of our problem."

Paid who? About what? Where did Cupcake fit into all this? Hunched down, all I could see through the vines and fence was a pair of dark loafers. They were nice, Italian maybe—at least they looked a lot like the Italian loafers in that Nordstrom's catalog KiKi brought over—but they were roughed up, with a dark smudge on the side, and not new. Raimondo probably wore Italian loafers, especially to this affair, and with him working in the garden, they wouldn't be polished. Of course, I couldn't be sure if Raimondo wore loafers tonight since my gaze had never traveled below his derriere. But Raimondo wasn't the only guy in Savannah to wear expensive loafers.

Loafer guy walked off, and I assumed Raylene did the

same. It occurred to me that there were a lot of clandestine payoffs going on around Savannah, and Cupcake was right smack in the middle. What was she up to besides stealing my husband (among others), threatening a minister, and winding up dead?

The fountain wobbled against my shoulder. I tried to steady it, the corner sinking deeper into the mushy ground. Lily pads, cute animals, and a lot of water tipped backward toward me, and I jumped out of the way to avoid being flattened. The fountain landed with a solid thump, murdering a mound of tulips and sending a metal frog rolling off into the daffodils. My dress was soaked, plastered to me like a second skin; my strappy shoes were ruined; and the pump made dry gurgling sounds.

The music stopped; everyone stared. My wet dress was more revealing than it had been when dry, and the red-polka-dot underwear I had on underneath probably explained the arched eyebrows, a few winks, and Auntie KiKi with her hand to her forehead, Lord-have-mercy style. Raylene looked as if she might have a coronary right there under the wisteria archway.

Embarrassment inched up my neck to my face, which now, undoubtedly, matched the polka dots. Where were tighty-whiteys when you really needed them? In the wash, that's where. I crossed the grass, the crowd parting as if I had the plague. At least the deviled-egg waiter was near the door, and from the grin on his face, I'd say he was a real fan of polka dots. I grabbed an egg and mentally bid farewell to my pride and a well-stocked fridge.

Three hours later, Mr. Sayjack, city bus driver for thirty years and now six months away from retirement, let me off right in front of Cherry House instead of the designated stop at the corner. It was a probably a pity stop because I'd told him about the fountain fiasco at Raylene's and using that blow-dryer thing in Leopold's bathroom to dry my dress before I met up with my ghost tour. No need to have my polka dots on display for the half of Savannah who'd missed the show over at Raylene's. More than likely, he let me off as payback for giving him the fries from the Happy Meal I'd picked up after my tour.

I watched bus taillights fade into the dark, along with a cloud of lung-clogging exhaust. I took off my ruined sandals, which had shrunk from the fountain dousing and were now killing my feet. I had just started up the walkway when I noticed two golden eyes peering from under the porch. The eyes were too big and far apart to be a rat or even a raccoon or cat. After having given a haunted tour, my ghost senses were on high alert, but these eyes didn't seem all that eerie. I caught a glimpse of a snout. "Dog?"

I got a doggy whine in reply. What was a dog doing here? I'd tried owning a cat once, Miss Fluffy, till I gave her a bath and she tore a hole clean through the back screen door, never to be seen again.

"I don't do well with pets."

This got another pitiful whimper, so I took a McNugget from my bag and, with the tip of my ruined shoe, pushed it under the porch. Immediately, I heard chewing. Hungry. I heaved a sigh, and my heart felt a little heavy. I knew all about hungry, and the poor fella was probably scared. I could relate to both. More times than I would care to admit over the last two years, I'd pulled the covers over my head and thought, *What am I going to do now?* That's when KiKi would bring over coffee and pastries with lethal fat content, and I felt instantly better. KiKi helped me; I could help the dog.

I sat on the grass next to the steps, pushed another nugget to my guest, then stuffed one in my mouth. "You should know that things are sort of lean around here."

"Who are you talking to down there?" KiKi asked as she ambled across the yard. She had on the blue lounging robe I'd given her for Christmas last year and a cup of something hot and steamy in her hand.

"There's a stray dog under my porch."

"Uh-oh." KiKi sat down on the steps. "Maybe you should call those SPCA people. Remember Miss Fluffy?"

"What happened after I left Raylene's?" I took the mug from KiKi and sipped coffee laced with Kahlúa. KiKi had lounging down to an art form.

"Things were downright boring after you hightailed it out of the party, though they had to give Raylene a few sniffs from Bernice Clark's portable oxygen pack to keep her from fainting dead away. Raimondo fixed the fountain easy enough, and two women wanted me to ask you where you got your underwear."

"Did you happen to notice if Raimondo was wearing loafers?" A starry night peeked down at us through overhanging cherry blossoms, and the warmth from the earth kept the chill at bay. Summer wasn't far off.

"Honey, when it comes to that man, I'm not looking at his shoes. Well, except for tonight. Raimondo had on loafers, and so did Urston and Baxter Armstrong. Now there's another delicious piece of eye candy, though he sure shuns the cameras. He leaves the limelight for Trellie."

Baxter Armstrong was a blond, blue-eyed boy toy from Atlanta, the new husband of Trellie Hudson (now Armstrong), one of the richest women in Savannah. That Baxter was twenty-nine and Trellie was fifty-plus did not bother the two of them one little bit, but it rivaled the Hollis-Cupcake extravaganza for top billing on the kudzu vine.

KiKi snagged a McNugget, and that was fine by me because she left me the Kahlúa. "Putter said he wanted loafers for his birthday, and he went on pointing them out so I'd get the expensive ones and not cheap knockoffs. I told him that-there putting green we're having installed was setting us back enough, and he'd jolly well have to wait for his loafers." She took a bite of nugget. "What's this all about? Are you consigning men's clothes, too?"

"That's a good idea. Most women buy for their husbands. The shoe thing is about me overhearing Raylene and a man arguing. They were on the other side of the fence when I was working on the fountain. Raylene said she paid off somebody, and it sounded like she meant Cupcake or that she paid someone to knock her off. Hard to tell. Loafer guy's answer got drowned out by the splashing water. All I could see were his shoes, but he's involved in a big way."

"We all know nothing drowns out Raylene if she's having a hissy." KiKi took the mug. "But why would she pay off Cupcake or want her dead?"

"Boone let it slip that there's more than one person involved with the murder. We know about Urston giving Cupcake money at the Telfair. There could be a connection from Urston and Cupcake back to Raylene, especially since Urston had on loafers tonight. Maybe they both wanted her out of the picture for some reason."

I handed off the last nugget to the big, pitiful eyes beside me now instead of hiding in the shadows. "Hollis told me today that Cupcake knew secrets."

KiKi took a gulp from the mug. "Blackmail? That's my guess. I can't imagine any hanky-panky going on with Raylene and Urston. Raylene would just as soon throw herself off the Talmadge Bridge than risk a divorce and losing the Carter name and money over the likes of Urston Russell. If Urston even thought about cheating, Belinda would skin him alive." KiKi turned to me, eyes wide. "But I think you're right, something is going on, and Cupcake had the goods. Cher says, 'If you really want something, you can figure out how to make it happen.' I think Cupcake wanted money, and blackmail was the way to get it. Do you think she had the goods on more people?"

"According to IdaMae, Janelle said Hollis would make her rich, and now I'm thinking it wasn't from selling real estate. Dinah Corwin's wake tomorrow night could be mighty interesting. Best I can tell, everyone thinks Hollis did the deed, case closed. The real killer should be right comfortable at the moment and might not feel the need to keep to the down-low. The killer could very well be Dinah Corwin herself. She sure didn't make a secret of her dislike for Cupcake. If Dinah had her way, she'd be dancing on Cupcake's casket all the way back to Atlanta."

"But she has a boyfriend now," KiKi reminded me. "She seems happy, not moody and resentful. I don't think she killed Cupcake one bit. She's moved on." KiKi looked down at the snoring dog. "Worst deviated septum I've ever heard. Sounds like a freight train coming through a tunnel. Too bad he's not some cute little fluffy puppy that fits in a purse.

Purse animals are very in. I suppose you could call him Calvin Klein. Slap a designer label on anything, and nobody will mind if he hangs around."

I eyed a muddy-brown, mangled ear and scarred snout. "Poor thing. The tip of his tail's missing, and I think he's missing a front tooth. He's pretty beat up for Calvin."

KiKi scratched behind his ears. "I do believe this here is Bruce Willis in a fur coat."

"I do not need a pet."

Contented snoring sounds surrounded us. "Honey, you've done been outvoted."

I ignored the outvoted comment but knew KiKi was right as rain. Bruce and I had broken McNuggets together. It was a done deal. We'd bonded. I gave BW a reassuring pat and decided to hit up KiKi while she was feeling all softhearted. "You know, what I do need is an excuse to visit the loafer boys and check out their shoes to see who Raylene was talking to. That would be a big help, and I could do it if I had an accomplice. In fact, it would be a snap if I had someone to be a distraction while I went off to find the bathroom, got lost, and happened upon a shoe closet."

KiKi made a sour face. "How did I get roped into this? Wait, you'd actually go through Urston's shoes?"

"He's our prime suspect because you saw him pay off Cupcake for whatever reason. Tomorrow we can stop by Urston's and ask to see his rose garden because you're redoing your backyard and need suggestions on landscape."

"Uh, how many rosebushes have you seen on a putting green, but I suppose I can cook up some excuse to go see Urston. The thing is, I can't see him or Raylene knocking off Cupcake."

"We're looking for a lead; that's all there is to it, nothing more. Maybe Urston will let it slip why he was handing Cupcake money." I said this to appease KiKi. Personally I believed Urston would knock off Cupcake in a heartbeat if he had to, and so would Sissy and maybe even Franklin. Reverend or not, he was human, and people got desperate and did desperate things. I watched those *CSI* shows, and I knew if the stakes were high enough, anything was possible.

If Cupcake threatened to spill the beans, and it became common knowledge that Franklin was doing the naughty with Sissy, he'd lose his congregation, respect, and probably his family. Raylene was into something big, or she wouldn't have been having a conniption fit right there at her own garden party. She could have filtered money to Cupcake though Urston. I figure Raimondo was innocent and just happened to have on the right shoes at the wrong time.

I had suspects, an invite to a wake, and a meeting with Urston's shoe closet. Was I on a roll or what? *Walker Boone, eat your heart out.*

"What are you grinning about?"

"What time should we visit Urston?"

Chapter Seven

A THIN sliver of moonbeam slipped though the dining-room windows and splashed across the pine floor between the display of jackets and blouses I set out. I laid the dress rack I was working on across two sawhorses and finished putting in the last screw. I'd concocted the thing out of leftover wood from the upstairs bathroom project and only nicked my finger twice with the jigsaw.

The Tybee Island Country Club had a bash next week, and the Rotary Club was planning a dinner event. The Oglethorpe Society always had some charity affair on the books. Spring was a great time for party dresses and accessories, and that should translate into good business for the Fox. Besides, I couldn't sleep, and building stuff relaxed me, least it did till I heard a dog bark right outside in my yard. I guessed it was Bruce Willis but couldn't be sure since

I'd never heard Bruce bark. Footsteps made their way across the front porch and stopped at my door.

Like any city, Savannah had its safe parts and the not-so-safe parts, except the robbers, rapists, and murderers sometimes drifted out of their designated comfort zones. The front door handle turned, and I held tight to my screwdriver. I was one mean dude with a screwdriver. The door opened, and Walker Boone strolled in, my heart dropping to my toes. "You scared me to death. Ever hear of knocking?"

"It's three in the morning. Why aren't your doors locked?"

"Every window is open, and getting through a screen isn't much of a challenge. I'm not too crazy about closed-in spaces if I can help it. Besides, if I screamed, Putter would be here in a flash, waving his fearful golf club. You're up at three; why shouldn't I be? And why are you opening the door to my house uninvited at three in the morning?"

He gave me a little smile. "Your lights are on, seems like a good-enough invite to me, and I got reason to be up at this hour."

"So do I. Things need to get done around here." I suspected Boone's reason to be up and about was a lot more fun than mine and probably included a hot date, cool drinks, and . . . other pursuits. "Are you charging me for this little intrusion?"

Boone canvassed the room, touching this and that. "You got nice stuff. You need an alarm system."

"I'll add it to the list right behind food and water. I bet you don't have an alarm system."

This time Boone gave me a steely smile. "I got me." He leaned against the newel post at the end of the stairs, looking a little unkempt and a lot mysterious. "Someone's out to not only murder Janelle but frame Hollis. The body wasn't tossed in the river or under a bridge but specifically planted in the Lexus. Someone's got it in for your ex big time, and you might be in danger too; ever think of that?"

"How do you know I didn't whack Janelle and frame Hollis? I had motive. I had so much motive I could write a book on motive."

"If you were going to whack someone, it would be me."

"Now there's a happy thought to hold on to in the middle of the night."

"You're over Hollis. You've moved on, but your getting involved in this murder could be bad for your health."

"You already gave me this sermon at the party."

"It was a really nice party." He gave me a knowing look that said he didn't mean the party at all but my visual contribution to it.

I ignored him and instead paid attention to my sleazy lawyer senses that were starting to tingle. "Why are you here in my house in the wee hours of the morning? Cherry House isn't exactly on your way home." I was thinking out loud, connecting the dots to what was going on. I arched my right brow. "You know something you didn't know before, and it brought you here. You want something."

Boone sat on the steps next to the pile of bills. "Like I said, you're not stupid." He did a little shrug. "Except when you married Hollis and signed the prenup, and now you won't let me handle Hollis's case. Those things are all pretty stupid." Boone leaned forward, his forearms on his knees. If he wasn't such a rat, he'd be marginally handsome. I took another look. Nope, forget handsome—all rat.

"I was at the police station," Boone said, leading up to

something. "Janelle was knocked over the head with one of those 'For Sale' signs Realtors use. The couple she showed the place to said she intended to put a second sign in the side yard that faced Lincoln, for more exposure. The police figure that when the couple left, Hollis showed up, continued the argument from the Telfair, and killed Janelle in a fit of anger. He wrapped her in the plastic, dragged her to his car, and stuck her in the trunk with the intent of ditching the body later on. Except you borrowed the Lexus and foiled his plan."

"Why wouldn't he just ditch the body right away? And why would he take the body when he knew someone surely saw his car at the house?"

"The police say stress makes people do dumb things, and since Hollis had that fight with his fiancée at the Telfair and then killed her in a fit of anger, he was under a lot of stress. We both know Hollis didn't do the deed. Janelle's murder may not have been premeditated, but framing Hollis was well thought out. The killer took the car, counting on the fact that it would be seen and that sooner or later someone would discover the body in the trunk. Or the police would go looking for Janelle and find her there. Everything pointed to Hollis."

"Someone wants Hollis out of the way. How did the murderer get Hollis's car?"

"Janelle's purse is missing, and Hollis said she had a key to the Lexus. He said you gave it to her. The killer must have used that key to get the Lexus. He saw the car on the street. and it wouldn't take very long to steal it, load the body. and return the car. It was parked on the street, and Hollis was working in his back office. He wouldn't have seen anything, and framing him was a piece of cake for anyone who knew of the fight he and Janelle had earlier."

"That means the killer must be a man. Bodies are heavy, and you're telling me all this because . . . ?"

"I want you scared. I want you to realize you're dealing with some nut-job who can kill and carry on with life as if nothing happened. I want you to back off looking for this guy." Boone gazed around the house. "Nice place, but it's not worth winding up dead over."

I folded my arms. "This is Walker Boone being polite and considerate? You're neither, least not to me. What are you up to?"

"I'm just a lawyer doing my job, trying to find the real killer and keep you out of it."

"You're a lawyer all right, clear through. You're not here because of me, Boone. You're here because of my mother. If something happens to me while you're defending her rotten, devious, lying bastard of an ex-son-in-law, it could go badly for you when you have a case to try in her court. Guillotine Gloria may not look kindly upon Walker Boone, attorney at law."

At least Boone had the decency to blush.

"Out!" I pointed my screwdriver to the door. "If you think I'm going to back off this case for your own personal benefit, you are out of your freaking mind. In fact, it makes me more determined than ever to stay with the case. I know stuff, lots of stuff. I can find the killer and not pay you one red cent."

"This nut-job is for real."

"And so is Judge Gloria Summerside." I threw a black evening bag at his head that he caught in midair. Good reflexes from dodging bullets, knives, and the occasional baseball bat. Boone put the purse on the steps and started for the door. He opened it to Bruce Willis standing on the other side. Finally something was going right. I had a dog, a big dog. I had protection! I had Cujo! "Get him. Bite him," I ordered, clapping my hands for emphasis.

BW looked from me to Boone, grinned—yeah, BW really did grin, I swear—and jumped up with his paws on Boone's shoulders. Tail wagging, he licked his face. It was that kind of night. The only good thing was, I could now tell that Bruce Willis was indeed Bruce and not Brucette.

Boone did the scratch-behind-the-ears routine, and Bruce got back on all fours, looking happy and content and completely nonthreatening. "If this is your protection strategy, I wouldn't give up on that alarm system if I were you," Boone said as he walked out onto the porch. This time I nailed him in the back with one of my blue flip-flops. Revenge is sweet, even if it does come at the hand of a rubber shoe. Boone stopped and looked back to me, his eyes dark and serious. "Get the alarm system, Reagan. I saw someone on your porch looking in your window. That's why I stopped."

"You're just trying to scare me again."

"Yeah, I am."

And he was doing a darn good job. BW followed Boone outside, my guard dog retreating to his domicile under the porch, and Boone's silhouette fading into the dark. Who would be on my porch at night? What did he want? Breaking and entering for used clothes made no sense at all. What was going on, and how did I figure into it? Then again, maybe Boone fabricated the whole thing trying to get me off the case so he could collect his hefty lawyer fee.

* * *

THE NEXT MORNING I WAS UP EARLY WITH BAGS under my eyes and a headache from too little sleep and nightmares about obnoxious attorneys in my house. That AnnieFritz and Elsie Abbott came in through the back door with sly smiles on their faces meant they knew about my late-night visit from Walker Boone and wanted the 4-1-1.

"What were you both doing up at three in the morning?" I asked as AnnieFritz set a cinnamon cake smothered in pecans on the dining-room table next to a display of costume jewelry. Elsie put down three mugs of coffee and wandered into my kitchen for plates. I knew their kitchen, and they knew mine. KiKi wasn't the only one who had pulled me out of the depths of divorce hell.

Elsie said, "Well now, sweet pea, we'll tell you what we were doing up at the wee hours after you tell us why that handsome son-of-a-gun Boone was here. Something like that we just can't walk away from. It wouldn't be neighborly."

I swiped a pecan from the cake. I didn't want to have this conversation, knowing anything I said would be held against me in the court of gossip, but there was cake, jam, and coffee to consider. "Boone thinks Hollis didn't kill Janelle, that someone had reason to frame him, and I could be in danger since I'm Hollis's ex."

Elsie cut a slab of cake and passed it to me, then cut sections for herself and AnnieFritz. "Took a mighty long time for Mr. Boone to get out that little bit of information."

AnnieFritz parked her ample girth on an antique chair that creaked under her weight. She exchanged knowing looks with Elsie. They were bookend sisters, being more alike then different. One taught religion over at Saint Peter the Apostle, the other at Notre Dame Academy. All that talk about sex, guilt, and keeping things covered and zipped had more influence on the sisters than their horny middle-school students, and neither married. They were great neighbors, true friends, and reliable gossips. What they said could pretty much be taken as gospel. I pulled out a chair.

"So," Elsie started, "maybe you should be paying attention to what Walker Boone is telling you. Last night at the Holstead viewing, some of that Seventeenth Street gang showed up. Seems Jerome Holstead has gone over to the dark side, but even the dark side shows up to pay respects when a daddy is laid to rest. They were all downright polite, nice as can be to everyone there."

As they cased out the late-model cars in the parking lot and sized up the jewelry, I added to myself. AnnieFritz took a nibble of cake and said, "I got to talking to Big Joey right there by the open casket. I said that no man should have to wear a pink paisley tie, even when dead and gone, and Big Joey agreed wholeheartedly. Then I said how sad it was that Janelle and now Mr. Holstead both passed right sudden like. Big Joey said Janelle's demise was not unfortunate one bit, and she had it coming, and good riddance to her."

The cake suddenly tasted like glue. "You were chatting it up with members of the hood?"

AnnieFritz took a sip of coffee. "He didn't wear any hood, honey, but he did have a nice tattoo on his forearm—a heart with 'Mother F' inside. I couldn't see the whole name of his mamma because his shirt covered it, but isn't that the sweetest thing? I figured anyone who thought that much of his mother had to be a fine person, no matter what anyone said."

I considered the "Mother F" reference. Probably his mother's name did not begin with *F*, but I decided to keep this to myself. If AnnieFritz hit it off with Big Joey, who was I to interfere?

Elsie sliced more cake. "Do you think the Seventeenth Street gang knows who did in Janelle? With a comment like that, it sounds like they sure know something. Up until last night, Sister and I were convinced Hollis was guilty as sin, but this got us to thinking that the boys—that's what they call themselves, *the boys*—might know who did the deed. It would be god awful if Hollis was convicted of a crime he didn't do, no matter how much we'd like to see the scallywag rot in jail for how he treated you."

I wanted leads to the killer, but did it have to be this sort of lead? Poking around Urston's house and Raylene's garden was child's play compared to "the boys," but if the boys thought Cupcake had it coming, then they knew why. I took a gulp of coffee to wash down the cake and choked. Annie-Fritz pounded me on the back hard enough to make my teeth rattle.

"Are you okay, sugar?" She looked at her watch. "Well now, I suppose it's time to be opening this here shop of yours. Elsie and I are in need of some new bereavement ensembles. The Dunwhitty funeral is tomorrow night, and we surely can't be showing up in the same thing time after time, now can we? What would people think? That would be downright bad for our business."

By lunch I'd sold enough to visit the grocery without having to dump my purse upside down on the counter, hunting for change. I had done that last week at the Kroger store, and once was enough. I filled Bruce Willis's water bowl, promised I'd bring home the bacon or something equally tasty, and locked the door. Auntie KiKi backed the Batmobile down her drive, stopped, and I took shotgun. The plan was to head to Urston's place first to check out his shoes. KiKi said, "So what was Mr. Hunky doing at your place at three in the morning?"

"Good grief, doesn't anyone in this city sleep?"

KiKi started down East Gaston and turned onto Abercorn. "We can sleep when we're dead; right now there's stuff going on. Spill it."

I couldn't tell KiKi that Boone wanted me off the case because she already thought I was off the case, at least the dangerous part. "He saw my light on is all."

"That's the best you got?"

"I'm hungry, I haven't had lunch, and I'm off to look at Urston Russell's smelly shoes. Give me a break." KiKi pulled to a stop in front of a neat bungalow on Liberty. Even if KiKi didn't know the address, I could have picked it out. Urston may not be the most handsome of men and might be involved in something he shouldn't be, but he and the Lord above sure could grow flowers. The front yard was pure Southern garden with old favorites like Georgia Blues, mountain laurels that framed the house, a gnarled pink dogwood, and splashes of daffodils in every color and combination of yellow and white. "Mercy," KiKi and I said together in complete awe.

We climbed the mossy stone steps, which gave the house a cottage-in-the-woods feel, and used the well-worn brass pineapple knocker.

"KiKi, Reagan," Urston greeted us as he opened the door, then stood aside to let us pass. "How is Putter these days?" Urston asked KiKi, then turned to me with, "I trust your mamma is doing well."

We followed him out to the back patio, which was overflowing with more tulips, hyacinths, and clematis and a stone bench and birdbath. I asked Urston where the powder room was, then headed off as he and KiKi talked about her backyard plans. Getting lost in a small house was tough to do. I eyed the bathroom at the far end of the hall and entered what looked to be the master bedroom, covered in flowers on steroids.

The pink hydrangea drapes matched the hydrangeas on the bedspread complimented the ivy on the wallpaper and the roses in the rug. A ceramic daisy lamp sat on the dresser next to matching candlesticks. I felt a little dizzy with all the patterns till I spied a red notebook on the antique cherry desk in the corner. It was *the* notebook, the one that held all Urston's notes from judging, the notebook that said who was winning Best of Show so far. It wasn't under lock and key but sitting right out there in the open air.

Not fair. I could resist broccoli and succotash and those Croc shoes. But I never met a sandwich or flip-flops I didn't want to try out, and now the red binder had that same tempting pull. What were the scores for best garden so far? Who'd win this year? There were others on the committee making the decisions, but everyone knew it was Urston's opinion that mattered most and swayed the other judges to think as he did.

Maybe a little peek inside? What harm could one little peek do? I wouldn't blab, I could keep a secret, and it wasn't as if my garden was in competition unless tallest dandelion and most robust crabgrass happened to be categories. I picked up the corner and opened the notebook to . . . nothing? Not one note or photo or sketch or comment. Blank. No impressions on the paper suggesting other pages were written on, then taken out. What kind of judging notebook was this? Maybe a decoy, but that made no sense with it being here in the security of Urston's own bedroom.

Maybe Urston had a photographic memory and knew the gardens that well without making notes? That seemed possible, but then why carry around his notebook at all? I fanned all the pages to check for notes in the back, and a computer printout slid to the carpet. *Aqueduct, one mile, claiming purse fourteen-hundred dollars, four-year olds and up, Sally Girl.*

I was not exactly the Martha Stewart of the garden world, but even I knew this was not flower talk and that Aqueduct was not so much a Roman waterway but a racetrack.

I didn't have time to think about this now. I needed to look for shoes. I tiptoed over to the closet and figured that if flowers fell out when I opened the door, I wouldn't be surprised. When I opened the door, there was nothing but clothes and shoes like any other walk-in closet. Women's stuff on the right, men's on the left, and a pair of brown loafers on a rack below. I hunkered down, balanced Old Yeller on my knees, and pulled off the right shoe to get a look at the side. It had the telltale black smudge that I saw at Raylene's, all right. So, it *was* Urston talking to Raylene. He also paid off Cupcake at the Telfair. Raylene, Urston, and Cupcake were connected. But why? Over what? And was it enough to murder someone?

I understood that Franklin would lose his congregation and probably his wife and family if his shenanigans with Sissy got out. That gave him lots of motive to get rid of Cupcake, but what would Urston and Raylene lose?

"What are you doing in here?" hissed a female voice towering over me.

I yelped and fell back on my behind. Old Yeller slid to my chest, and I dropped the shoe on the floor. I gazed up at Belinda Russell, who looked like my third-grade teacher when I drew a devil face on her grade book. Belinda growled, "What do you think you're doing?"

I could go with the lost-in-your-house premise, except I was lying in her closet with her husband's shoes. "I'm sorry to be here without asking anyone, but my uncle admired Urston's loafers at the garden party last night, and I wanted to get him a pair for his birthday."

Belinda lips thinned. She wasn't buying it. "Urston said you and KiKi were coming over to talk about recommendations for her back gardens. You could have asked Urston about the shoes then; wouldn't that have been easier than sneaking around my house?"

KiKi was right. I needed to get better at lying. Belinda's eyes knit together in thought. "I should have you arrested; what would your mother think of that, and why does she let you run around with hair like that?"

"Raylene was talking to Urston at her party last night, and I noticed Urston's shoes is all."

Uh-oh. As soon as I babbled the words, I knew I'd given away too much information, connecting Urston and Raylene. Belinda's eyes cut to the notebook on the desk, and little red blood vessels strained in the white part of her eyes. She picked the candlestick off the dresser and shook it at me. "Get out of here, and mind your own business!"

Thoughts of Miss Scarlet in the bedroom with the candlestick flashed though my brain. "I should go."

"And don't come back!"

I pushed myself up, snatched my purse, then edged past Belinda, still holding the candlestick. "Tell Auntie KiKi I'll see her back at the shop."

"That old bat probably had something to do with you snooping around here in my house. Everyone knows you two are thick as thieves."

I felt a few blood vessels of my own start to pop. "Auntie KiKi is not an old bat. She came here for a nice visit, and I was admiring your décor and took a look at the shoes. That's all there is to it." I did the pregnant pause thing for effect. "Unless, of course, that's not all. Is there more?" This time I cut my eyes to the notebook. "Are you and Urston going to the wake at the Marshall House tonight for Janelle Claiborne? Heard tell it's going to be a real wingding affair."

Belinda's face went white, and her jaw clenched tight. "Why should we go? Dear Lord, we didn't know Janelle. Not at all, except for the Homes and Gardens Committee, of course. Just the committee."

Those were a lot of words for a simple yes or no answer. At least I wasn't the only one who babbled when nervous. Belinda following, I headed down the green hall, which was stenciled with big, white magnolia blossoms, then stepped out onto the porch. The door slammed behind me, making the pineapple doorknocker bounce. I sat on the bottom stone step, next to the dogwood, to think about what had just happened.

I knew what Cupcake had on Franklin, but what did she

have on Urston and Raylene? She definitely had something because Urston gave her money, and Raylene was involved. My guess was Raylene paid off Urston to win Best of Show. I had no proof of that, just a hunch from seeing the blank notebook.

Dinah Corwin made no bones about being tickled to her toes that Cupcake had bought the farm, but why were Big Joey and the boys overjoyed Cupcake had joined the heavenly choir? Why did they care that some uptown chickie was dead? So many questions, so few answers, and all the while Walker Boone racked up big bills I'd have to pay.

A bus stopped farther down on Liberty. I had time before the Fox reopened and could hop on down to the Piggly Wiggly and get groceries, or I could catch the bus going the other direction and visit the heartland of Big Joey and friends and maybe get some answers. I'd never take KiKi to that part of town, and I shouldn't go there either, but what the heck. It wasn't a dark night in the pouring rain, where anything could happen. It was noon, and the sun was shining, birds chirping, and not a cloud in the sky. How scary could the hood be in broad daylight? It wasn't as if I wanted to horn in on the boys' territory. In fact, I was only marginally sure there was a territory, and that hinged on gossip involving an infamous tattoo and a badass lawyer.

If Big Joey saw fit to converse with AnnieFritz Abbott he'd do the same with me, right? All I wanted to know was what Cupcake did to tick him and his buddies off. Whatever it was, a little voice added inside my head, I had to be real careful not to do the same thing. There were hornets' nests, and then there were sincere and downright dangerous hornets' nests.

Chapter Eight

"YOU'RE sure this is where you want to get off?" the bus driver asked me as she pulled to a stop at Ogeechee and Seventeenth. Shaking her head in disbelief, she looked me over head to toe. "Girl, this here is not a place where you need to be this afternoon."

"I'm doing research."

"Try Google." The hinged door wobbled closed, and the bus lumbered off in a gray cloud. I started down the street, holding tight to the theory that nothing bad would happen in broad daylight under a blue sky with spring flowers, except there was a definite absence of flowers. The run-down frame houses were surrounded by red mud and sand instead of grass, and the sun hid behind the trees. Seventeenth Street was no-man's-land empty. None of the boys were out showing off do-rags and tats. Guess they liked their afternoon nappy time to rest up for evening activities of beating other gangs to a pulp. I felt like a fish at an alligator farm.

"Yo, white woman. You lost?" said a voice behind me. Least I think that's what the voice said. I was distracted by the sensation of every hair on my body standing straight on end. I turned and faced the heart tat Elsie Abbott had described, except no shirt sleeve hid the full inscription. Pay dirt! My eyes traveled up a rock-solid ebony chest with more tattoos to the beefier, African-American version of Walker Boone. "Big Joey?"

"Who want to know?"

Some idiot from the Victorian District trying to save her house. "I was hoping you could help me."

Rocking back, Big Joey folded his arms, his biceps bulging even more. He gave me a smile I doubted he gave to Elise Abbott. "What you have in mind, and if you don't think of nothing, bet I can."

"Last night you were talking to a friend of mine at the Holstead funeral, and you happened to mention that Cupca—Janelle Claiborne wasn't exactly a friend of yours and you were glad she was history."

"You mean dead." Big Joey said the word like he meant it.

I swallowed and nodded.

"Your friend talks too much."

"You have no idea."

Big Joey took a step toward me, and my stomach jumped all the way up my throat. "I'm a friend of Walker Boone." Amazing what pops out of my mouth when I'm scared and think name-dropping might save my behind. A smile pulled at the corner of Big Joey's mouth, a gold tooth catching a stray bit of sunlight.

"You not his type. He's into classy broads, not ones with striped hair and a cheap purse." Big Joey gave a quick look around. "What's your ride?"

"That would be the Chatham Area Transit system. I've sort of fallen on hard times." I raked limp curls from my face, nervous perspiration sticking hair to my forehead and neck. "My ex is accused of killing Janelle, and he's going to sell my house to pay Walker Boone to defend him. The only good thing I got out of a marriage was that house that I've rehabbed. I need to find the real killer myself so I can keep my place."

"You're here thinking you can get me to confess to murder so you got a place to live?" Big Joey laughed through a string of swear words that would do HBO proud. This brought some of the boys out onto porches to enjoy the afternoon festivities.

"You hear things that I don't," I rushed on. "I just need a name of someone who you think might have done the deed."

"Do the murder."

"Yeah, murder."

"You are one mighty stupid woman."

This time the boys laughed. Big Joey took another step toward me. I took two steps away, sweat slithering down my back. "What if someone tried to take your car or something you valued, something you worked on to make it yours. Wouldn't you fight to keep it?"

The grin returned, along with a few more colorful expletives. "I get the point, and 'cause I do, I'm gonna tell you to get out of here instead of show you the way myself."

"What about Janelle?"

"She got what she deserved, but not from me or the boys here. She was in a bad business that caught up with her."

"Blackmail."

"And she do it to the wrong person. Make a lot of people unhappy." Before I asked another question, Big Joey grabbed my arm. I gasped. My heart stopped. He turned me around and gave me a little shove. "Git."

End of interview. The porches emptied, the boys drifting back inside, matinee show over. I headed up Seventeenth, amazed that I didn't have to sit down to keep from fainting dead away.

"Good luck with that house. Tell Boone *hey*."

If Big Joey had fired warning shots over my head, he wouldn't have surprised me more. I stopped and glanced back. "Thanks for the information." I bit at my bottom lip. "Why did Boone leave here? Why become a lawyer?" I don't know where that came from; the words just came out all by themselves.

Big Joey pulled a cigarette or something smokable from his jeans. "That best come from Boone." Joey lit up, then took a deep drag. His demeanor relaxed now, and our eyes locked across the pockmarked street. He gave me a nearly indiscernible nod. I figured the one thing we had in common, and the reason I was leaving with all body parts intact, was that we both knew Walker Boone. That didn't exactly make us bosom buddies, but we had a connection all the same.

I caught the bus, the driver as surprised picking me up at this location as the other driver had been at dropping me off. While getting chauffeured around the city, I thought about Big Joey and his band of merry men. I wasn't an authority on gangs, but I thought Big Joey was telling the truth that he hadn't murdered Janelle. There was no reason to lie to me. It's not like I was the police, so confessing to me was pretty much like bragging rights. My guess was the boys did that every chance they got—they didn't strike me as the humble type. If they did the deed—the murder—they would have gloated.

Another thing to consider was that stuffing a body in a car trunk didn't smack of gang ritual. I imagined they had far more creative ways of disposing of a body in our geographic location, which was surrounded by swamps, marshes, and an active alligator population.

On the other hand, the idea of Urston, Raylene, and Belinda wrapping a body in plastic and stuffing it in a Lexus made a certain kind of sense. It was neat, clean, and a snobby ride. I exited at Gwinnett and crossed the street to the Kroger's grocery store. I grabbed a bag of doggie kibble, a few groceries to keep body and soul together, and a Perky Blonde hair-dye kit. I hoofed it back to the Fox by one thirty. Two customers waited on the porch with clothes to consign. I apologized for being late and brewed the last bit of cinnamon coffee I had to make up for my tardiness. Happy customers spent money; at least that was the theory. Too bad today it wasn't a reality.

After they left, I went outside and looked under the porch for Bruce Willis. Two eyes stared back. I heard thumping sounds from a wagging tail hitting the ground. Bruce seemed happy. Not quite ready to give up his monastic life under the floorboards, but better. I filled a bowl with food and refilled the one with water as the sultry beat of a rumba drifted out from KiKi's house. That meant she had made it back from Urston's without the wrath of Belinda doing her in and that the couple taking dance lessons was older. My guess was the Paxtons were doing one last run-though for their twenty-fifth-anniversary shindig out at Sweet Marsh Country Club tonight. Not that I was invited. I would have been if I was still Mrs. Hollis Beaumont the third, but now instead of rubbing shoulders with the rich and mighty at the club, I exchanged pleasantries in the hood.

I stayed open until seven thirty, hoping to catch the working-girl crowd, but it didn't happen. Business was spotty, bills were due, and I had an extra mouth to feed. I needed to advertise. Problem was, advertising cost a lot of money. I ran upstairs to get ready for the wake and lose the skunk look. When gang members saw fit to comment on the condition of my hair, it must be really bad.

I draped my bathroom with an old sheet to catch splashing dye. The place was now celery green, with Irish-cream-colored tile and a claw-foot tub that I found dirt cheap over in Garden City. The room used to be rust brown, and not from a paint job but from dripping water, with old fixtures dangling precariously on a cord from the ceiling, crumbling tile, and a mildew smell that would knock your socks off.

I worked goo into my hair per the directions and spent the time needed to turn me perky blonde painting my toe-nails Hot Chili Pepper red. Somehow, before, I'd always managed to scrounge up enough money from the bottom of my purse, under my car mats when I had a car, between the cushions of my sofa when I had one of those, to afford to get my hair done by Jan, down at the Cutting Crew. Jan was a hair diva, her name mentioned in reverent tones. No one did hair like Jan. Those days were behind me. At least until I could get the Prissy Fox to turn some sort of real profit and secure Cherry House from the clutches of Walker Boone.

Forty minutes later, I jumped in the shower, shampooed, dried, then checked the mirror. I was blonde again, sort of, with the skunk stripe now the color of my old bathroom and the rest of my hair a match for Urston's doorknocker. This two-tone look never happened on those hair-dye TV commercials. There the girl swished around her newly colored locks, and some handsome dude took her to dinner in a Jaguar.

I clipped my hair up on top of my head and hoped the bicolored effect wasn't so obvious. I dressed in funeral-black capri pants and a black blouse with taupe trim. I slipped on my best flip-flops, which I saved for special occasions, to show off my new toes. The shoes were so cute, with little flowers and rhinestones. Maybe no one would notice the hair.

I couldn't hitch a ride to the wake with KiKi and Putter, because they were at the Paxtons' party—I would simply meet them there. I decided to forgo the bus, save two bucks, and walk. I started up Drayton alongside Forsyth Park, which was brimming with flowers, blooming tress, joggers, walkers, and the Confederate Monument, with soldier Archibald McLeish atop, facing north to the enemy. In Savannah, some things are never forgotten.

Streetlights flickered on as I rounded the corner onto Broughton. Up ahead was the Marshall House, with distinctive black wrought-iron railing across the second floor. The white-gloved doorman tipped his hat and said, "Good evening." I headed for the bar area, which was even more crowded than usual.

The Marshall House was a bed-and-breakfast that had

been everything from a boardinghouse back in the early eighteen hundreds, to a hospital for Union soldiers when Sherman had his change-of-address cards read Savannah. When I was in high school, the place was rehabbed. To the delight of kids and ghost tours, amputated body parts were found buried in the basement. Over the years, I've heard ghostly stores of pictures falling off walls, electrical systems failing, alarms going off in the middle of the night, guests getting locked in their own rooms, and apple pie flying across the kitchen. Wish I'd been around to see that one. All in all, the elegant Marshall House was the perfect place for a wake.

"I'm so glad you could make it," Dinah Corwin gushed, as she breezed over to me in a red dress and ruby shoes. She snagged a glass of champagne from a tray and slipped it into my hand. "Drink up, girlfriend. The wicked witch is dead."

Dinah danced between the tables of those she recognized and the regular customers, though some could have been there to celebrate as well. Hard to tell. Not everyone wanted his or her name connected with a dead cupcake. Dinah chatted with IdaMae, AnnieFritz and Elsie, and Auntie KiKi and Putter, with his golf club. I said hi to Jan, from the Cutting Crew, and suspected Cupcake had her manis and pedis done there. Sarah, from Shoes by Sarah, sat next to Jan, both with martinis in their hands and smiles on their faces. I headed for KiKi's table in the back and caught a glimpse of Sissy Collins. The reverend wasn't there, but Sissy wore a dopey smile and was obviously soused from a little too much celebrating. When she spotted me, the smile morphed into a glare. She downed the rest of her martini and hustled out the side door. I guess I wasn't loved by one and all either.

"Where in the world did you go off to this afternoon?"

KiKi asked in a rush as I sat down in Putter's chair while he refreshed his martini and talked wedges and irons with Raimondo and Baxter Armstrong at the bar. KiKi picked up a strand of my hair. "Honey, you've been striped."

"Things happen."

"To some of us more than others." She let out a resigned sigh, then leaned closer and whispered, "Why didn't you come back into the garden with me and Urston? Belinda said you weren't feeling well and had to leave right quick, but I didn't buy that little fib for one second. She lies worse than you, with her lips twitching and eyes blinking as a dead giveaway she's up to something."

KiKi glanced from side to side to make sure no one was listening before continuing. "So, did you find the scuffed loafers?"

I did a thumbs-up. "Now we know Urston and Raylene were the ones arguing at the party, and they're connected to Cupcake. There's more. Get this, I saw Urston's red notebook. *The* notebook. It was right there in his bedroom on a desk, and not locked up like we all think."

"Honey, if you didn't take a look inside that book to find out who's winning Best of Show so far, I'm having a stroke in this very chair."

KiKi grabbed my hand tightly and leaned closer, her voluptuous cleavage nearly spilling out onto the table. I prayed she had the girls pulled in tight or there'd be more celebrating going on than the end of Cupcake, and we'd have a new Best of Show right here in the Marshall House.

KiKi added, "I heard at the country club that Raylene's made reservations at the Pink House. That means she thinks she's going to win again and showing off with a fine, expensive dinner—of all the nerve." KiKi was so close our noses nearly touched. "So, is she going to win?"

"I don't know."

KiKi jolted back in her chair. "Whatever do you mean you don't know?"

I pulled KiKi back to hush-hush position. "There was nothing in the notebook about the gardens. The book was blank! If Raylene is making noises like she's a shoo-in, and Urston isn't making notes on what garden is best, then something fishy's going on in Savannah."

"I do declare. It's like maybe Urston already knows the outcome and so does Raylene? Why on earth would Urston get himself involved in such a thing?"

I said to KiKi, "Remember when you told me that Urston had a love affair with the ponies? I found a racing form tucked in the notebook. My guess is Urston's run up gambling debts and needs money, and Raylene's paying him off so her garden wins. We all know Urston is the one who persuades the rest of the judges to do things his way, and Raylene has no problem flashing her checkbook around when she wants something bad enough."

"Cupcake was part of the Homes and Gardens meetings. She must have been digging up dirt on people. She found stuff on Franklin and Sissy, and she got the goods on Urston and Raylene." KiKi giggled. "This is all mighty fine dirt, too, and we're the only ones who know."

I sucked air through clenched teeth. "Not exactly. Belinda found me in her bedroom, and I got sort of nervous and might have let it slip that I saw Raylene and Urston talking at the garden party. Now she knows that I know about the notebook and I might have figured out what Raylene and

Urston are up to. I decided to leave the premises when Belinda picked up a candlestick and looked as if she knew how to use it for more than just holding candles."

"Mercy! Cher says, 'If you really want something, you can figure out how to make it happen,' but this is going too far." KiKi plucked the toothpick out of her martini and slurped the green olive right off the end. "What ever happened to you flying under the radar? I think you just crashed and burned."

"I've asked a few questions, but being that Hollis is my ex and the prime suspect, I don't believe anyone entertains the thought that I'm after the killer. Most assume I'm happy as can be Hollis is in a mess and that he's got it coming. I bet Belinda just thinks I stumbled onto some information about the Homes and Gardens Tour is all."

"Cupcake stumbled onto that very same information and look where that got her. Belinda may not be the brightest bulb on the Christmas tree, but even she knows people don't go snooping in closets and notebooks without being up to something. Thank the Lord above you're taking all this to Boone and letting him handle things from here on out. Now you can concentrate on the Prissy Fox and stay out of trouble. It's time for you to back off."

"Back off what?" IdaMae asked as she sat down across from KiKi.

I held up KiKi's glass. "Martinis."

IdaMae's eyes laughed. "Well, she can't do that tonight. This is a mighty good party now, isn't it? I suppose I shouldn't be saying a thing like that when poor Janelle is in a big, old black hearse this very minute, careening across Highway 16 on her way to Atlanta."

KiKi quirked a brow in surprise, and IdaMae added, "Hollis asked me to take care of the arrangements. Janelle's mamma is simply too distraught to handle funeral affairs though, best I can tell, there's not going to be much of a funeral. She doesn't want the press sniffing around and asking a lot of nosy questions about the murder, and, of course, Hollis can't attend. Just plumb awful the way he was hauled off to jail like that. Who would have thought?"

"How did your house showing go?" I asked. It wasn't a very subtle change of subject on my part, but IdaMae brightened right up.

"Well, my goodness, do you believe I went and sold my very first piece of real estate? When Hollis called me about the funeral arrangements, I told him about the house. He was all atwitter. Said it was nice to have someone bringing in money, and I was pretty much running the place now. Everything's going to be better than ever when he gets home. Poor Hollis. I feel so bad for him."

Home! I pictured Hollis's town house full of dead vegetation and stinking like a swamp, all because of me. "I forgot to water his plants."

"Don't you worry about a thing," IdaMae said to me, patting my hand. "I went and got the complex manager to let me inside Hollis's place. I knew you were busy with your shop, so I took care of it. That's what I came over here to tell you."

I promised IdaMae I'd take over watering duty. I thanked Dinah for a lovely party and told KiKi I'd catch up with her tomorrow. Not everyone was at the bar for the wake, of course, with Marshall House being a popular Savannah watering hole. I said good-bye to Uncle Putter, with his trusty putter; Raimondo, taking a break from work and with withered petals by his left foot; and Baxter Armstrong, taking a break from being married and with his Porsche convertible in the parking lot. Golf was the great equalizer around here and made for eternal male conversation. Saint Peter probably played golf.

After last night's activities of building display racks and booting Walker Boone out of my house at three in the morning, I needed sleep. I grabbed Old Yeller and headed down Broughton. Traffic was heavy, with everyone out enjoying the weather. I turned onto Abercorn and ran into a ghost tour at Colonial Park Cemetery. The place dated back to before *the* war, and, of course, there was only one war talked about around here. I crossed to East Charlton, which had oaks so dense they formed a canopy overhead. Side gardens with trickling fountains, flickering gas lamps, and raised porches to avoid dust from once-upon-a-time mud streets made Savannah picture-perfect Old South.

The shadows deepened to near black, but I'd walked this way often enough to know where tree roots and lose sand made for uneven cobblestones. An open-air orange tour bus rumbled by, spouting the glories of Oglethorpe and his loyal followers, and I was suddenly yanked from behind by my purse strap and pushed into a narrow alley between two of those perfect Southern houses. I hit my head against one of the stone foundations and stumbled to the ground, getting a mouthful of dirt. My heart stopped, and I couldn't breathe. Glass and gravel dug into my knees and elbows, and all I could see were rocks and weeds. *Scream*, my brain demanded, but nothing came out.

My purse was yanked hard, no doubt to get at my money,

but I held it tight to my chest. I had about three bucks in cash, but I couldn't afford to replace my bag, even if it was a Target special. Another big tug came on the strap, but I had a death grip. I hoped that didn't turn out to be a literal description.

"Mind your own business." The voice was rough and throaty, and I had no idea who it was. I suppose that was the whole point. Footsteps hurried off, and I lifted my head as the rotten, no-good pig in a big black coat disappeared around the back of the house. I was scared, shaking, fighting to catch my breath, and thanking my lucky stars my attacker left me alone. I cut my eyes to the front of the alley where I'd nearly been purse-napped and spied another big thug coming right at me. That's why pig attacker left. There was someone else wanting a piece of the action.

Enough action! This time my vocal cords and adrenaline rush worked perfectly. I jumped up, yelling stuff that sounded remarkably like the expletives I heard over on Seventeenth Street. I charged for all I was worth down the narrow alley, swinging Old Yeller with both hands.

"Ouch! Ouch! What the heck!"

I knew that voice. Anger pooled in my gut, but I didn't think my life was in danger. I tried another swing, but my arms got pinned to my sides, rendering my purse flailing ineffective. I was flattened against the side of a house by a hard male body. Granted, it had been a while since I'd felt one of those, but I had a pretty good recollection. Slowly, I looked up and came eye-to-chin with Walker Boone.

Chapter Nine

"You scared the liver out of me!" I wanted to continue beating Boone with my purse for taking ten years off my life in sheer terror, but he had me so I couldn't move, and his stubble was sandpapering my nose. "Do you mind backing off? Do you ever shave?"

"Yes, I shave, and I do mind. You're a raving wildcat. I think you chipped my tooth."

"Well, someone just tried to mug me in an alley, then you came along, and I was overwrought." I tried to wiggle free but it was useless. "You're squashing me here."

"I'm considering doing a lot more. Why were you over on Seventeenth Street? Do you have a latent death wish? And who gave you permission to be throwing my name around?"

"For your information I wasn't throwing, more like a little toss." I ducked under Boone's arm and slid free. "And why do you care what I say, anyway?" I parked my hands on my hips in defiance. I'd had enough bullying and being scared for one day.

Boone took my hands and held them, palms up, his eyes blazing mad. "You're bleeding, and you're shaking. What happened in that alley?" He looked down. "Where are your shoes?"

"Someone tried to snatch my purse, and I sort of lost my shoes." I nodded back down the alley.

Boone handed me a handkerchief, then picked my purse off the ground as if it were a dead rat. "You got mugged for *this?* Just give them the thing next time and consider it a blessing in disguise."

I tried to grab back my bag, but I didn't have the strength. Instead I held out my hand. "Give me my bag so I can go home, okay?"

"I'll drive you."

"I'll walk."

"Not without shoes." Boone went into the alley, and I watched as he picked up one flip-flop, then the other, then came back, dangling them off the tips of his fingers. "These aren't shoes. These are things you wear in the shower at camp so you don't get jungle rot and your toes fall off."

"*You* went to camp?"

"Boot camp for badasses." He gave a slight smile as I snatched my flip-flops, with the little flowers now smashed. "Your mother sent me there instead of the slammer. I'm taking you home before something else happens and I get the blame."

Boone took off down the street with Old Yeller, and I hopped after him on one foot, then the other, while slipping on my mangled shoes. "Hey, that purse is mine, and what do you mean, *my mother*?"

"The one who gave you birth, kissed your boo-boos, and wears a black robe sans pointed hat, though there are those of us who think she keeps it in the closet next to her broom." Boone stopped by a vintage red Chevy convertible, top down, with a pristine white interior.

"I think my granddaddy Milton had a car like this," I said, giving it an appreciative once-over. "I also think there are a lot of things Mamma doesn't tell me."

"I bet that cuts both ways." I went to open the door, but Boone stopped me. "Don't get in just yet. You're really a mess, and you smell like the stairwell in a parking garage." He unlocked the trunk and pulled out a blanket, then spread it over the passenger seat. He opened the passenger door. "Try not to touch anything."

"I feel so welcome."

Boone handed me my purse, then took the driver's side and cranked over the Chevy. It was good to be safe and sitting in a nice car. The company left something to be desired, but you can't have everything. "How did you find me?" I asked as Boone headed across East Charlton. "I have a hard time believing this was a chance encounter. Are you stalking me?"

"Don't have to. You're like the cops, always around when you don't want them. Big Joey took great pleasure in telling me you paid him a visit. I thought you and I needed to chat. I heard about Dinah Corwin's wake over at the Marshall House and figured you'd go. Your auntie KiKi said you were walking home. I saw you, parked the car, and then you were gone. I took a look around, and you were facedown in the alley with someone standing over you." Boone plucked a Kit Kat wrapper from my hair. "How do you keep getting into these messes?"

"It's a knack."

"Big Joey and the boys are not to be messed with."

I turned sideways in my seat to face him. I wanted to see his reaction to my next question. Boone always knew more than he let on. "Then you tell me why Big Joey's all cheery about Janelle's demise. I can't imagine those two even knowing each other, and them running in the same social circles doesn't compute. My guess is she did something to tick him off, and Big Joey does not seem the sort to take ticking lightly."

"Why don't you just play with your little store and mind your own business."

"It's not gonna work, Boone. I know you. We've done battle for two years, and I know when you're pushing my buttons so I get all huffy and bent out of shape. Then I storm off and sulk and let you get your way." I folded my arms. "My sulking days are over, and I'm not going anywhere. Big Joey told me that Janelle went after the wrong people and that's why she's dead. That means he knows she was into blackmailing, so my guess is Cupcake was blackmailing somebody Big Joey cares about. How am I doing so far?"

Boone stopped for a light, and I leveled him a hard look. "Who was Janelle blackmailing that Big Joey would take serious issue with? You?"

Boone barked out a laugh, his dark eyes lit with humor. I'd never seen this side of Boone. As far as I knew, the only thing he ever barked was orders. It was a little unnerving to see him genuinely . . . happy? "Savannah gossips know all about me," Boone said. "Or at least they think they do, and what they don't know they make up. Blackmailing me is a waste of time." Boone sobered. "So, you think you know everyone Janelle was milking?"

"I'm working on it."

He rubbed his hand over his face, then motored through the green light. "Virgil Franklin has his faults, to be sure, but he helps a lot of people. He doesn't care if they're from the hood or the country club; he steps in and saves marriages, gets people in AA, rehab, finds kids homes, gets food on the table where there isn't food or a table. Big Joey and Franklin get along, and Joey wasn't happy when he got wind that Janelle was blackmailing him about his little . . . shortcoming. Franklin is the sacred cow around here. Hands off. Big Joey didn't kill her."

"Someone else beat him to it?"

"That would be my guess."

"Why are you telling me this?"

Boone's eyes were back to business black. "So you stay off Seventeenth Street, and if you had two ounces of sense, which I know you don't, you'd stay off this case."

Boone pulled up in front of my house and did the quick look-around. "Where's your furry friend?"

I clapped my hands, and a doggie head appeared from under the porch. "We're making progress. You're the only one he's ever come out to see."

"We badasses hang together." Boone climbed out and opened the door on my side. I stepped out and grabbed my purse. Bruce Willis trotted up to Boone and licked his hand. Boone did the ear-and-head-scratch ritual.

"I don't believe this. He doesn't come out from under the porch for me, and *I* feed him."

Boone climbed back into the Chevy, then pulled away from the curb. He stopped and looked back. "He likes hot dogs. He's been living out of Dumpsters and needs a break from all the healthy crap you no doubt dump in his bowl each day. I gave him part of my dog from Dog and Deli when I was here last night. We bonded."

"How much is Hollis's bill so far?"

"Beats me—I suck at accounting."

"Boone."

"What."

I had to do this no matter how much I didn't want to. I took a deep breath and clenched my fists at my sides. "Thanks for showing up tonight."

"Now, was that so hard?"

"Yes!"

He gave me a little salute. "Remember to lock up."

He sped off, and I switched my attention to the traitor at my side. "A hot dog? I give you Science Diet at thirty-five dollars a bag while I eat cheese sandwiches. You eat healthier than I do, and then you spoil it all with a hot dog?"

Bruce smiled up at me, tail wagging. "I try to be a good doggie mommy and this is what I get?" There was more tail-thumping happiness. Defeated, I started up the steps, and Bruce reclaimed his perch under the porch. At least he came out once in a while, even if it was for artery-clogging food.

I went inside and switched on the lights. As I stood in the hall I smelled . . . dog poop? Except Bruce was outside, and I was diligent about scooping. Oh for the love of . . . *I* was the one who smelled like dog poop, and this was my favorite blouse because it didn't need ironing. Maybe my shoes had been defiled? My capris? No, I loved these capris! I unbuttoned my blouse, slid off my pants, and tossed them out on the porch, followed by my flip-flops. I bet Cupcake never had these kinds of problems. Then again, Cupcake was dead. She had serious problems; I was just relegated to my bra and panties. Things could be worse.

I wiped off my Old Yeller, one of the joys of shiny plastic, and scrubbed myself under a steaming shower till the hot water conked out. Exhausted, I fell into bed but was instantly wide awake. Did I remember to lock the doors and close the windows? Of course not. I never did these things. I dragged myself off my nice comfy pillow-top mattress, something dear old Hollis left behind that I could actually use, and made my way downstairs. I secured everything that had a bolt or latch and even wedged a chair under the back door-knob for extra protection. I pulled the blue gingham curtains closed so no one could see in.

I kept two lights burning, in the dining room and kitchen, then got out my trusty baseball bat. I sat on the second step next to my bill pile and stared at my neat little shop, not really seeing the clothes, shoes, and jewelry. I didn't want to think about what my purse snatcher said tonight, but the words kept running around in my head and wouldn't go away. I wasn't all that well versed in the behaviors of muggers, but I was willing to bet that "Give me your money" fit the profile of a purse snatcher a whole lot better than "Mind your own business."

My mugger wasn't a purse snatcher. I'd ruffled someone's feathers, and considering my activities these last few days, that covered a lot of territory. If Boone hadn't come along when he did, who knows what would have happened in that alley. Someone wanted me to stop snooping around. It could have been Urston or Raylene or, more likely, someone they hired. Maybe it was Sissy, and she waited for me after the wake? Big

Joey and the boys didn't want me hanging around for sure, but as far as I knew, a black trench coat didn't fit with typical gang garb. Somehow I'd gotten close to finding Cupcake's killer, and this was a warning shot over my bow to back off.

Whoever it was meant business, and sitting here on the steps alone in the semidark with just a baseball bat gave me a bad case of the willies. I had to get a phone, and I'd have a little woman-to-dog talk with Bruce Willis about guard duty and not falling for every guy who wagged a juicy hot dog in his direction.

AT NOON THE NEXT DAY, AUNTIE KIKI HUSTLED through my back door with two glasses of sweet tea and stopped right in the middle of the kitchen, eyes bugging. "Lord have mercy. Every day you look a little worse, honey. What in heaven's name happened this time?"

"I had a run in with a purse snatcher."

KiKi plopped the glasses on the counter and clutched her bosom. Scarlett O'Hara couldn't have done it better. "What is this world coming to? Are you all right?" KiKi took in my scraped knees and hands, then gave me an auntie hug, patting me on the back like she did when my soccer team lost the state finals.

"It's just a phase," KiKi soothed. "Ever since Cupcake came on the scene, things have been a mite rough for you. But it'll get better; you just wait and see. Walker Boone came looking for you last night at the Marshall House; did he ever find you?"

"He's the one who scared off the mugger."

"Why, see there," KiKi beamed as she let me go. "Things

are better already. Boone did you a good turn for a change, and who would have thought that would ever happen?" Her brow furrowed again. "But is there some particular reason why you're all splattered with yellow paint?"

I led the way to what used to be my pantry off the kitchen. "Ta-da," I said as I opened the door to sunshine-yellow walls, a cute vintage crystal light fixture salvaged from one of the bedrooms on the third floor, and a gilded cheval glass from the attic.

"How did you do this? You hate getting into little places."

"I left the door open, and since I have no food to put in here, I decided to make it into a dressing room for the customers, *if* I had customers." KiKi and I listened to a house void of shopping noises.

"You know," KiKi said in a sympathetic auntie voice, "you could sell Cherry House and start over. You're young; you can do that. There might be a teaching job for you out there; the city schools are always looking for substitutes. You could move in with your mamma or Putter and me. We'd all love to have you; you know that. We're family. We support each other through thick and thin."

Visions of being trapped in a classroom with a bunch of mean little kids ran though my brain, followed by more visions of Mamma's perfectly ordered house, where everything had a place and never moved. Or maybe there was Uncle Putter, darting through hallways in his boxer shorts while a wild tango vibrated up through the floorboards, with KiKi saying, "One-two-three, one-two-three."

I couldn't move in with Mamma or KiKi. There wouldn't be out-and-out bloodshed or a homicide; it wasn't the Summerside way. There *would* be dinners where I had to eat my carrots if I wanted dessert and long silences over morning oatmeal. I hated oatmeal and never understood how a carrot—a vegetable with great color—could taste like dung dunked in sugar.

"Flyers," I yelped, feeling a wave of inspiration—or was it desperation?—wash over me. "Like when we advertised car washes at church. If it works for the good nuns at Saint John's, it can work for me."

"Well," KiKi said, not sounding all that convinced, "I suppose we can try flyers to draw attention to the Fox; that's one way of doing it. Cher used sixteen changes of sequined-enhanced clothing, ten wigs, five drag queens, and a mechanical bull to get attention."

Neither of us were drag queens or had access to a mechanical bull, so, a half hour later, KiKi and I were handing out flyers I'd made on her computer.

"My feet are killing me," KiKi said as we came out of Dottie Freemont's Modeling and Finishing School. "Remind me again why I'm doing this."

"You're the one who said we support each other through thick and thin. I appreciate your help; I truly do."

"I wish my big toe did," KiKi said to me, then pointed across the street to Shoes by Sarah. "We should visit Sarah. She's a good bet for pushing a consignment shop. If gals sell their lightly worn designer shoes at your place, they're more likely to buy new shoes at hers, and I could do with some sandals that didn't give me blisters."

We crossed Abercorn, and I opened the boutique's lavender door to plush carpet, cream-colored walls, and little French chairs with tapestry upholstery. Something by Mozart played in the background. Displays of evening clutch bags, designer heels, and sporty flats dotted the store, and I spotted a pair of pink-and-white peep-toe pumps that screamed *Buy me.*

"I know you," the woman with "Sarah" on her nametag said to me as she came to the counter, where KiKi and I stood. She was dressed in the boutique uniform of white blouse and black skirt. "You were at that wake last night. You're the ex." She stared at KiKi. "You were there, too."

KiKi took off her shoe and rubbed her toe. "I was there for the martinis."

Sarah leaned across the counter and whispered, even though no one was around. "I suppose you're happy as a clam that Janelle's pushing up daisies."

"I take it you're another clam," KiKi whispered back.

"More than once that woman returned shoes with some half-baked story about them being defective and demanded another pair for free. Said if I didn't do right by her, she'd put the word out that Shoes by Sarah was a store not to do business with. Boutiques have a hard enough time as it is, competing with the mall. In this pitiful economy, we're all hanging on by a thread. I gave that little witch what she wanted, but I'm here to tell you I'm mighty grateful she's not around to bother me anymore."

KiKi nodded at the pile of shoes on the counter. "Well, someone sure enough likes your store. They have quite a selection picked out."

Sarah put her hand to her heart and gazed skyward in devout prayer. "Thank the Lord for Trellie Armstrong. That fine woman's just the opposite of you-know-who. I do declare Trellie keeps half the boutiques in Savannah afloat. She would have bought even more shoes if she didn't need to get herself presentable for her dear Baxter. She said he plays golf every day at the country club, then comes home and takes her out to dinner." Sarah winked. "On her dime, of course. Baxter sure did marry well, I can tell you that much, and Trellie got herself one fine-looking man to wake up to each morning."

KiKi looked thoughtful for a minute. "In all fairness, I have to say I've never seen Trellie happier."

"I do believe you're right," Sarah agreed with a genuine smile. "Right as rain."

After KiKi bought comfortable navy sandals and Sarah promised to spread the word about the Prissy Fox, we cut across Broughton, passing out more flyers. KiKi's blister looked red and angry even with the new shoes, so we took a shortcut home, cutting though the alley by the Marshall House. I sidestepped a loose cobblestone, and KiKi suddenly flattened me against the side of a huge green Dumpster. "Baxter," she mouthed, and pointed around the corner.

I took a quick peek. Good Lord, it *was* Baxter coming out the back door of the Marshall House! I wouldn't have recognized him in a beat-up Braves ball cap, thick horn-rimmed glasses, ragged polo shirt, and cheap Levis. Sarah had just said he was playing golf at the country club. But lo and behold, here the man was right in front of us in an alley.

I craned my neck for another look to make sure. Yep, it was Baxter Armstrong all right. KiKi stuck her head below mine. Baxter dropped a suitcase in the back of an old, rusted black pickup, then jumped in the driver's side and brought the truck to life. For a split second, his gaze landed on us. I jumped back, pulling KiKi with me as the truck tore out of the alley.

"Heavenly days," KiKi said, puffing out a shaky breath after the truck left. "Do you think he saw us? What was that all about, anyway?"

"I doubt if Baxter realized we're here. This isn't the usual stomping grounds for KiKi Vanderpool and Reagan Summerside."

"Honey, this isn't the usual stomping grounds for Baxter Armstrong either, and yet here he was in the flesh, right in front of us. Why on earth was the man sneaking out of a hotel when he should be on the tenth hole with a driver in his hand? Maybe that was Baxter's evil twin brother, like on *Days of Our Lives*. Maybe it was Baxter planning a surprise party for Trellie, and that's why he's here being all secretive. He could be working on one of the fund-raisers Trellie heads up. There could be a million reasons why he's here and not playing golf today."

"Except why is he dressed the way he is and coming out the rear entrance? For sure he didn't want to be recognized with those glasses and that hat."

KiKi bit at her bottom lip and made the sign of the cross. "I hate to even say this, but maybe he's cheating on Trellie. Do you think he really did marry her for her money like everyone thinks?" KiKi stomped her foot right there in the alley. "I like Trellie, and up until now, I liked Baxter. Every time Putter and I meet up with them, Baxter's nice as can be and so attentive to Trellie. Why is he doing this to her? What a rat!"

"Last night I saw Baxter right here at the Marshall House, having a drink at Cupcake's wake. I thought the Marshall House was his usual watering hole, and his being there was a coincidence. Now I'm not so sure. I think Cupcake might have found out what we just found out. Not that we really found out anything for sure, of course, but we have definite suspicions."

KiKi leaned against the Dumpster to rub her foot. "You think Cupcake knew Baxter was stepping out on Trellie?"

"We found out, and we weren't even looking to find out. Cupcake was on the hunt to add unsuspecting wayward individuals to her blackmail list. I think she discovered what Baxter's doing and that's why he was at the Marshall House last night—to celebrate."

KiKi held up her hands as if warding off a herd of charging cattle. "This is crazy talk. We're making assumptions that could end up hurting a lot of people. If Baxter really does play golf every afternoon like Trellie thinks he does, or even if he just plays once in a while, Putter will have the skinny on him top to bottom. Putter doesn't know what color our living room is or if we've had chicken three times in a row for dinner, but if there's a golf ball involved, he knows name, rank, and serial number."

KiKi suddenly looked happy, and with the blister situation, she hadn't smiled all afternoon. "You and I should meet Putter for dinner at the club and get this straightened out. It's crab-cake night in the dining room, and I'm dying for a good crab cake and maybe a piece of chocolate cheesecake. This is all in the interest of getting our facts straight, of course. Put on something nice and do up your hair, honey. We need to leave by five sharp."

Chapter Ten

By the time we got back home, KiKi was barefoot and saying unflattering things about every shoe ever made. She hobbled to her house to tend to her poor toe, and I opened the Fox to three new customers and Dinah Corwin waiting for me on the front porch. Dinah had on huge sunglasses, no doubt to hide the aftereffects of one too many dirty martinis the night before.

"Great party," I said to Dinah as another customer strolled through the door, making my heart do a little tap dance in anticipation of money coming my way.

"That it was," Dinah said in a weak voice as she sank into a chair. She held her head with both hands and made little gurgling sounds deep in her throat. "You wouldn't happen to have two aspirin by any chance?"

I went off to get the pills and a glass of water and collided with Chantilly, rushing in through the front door. "I almost didn't recognize you," I said, taking in her appearance. She had on skinny jeans, swanky boots, a yellow tank top with little rhinestones, and no sign of a brown uniform anywhere. "If UPS knew you looked this good, they'd give you special dispensation on wearing brown."

Chantilly laughed. "I have the day off and came over here to go shopping at the best little shop in Savannah. I'm in need of something real nice to go with this little old thing!" Chantilly thrust out her left hip along with her left hand, which sported a sparkling diamond on the third finger.

"You're engaged?"

"To the finest man on earth, I do declare," Chantilly squealed, grabbing me in a hug. "Am I lucky or what! I'm so excited I can't stand it. I wanted you to know so that you don't give up on men like I almost did."

"I am so over men."

"Nuh-uh." Chantilly shook her finger at me schoolteacher style. "You can't be doing that. I was engaged once before to a complete loser. He emptied my bank account, sold my stuff at that flea market out there by the airport, and cheated on me with Cousin Rachael and Cousin Ralph. Obviously, I didn't know my fiancé as well as I thought I did. That was two years ago, and just look at me now. Simon is different. Simon is way different. The man treats me like gold." Chantilly gave me a wicked look. "And he's gorgeous as all get-out."

She retrieved her iPhone from her purse and showed me pictures of the engagement party. The engagement ring was nice, the man nicer, but what I envied was the iPhone.

Chantilly sashayed her way over to a sexy black dress, and I went off in search of pills. When I got back, Dinah had picked out a pink sundress with a beige jacket. No matter how poorly a woman felt, she always had enough residual vitality to go shopping; it was the law of the universe.

Dinah downed the capsules and massaged her forehead a few times. "I think I might live after all." She held up the dress. "It's perfect for the interviews I have out at the country club later on, and I can wear it on my cruise. Henry, that's my new honey in Atlanta, called last night. We're going to Cabo."

She laughed, then made a face and held her head again. "I put myself in your hands. Make something match this dress."

AT FIVE SHARP, KIKI HAD THE BEEMER OUT OF THE garage, honking every two seconds for me to get a move on. "We're going to be late," KiKi said as I climbed in the car, still buttoning my navy linen skirt. It was old but one of my favorites, and navy linen with a cream blouse took you anywhere in the South in springtime. KiKi booked it down East Gaston like the devil was in the rearview mirror. "They only make so many of those crab cakes, and I've been thinking about them all day long."

"What about the cheesecake?"

"Been thinking about that, too."

"How's the foot?"

"It'll be much better once I have crab cakes and cheesecake in me. Notice how all good things have the word *cake* in them—except fruitcake. Even Paula Deen doesn't do fruitcake."

Fifteen minutes and one hair-raising ride later, KiKi

squealed into the Sweet Marsh Country Club parking lot, tossed the valet her keys along with a five-buck tip, then limped her way up the steps to the club restaurant and bar.

Sweet Marsh was one of the oldest country clubs in Savannah. It was hard to get into and easy to get kicked out of. You needed sponsors to gain admittance, social standing to be accepted, and a hefty stock portfolio over at Goodman, Sears and Young if you intended to stay around for a while. Or you could inherit membership from a dead relative the way Hollis had, though I suspected being in jail and deprived of a portfolio would have him kicked to the curb soon enough.

I wasn't in the mood for crab, mostly because I couldn't afford crab, and I hated to keep sponging off KiKi and Putter. I lied to KiKi and said I wasn't hungry. I told her I'd ask around about Baxter and meet up with her later. I pilfered cheese and crackers from the bar area, which was done up in white wicker, ceiling fans, and big palms. This appeased my growling stomach for the moment, and it gave me a chance to ask the bartender if Baxter Armstrong was at the club today. The bartender didn't know Baxter and neither did two of the servers.

If Baxter played as much golf here as Trellie said he did, then these folks would know him really well. Golf wasn't just about driving carts and hitting little dimpled balls over short grass. It was about camaraderie, being part of the *in* crowd. Golf was something spiritual, talked about in reverent tones over drinks or cussed about in loud voices, depending how your game went on a particular day. I figured golf was to guys what shopping and doing lunch was to women.

I spotted Dinah Corwin standing in the stone and

mahogany lobby, wearing the dress she'd bought at the Fox. She chatted with some of the club regulars, who were all decked out in perfect spring dinner attire. No white just yet. That didn't come till after Memorial Day, then got tucked away again after Labor Day. Rules were rules. The club was clearly a place to see and be seen, especially on crab-cake night.

Dinah gave me a little wave, then headed in my direction. "We'll I'll be, I didn't know you were a member here," she said, looking much better than when I last saw her at the Fox.

"I'm a guest, but you seem to be fitting in right well."

Dinah gazed around at the milling crowd. "Now maybe I do, but it sure wasn't that way when Janelle was alive and sucking air." Dinah leaned close. "When I first got here, no one would give me an interview for my TV spot. Janelle had spread the word that I had a bad reputation back in Atlanta. That I made people look stupid on TV and did bad interviews. My boss at WAGA was ready to fire me, until Urston and Raylene stepped up, bless their hearts. I don't think they liked Janelle any more than I did, and going against her recommendation worked just fine and dandy with them. It sure saved the day for me, I can tell you that."

If Raylene and Urston helped Dinah out, then there was a good chance Baxter did too *if* Janelle was blackmailing him. No matter what form it took, revenge was always sweet. "What about Baxter Armstrong?" I asked Dinah. "I have the feeling he didn't care much for Janelle."

"Oh, that is so true. I forgot about Baxter. He's kind of the strong silent type—you know what I mean. Once when we were talking here at the club after dinner, Janelle came over, and Baxter just got right up and left, as if she had the plague or something. Trellie and I didn't know what to make of it." Dinah checked her watch. "I have an interview with the mayor in the club's rose garden at sunset; it should be positively lovely if I do say so. This series I'm shooting here in Savannah will be great for my ratings. Janelle's demise came at the best possible time. It put her under a cloud of suspicion, and the ugly rumors she spread about me don't matter now. I have more interviews than I know what to do with. I better find my cameraman and get things set up for the mayor."

This was one of those times when I was right and wanted to be wrong. None of the employees at the club knew Baxter, and that meant he wasn't at the club playing golf. Baxter gave Dinah an interview, meaning he knew Janelle for the evil person she was. It seemed to me that Cupcake was blackmailing Baxter because she had evidence he was sleeping around. She probably threatened to tell Trellie, and if Trellie found out, she'd divorce Baxter. That meant bye-bye expensive wardrobe, designer salons, and red Porsche convertible.

I took a second swing around the cheese and cracker tray, then hid behind a row of potted ferns to scarf down my dinner. Most people took one dainty cube of cheese to have with their wine, not a plateful piled high. I bit a chunk of cheddar off a toothpick with red plastic ruffles on the end and noticed a small plaque in the spiky pink fern pot that said "Tillandsia Fasciculata—Plants maintained by Raimondo Baldassare." I didn't envy Raimondo taking care of greenery with points, even if they were pretty and pink. Raimondo was scheduled to start work on Uncle Putter's backyard sometime this summer. I smiled in anticipation. Lord knows

I couldn't afford Raimondo, but I'd get the benefit of watching the Italian hunk run around KiKi's yard, digging, pruning, sweating, and—

"Why are you grinning like a lovesick cow?" Boone asked. I jumped and yelped in surprise, dropping my little plastic plate of goodies. Heat inched up my neck and settled in my cheeks at being caught by Walker Boone, eating cheese behind a potted plant.

"Hungry?"

I bent down and scooped up the mess. "This was dinner."

Boone bent down beside me. "Let me buy you a real dinner."

I had a dream where I was naked, running down Bay Street, and far less embarrassed than I was at this moment. "What do you want? Why are you here? How did you get into this place?"

"I'm a member."

"You have on jeans; they never let people in here with jeans."

Instead of an answer, we stood, and Boone gave me a little shrug along with a smug smile. He took my plate, handed it off to a passing waiter, and nudged me back into the nook of palms. "I just had an interesting talk with your auntie KiKi. We were watching the mayor's interview. Nice woman, your auntie. She cares a great deal about you. She wants the best for you."

Uh-oh. I had a bad feeling in the pit of my stomach where this little speech about the virtues of KiKi was headed and it was all downhill.

"Imagine my surprise," Boone pushed on, his voice low,

"to find out that you and I are working together. KiKi said you were meeting with me about who the real killer is and that you have some good leads." Boone stuffed his hands in his jean pockets and rocked back on his heels. "Want to tell me about those great ideas?"

"At hundreds of dollars an hour, I can't afford to tell you anything. I'll take my chances finding the killer on my own, thank you very much."

"Unless the killer finds you first. My guess is that's what the mugger in the alley was all about. Charlton Street isn't exactly a hotbed of burglars and thieves around here. You getting dragged into the alley smacks of a warning to back off whatever you're doing. Maybe you should listen."

"Would you listen?"

"I'm not you." Boone's cell chirped, and he answered it, his unreadable lawyer face firmly in place. He was good at that except for those times when his eyes got all mysterious or his hands balled into fists at his side like they were doing now. Something was up in lawyer-land, and if it got a reaction from Boone, it was serious.

"What?" I asked as he disconnected.

"That was the police. Hollis's town house was broken into. Someone picked the lock, and the place is turned upside down. The caretaker saw a flashlight darting around inside and called the cops."

"My guess is it's somebody looking for Janelle's blackmail information."

Boone arched a surprised brow. "Information?"

"Incriminating pictures, letters, tapes, whatever. Any blackmailer worth two cents has that info stashed somewhere. There must be a lot of people looking for that stuff.

If it falls into the wrong hands, the people being blackmailed keep getting hit up for money, even with Janelle out of the picture. The killer would want to make sure he's not discovered. I bet that's some interesting pile of information."

Boone peered at me hard. "You're like a ten-year-old driving a Ferrari. You have no idea what you're getting yourself into. You're digging up critical information, and people aren't going to sit by and watch you make mincemeat of their lives. If just one of the people being blackmailed realizes you're looking for dirt on him—or her—he will want to stop you any way he can. Get out of this now, Reagan, before it's too late. Tell me what you know, and I'll take it from here."

"You think I know things you don't?"

"You live between the dancing kudzu vine and the gossip girls. Rumors aren't exactly hard evidence, but it's a good place to start looking around." Boone folded his arms. "We can work something out."

"Oh yeah, like with my divorce? I remember how that worked out. You got all the money; I got all the grief. This is not divorce part two. I'll see you at the town house."

"Why do you want to go to the town house anyway? What do you think you'll find? If the intruder got what he was after, the deed is done."

"And if he didn't, that something is still there. I'm not giving up, Boone," I said, keeping my voice low so as not to draw attention. "Someone is after whatever Janelle had on him. The question is whether this person found what he was looking for. If the dirt isn't at the town house, where is it? A safe-deposit box? At Hollis's office? Buried out at Bonaventure Cemetery next to the statue of little Gracie?"

"Keep this up, and that's were I'm going to find you."

"Not if you wind up there first. You're not Superman, you know." His brow arched, suggesting some would disagree. My guess is they were all women. "If someone is upset with me digging around, they feel the same way about you."

"But I'm not the one who got dragged into the alley." Boone took the steps out to the parking lot. He was on his way to the town house, and I probably wouldn't get there for another hour. I needed to make up an excuse to KiKi for not hanging around and then find a ride. I wondered when the crime lab would be done with Hollis's Lexus; I could really use that Lexus. Gas for it was another problem.

TWO HOURS LATER, I TRUDGED UP THE SIDEWALK TO Hollis's town house, on East Macon. I'd hitched a ride with one of the beverage distributors who'd made an emergency run out to the club with more Moon River beer. It was an unpardonable sin to run out of local brews, and Moon River was the beer of choice no matter if you were drinking out at the country club or at Wet Willies down on River Street.

A steady breeze kicked up from the east; a rainstorm was brewing off the coast. We'd have a downpour by morning. The air felt chilly with the last touch of winter, the dampness seeping into my bones and making me shiver. Linen looked great in the day but didn't offer much warmth at night. There were no cop cars or Boone's '57 Chevy parked out front, and 3080 East Macon wasn't decorated with crime-scene tape. Breaking and entering was small potatoes in the smorgasbord of Savannah crimes.

I took the bricked walkway, flanked by boxwoods,

azaleas, and a blooming pink dogwood. I fumbled around in Old Yeller for Hollis's keys, which I carried with me for watering purposes.

"I'm the caretaker around here. Can I help you?" said an unfriendly voice behind me.

I turned to face a tall, youngish man who apparently didn't see the necessity of shaving but sure did see the necessity of working out. The guy was ripped. He gripped a crowbar in his left hand and a Budweiser in the other. Not a great mix from my viewpoint.

"This is my ex's town house," I said to him in a sweet little-girl voice. "I'm sure you know it was broken into. With Hollis being in jail and all, I was checking to see if anything was missing."

"You mean besides his fiancée? Do you think he killed her? She sure was some hot babe—I'll tell you that." Ripped guy gave me the male once-over that said I wasn't a hot babe, but I must have looked harmless because he unlocked the door.

"Thanks."

"That attorney guy was here earlier," the caretaker said as he pushed open the door. "He told me if a woman with striped hair showed up to let her in. That's you. Not many women with striped hair. Said if I didn't let you in, you'd break a window. I've got enough to do around here without fixing windows. Lock up when you're done, and don't break anything else."

The place was dark, except for streetlights slipping through the shades. Feeling along the wall, I flipped the switch, and two broken lamps on the floor came to life. A security box with a keypad sat next to the bank of light switches in the entrance hall. Why didn't the intruder get caught by that? Then I considered the fifty-bucks-a-month activation fee that went with the system, and the fact that Hollis was strapped for money.

I wondered if Hollis was too strapped to have a cleaning lady. The place was a holy mess. Somebody was sure after something, with drawers upended, cabinets overturned, cushions sliced open, and stuffing strewn everywhere. Molting season at a chicken farm, not that I'd ever been to a chicken farm, but I bet this was it, only with better furnishings. A short hall led past a laundry room to the master bedroom, which was in even worse condition, with a butchered mattress, chairs the same, a ripped-apart area rug, and overturned nightstands.

The walk-in closet was untouched and had one of those built-in systems with drawers, shelves, and racks. Either the intruder found what he was looking for or he was interrupted. I recognized the two wood crates on the floor across the back as Uncle Cletus's gun collection. On the right side of the closet, Hollis's suits hung on wood hangers, all facing the same direction, an inch and a half apart. His shoes were perfectly polished and poised with the right one first, then the left; belts in neat coils; shirts fresh and folded from the cleaners with only the first two buttons fastened. During our married years, Hollis spent hours in his closet. The term *inner sanctum* took on a whole new meaning.

Cupcake's side of the closet seemed more real, with dresses mixed in with jackets, sweaters more tossed than folded but still orderly. I felt a little weird looking though Cupcake's life like this. She was far from being my BFF, but she was dead, and some respect went with that. I made the sign of the cross for Cupcake, then heard the front door open. I made another sign of the cross, this one for me. I grabbed one of Cupcake's stilettos, the most lethal thing I could find in the closet, unless I suddenly came across a crowbar to uncrate the guns.

I picked my way around the flipped-over nightstand, then over an ironing board. An ironing board? Cupcake ironed? No wonder Hollis wanted to marry her. My foot caught on one of the ironing-board legs, and I reached for something to catch myself but fell onto the nightstand with a solid, bruising *oomph*.

The lights in the living room went out.

Not good. "Hello? Boone? Is that you?" Maybe he came back to do battle with me on coughing up what I knew abut the murder. Except Boone would not turn off the lights, or if he did, he'd turn them on once he heard me call his name. The place stayed dark and dead quiet—bad choice of words under the circumstances. I had two choices. I could stay out of harm's way and find out nothing or sneak a peak and add another name to my list of suspects. Hiding had definite appeal, but I hadn't ridden two hours in a stinking beer truck for nothing. Quietly, I pushed myself up, threaded through the rubble, and made my way out into the hall. So far so good, until someone shoved me down, then dashed for the front door. I staggered to my feet and stumbled outside to a white horse-drawn carriage with lovers cuddled in the back and a pub crawl meandering its way from The Lion's Den down on Bull Street up to Pinkie's on Drayton.

Where did he go? It was definitely a he, or a woman on steroids. And whoever it was probably wasn't the killer, or he would have done more than just shove. Lush landscape circled the building to the back, giving the intruder a good hiding place and a way to escape. He could have also fallen in with the pub crawlers, who were too drunk to know if someone had joined their group. I ran my fingers though my hair in defeat and fought the urge to scream. Bruised shins and a long beer ride for nothing.

A red '57 Chevy convertible, top down, pulled up to the curb. Boone had company; a tall blonde with heavy makeup and a red-sequined dress occupied the passenger seat. She was just his type, with enough boob to attract attention from fifty paces and lips red enough to stop traffic at every intersection. Boone tapped his watch. "Took you long enough to get here."

"You could have given me a ride, you know."

"I hoped you'd come to your senses and stay away. I've got to get Conway here to work; his car died. I'll be back in a minute."

"His?" The word slid out before I found the good manners to keep it in. Normally, my social graces were better honed, but my life hadn't been normal in quite a while and showed no signs of improving in the near future.

Conway gave me a big wink, a wide grin, and a little finger wave, complete with flawless manicure. "Hello there, dollface. I'm Cinnamon Sugar."

Drag queen. A very well-made-up drag queen. Club One over on Jefferson had the best drag show in three states, made infamous by that *Midnight in the Garden of Good and Evil* book. Cher was right-on about drag queens being much better at getting attention than flyers ever could. I said to Cinnamon Sugar, "Great nails. What polish do you use?"

"Come around and see me sometime, honey, and I'll give you a bottle. I get it made up special."

I said I'd try and make it to a show, told Conway to break a leg, and then Boone sped off. I didn't want to be here when Boone came back, but I needed to look around the town house. I figured the intruder was hunting for evidence and probably hadn't found it or he wouldn't have come back a second time. I didn't see him, but maybe I could find what he was looking for. Least it was worth a shot.

I went back inside and surveyed the wreckage. The only way to find anything was to straighten up. It irked me to clean Hollis's love nest, but kicking around stuffing and broken furniture and dishes wouldn't get me anywhere. Righting the leather couch was out of my league by about fifty pounds, and thank heavens the three big plants and the Eastlake secretary that Hollis's uncle had given him were all still standing and unharmed. Not only were they the heaviest things in the place, but also hands down the most expensive.

I set up chairs, the coffee table, and matching end tables and balanced the broken lamps between books that I picked up off the floor. I piled ruined cushions by the door to take out later, then found a broom and swept up broken pieces of Moss Rose china—Grandmother Summerside had the same pattern, which she used every Thanksgiving and Christmas—magazines, junk from drawers, glasses, smashed DVDs and . . .

Glasses?

I stopped sweeping and stared down at the pile. Hollis didn't wear glasses and neither did Cupcake, least not these glasses. They weren't those cute half-size yuppie glasses for reading expensive menus; they were big and thick. I stooped down. They were horn-rimmed. Holy mother of pearl—I knew these glasses!

The door opened. "Reagan? You still here?" came Boone's voice from the entrance hall. I slid the glasses into my skirt pocket and stood.

"What's going on?" Boone asked as he came in.

"Nothing," I said too quickly, sounding guilty as all get-out. I tried to smooth things over with, "You try cleaning up your ex's place and tell me how it feels. It's a little unnerving."

Boone flipped up the couch as if it were a toy. He sat on the overstuffed arm, staring off into the room, thinking who-knows-what. I took the opposite arm, thinking about my cheese and crackers back at the club.

"You suppose whoever did this found whatever Janelle had on them?" Boone asked in an offhanded manner.

"He didn't, because the person who picked the lock and let himself in came back while I was here. I figure he wanted to take another look around because he didn't get the job done on the first pass, and the chances of two different people coming to the town house on the same exact night are slim to none. I'm telling you this because you saved my bacon in that alley, and now we're even."

Boone gave me a long, steady stare. I'd surprised Walker Boone and was willing to bet that didn't happen often.

"Did you see who it was?"

"If I tell you anything else, that would make us uneven, and I sure don't owe you that much."

"You should tell me everything."

"I can't afford you."

"This person had a reason for coming back. He had to get something out of here right now, or maybe he found what he was looking for and didn't get a chance to get to take it."

Boone stood, walked around the room, then stopped in front of me. "I don't know if you saw this guy or not, but I got a real bad feeling he saw you. Whoever broke in here may be the killer. All the people being blackmailed are desperate to get back what Janelle had on them and make sure no one else gets that information. That puts you right in everyone's crosshairs."

A little shiver crawled down my back, and it had nothing to do with the temperature outside and everything to do with the too-quiet tone of Boone's voice. He tucked his finger under my chin, tilting my head, our eyes meeting. His were black and serious. "I told you to back off. That your house isn't worth the risks, but that ship has sailed. Too many people know you're involved in this case, snooping around and unearthing God-knows-what. You're in this up to your armpits."

"Hey, so are you."

"Yeah, but I have resources. You just have Auntie KiKi. Go home, lock your doors, and don't come out till this is over. Someone's out for blood. Yours." Boone turned for the door.

Chapter Eleven

"**Y**OU'RE not going to scare me off," I yelled after Boone, the door closing behind him. I picked up an already cracked plate and threw it against the door, smashing it into even smaller pieces. What was this about blood? I looked at my scraped hands. I did not need more blood.

I took the horn-rimmed glasses from my pocket, gaining some confidence that I knew things Boone didn't. Baxter Anderson had been here in the town house tonight. These glasses were distinctive, memorable, and fearful ugly. What was the man thinking? Considering Baxter's usual attire, I would have thought he'd have better taste even when traveling incognito.

I didn't have enough energy to go on cleaning and looking for evidence, whatever it was. Truth be told, it was a little creepy being in the town house all alone after Boone's speech. Baxter knew I was here. He knew I might have seen him, and I probably had his glasses, the ones he dropped. If he did see me and KiKi that day at the Marshall House coming out the back entrance, he knew I could connect him to his clandestine female activities there. I could tell Tillie, and that could lead to divorce court and end the easy life as he knew it.

I dropped the glasses in Old Yeller, flipped off the lights, and stepped out onto the stoop, hoping to feel safer in the company of traffic and late-night walkers. Except the wind blowing through the trees and lightning flashing over the ocean had chased everyone inside. The streets were deserted, with only an occasional car, the carriages and tour buses calling it quits. Leaves somersaulted across the sidewalk, and flowers tossed their heads in all directions. I could wait for a bus, but they only ran every hour or so this time of night, and a storm was brewing. It was about a fifteen-minute walk to Cherry House, fifteen lonely minutes, and I did it in ten, walking mostly in the street, avoiding shadows, listening to the wind blow though the trees.

Home looked especially good as I trudged up the walk. I took a hot dog I'd gotten at Parkers and put a chunk of it on the steps. I clapped my hands. "Look what I have, Bruce Willis," I singsonged. "Come and get it, the big surprise."

Bruce stuck his nose out from under the porch, spied the hot dog, then came all the way out and scarfed it down. I put another piece on the next step and Bruce ate that, then the next step, and all the way across the porch to the front door. "You wait right here." I handed off the last bit of hot dog. "I'll be back."

I got a blanket in hopes of enticing BW to stay on the porch as my four-legged alarm system, but when I got back outside, there was no doggie. I looked in his usual residence, finding two eyes and a thumping tail. "What happened to being man's—and woman's—best friend? What happened to protecting your turf?" I patted the steps. "This is your turf."

Thunder rumbled in the distance, and another gust tangled my hair around my face. "I'm your turf. I'm the hand that feeds you." I scratched him behind the ears. "See you in the morning, big boy. Bite anything that moves."

I went back inside, turned on every light, and locked and braced the back door. I curled up in a chair by the front door with the baseball bat as a pillow and my Old Yeller beside me as a backup weapon. It occurred to me that my life was not improving. It also occurred to me that I was still living in the house I loved, and for the moment, that seemed good enough.

SUNLIGHT STREAMING THROUGH THE WINDOWS IN the dining room proclaimed it was morning. I tried to unbend myself from the chair. My left arm had that tingly feeling from being squashed, my neck wouldn't straighten, and my head was listing to one side. I looked like a Picasso painting, probably the blue period. There was a knock at the front door, and I opened it to Auntie KiKi with her arms folded, foot tapping, her eyes glaring holes right though me. "Good, you're up and dressed," she huffed. "I'd hate to be yelling at you in your pj's. Want to tell me what's going on with you and Boone?"

"You'll have to narrow it down a bit." I stood back to let Auntie KiKi inside.

"How about the bit where you looked me right in the eyes

and told me you shared information with Boone, that you were letting him take the lead in snagging the real killer. That you were backing off of Hollis's case. When I saw Boone at the country club last night, he had no idea what I was talking about. I felt like a fool."

"I didn't want you to worry, and I knew you would." KiKi and I sat on the stairs. "I think I know more about who may be the killer than Walker does. I can find him quicker, and I don't charge three hundred bucks an hour to do it."

"Great. Your savings can buy your tombstone."

"He ticked me off. He said he could take care of things because he has resources and I just have you. He called you the dancing kudzu vine."

KiKi's eyes shot wide open. "He called me what!" KiKi jumped up, all five feet five inches shaking in outraged indignation. She poked herself in the chest. "I do declare, who does that middle-Georgia redneck think he is, talking about me that way?" Her eyes got beady. "I did gigs with Cher, I danced the rumba with Arthur Murray, and I married Putter Vanderpool the fourth and helped put him through medical school by giving dance lessons." She jutted her chin. "I'm KiKi Summerside Vanderpool and I am not a 'just.' "

Uh-oh. I'd wanted to get Auntie KiKi's support so she wouldn't pressure me into handing the case off to Boone. I thought she might be ticked that Boone had downplayed our abilities, but I hadn't counted on an out-and-out hissy fit. I took Auntie KiKi's hand. "That's pretty much the way he makes me feel all the time. You'll get over it."

KiKi swiped her hand back. "I will not get over it, and no one picks on a Summerside without spoiling for a fight." She jabbed her hands to her hips. "The way I see it, we got ourselves a pretty fair list of people who wanted Cupcake dead. Now we figure out which one did the deed, and we tell the police. To do all that, we need sticky buns and pecan coffee. The brain works much better with a good old sugar rush."

She pulled me up, my joints not happy about moving. "And I got both at my house right this very minute."

I followed KiKi out my door to hers, surrounded by yellow buttercups and purple wisteria. I brought the blue-enamel coffeepot and Spode cups to the table, KiKi snagged the sticky buns from the antique pie safe in the corner. Even as a kid I thought a safe for pies had to be the best idea ever—as long as I had a key, of course.

KiKi got a pen and paper. Things were getting serious if lists were involved. There was no way I could get my dear auntie to back out of finding the killer now, but Boone was right in that it was dangerous. I didn't mind putting myself in harm's way, but it wasn't right to do that to KiKi. If I lost my house, that was one thing, but if anything happened to my auntie . . . Well, that simply wasn't an option.

KiKi plopped two cubes of sugar in her coffee, gave a quick stir, then picked up her pen, which had a little plastic tulip sticking out of the top. At KiKi's house, nothing was simple; everything was a bit over the top.

"For suspects so far we have Urston and Raylene, Sissy and Franklin, and Dinah Corwin." KiKi stopped writing. "I forgot to ask, did you find out anything at the club about Baxter? Is he playing golf like Trellie thinks he is, or is he playing bedroom bingo over at the Marshall House like we think?"

I took the pen and paper and added Baxter Armstrong.

"The bartender and servers had no idea who Baxter Armstrong was, and there's more. Last night Hollis's town house was broken into. My guess is by one of the people Cupcake blackmailed. I went over there to look around and found—you're going to love this—horn-rimmed glasses."

"Baxter's!" KiKi said in a gasp.

"How many people have you seen in glasses like that? Hollis wouldn't be caught dead in the things, and they surely aren't from Cupcake's accessory drawer."

"Well, blast his cheating hide!" KiKi fanned herself with a yellow napkin. "Cupcake found out Baxter was messing around with other women and blackmailed him." KiKi sat back in her chair, took a bite of sticky bun, and said around a mouthful, "I don't rightly know what to do now. This will break Trellie's heart if she finds out, and you know she will."

KiKi finished chewing, her eyes fixed in deep concentration. She slapped her palms on the table, making the paper, pen, and me jump. "We should tell that lily-livered cheater that we know what he's doing, and he needs to put a stop to it right this very minute."

"He could be more than a blackmail victim," I added. "He could be the killer, and if we confront him, he could add us to his list."

"Trellie was there for me when my daddy passed, and I remember when her Frank dropped dead so sudden-like on the sixteenth hole over at Sweet Marsh. She was so sad that I didn't think she'd ever get over it, and then she met Baxter, and the twinkle was back in her eyes. I can't let her heart get broken all over again, now can I?" KiKi stood up. "First thing we'll do is follow Baxter and see what he's up to, and then we knock some sense into him. Go get your bat."

This was like trying to stop a runaway train.

KiKi added, "You need to get the Fox ready for the week. While you're doing that I can follow Baster." Her eyes got steely, just like the time she set her mind to do the 5K walkathon for breast cancer. That she hobbled around for months after was of little consequence.

"You have to call me every hour and check in, and we confront Baxter together, remember that word—*together*. There's safety in numbers."

"Honey child, calling's going to be a mite hard since you don't have yourself a phone, now do you. Maybe you can use Hollis's; he doesn't have any use for it."

Duh! Hollis's phone. All this time I hadn't even thought about that option. "I'll run down to his office and see if it's there and call you with the number. I'll close the Fox at noon, and we'll meet up then."

"I have a tango lesson at one, so you can take my place following Baxter, and I'll go on back home." KiKi pursed her lips. "You know, I truly can't see Baxter Armstrong as the killer. If he was, he'd have knocked off Trellie by now for the money."

"How do we know she's not next on his list?"

KiKi made the sign of the cross, and I left her with that less-than-happy thought and went back home to grab a quick shower. I needed to get to IdaMae for the phone before I opened the shop. I pulled on my last clean pair of underwear, the ones I liked least, the ones that had lost their elastic zing and now classified as droopy drawers. I slipped into jeans too tight from eating too many sticky buns. Bruce Willis's bowl sat on the second step, and I filled it with food mixed with a hot dog. With a little luck, he'd stay on that step, and sooner or later I'd work him up to watchdog position. I clapped my hands. "Come and get it, boy."

Bruce charged out, eyed his bowl, and chowed down, looking like me and cranberry stuffing at Thanksgiving. I didn't like cranberries but suffered though them to get to the rest of the stuffing, which was simply sublime.

At the office, IdaMae was typing away at the computer but at Cupcake's desk. IdaMae had two pink African violets in full bloom, a candy bowl, a caddy of matching pens, and a framed picture of her cat, Buttercup.

"Reagan, honey!" she gushed. "You look lovely today, I must say."

"Truth be told, you're the one who looks lovely."

"It's the hair." IdaMae blushed and fluffed her soft curls, now a honey blonde with subtle highlights. "I went to that Cutting Crew place Janelle frequented, and they fixed me right up. They didn't have much good to say about Janelle—I can tell you that."

"And new lipstick and makeup?"

"Those Clinique girls out at the mall know their stuff. I got new shoes." She stuck out her foot from behind the desk. "Sensible but stylish, that's what the lady at Macy's said. I figured I best be looking professional if I'm in charge of the office till Hollis gets himself back home. I have to spruce myself up if I'm showing houses and all." She held up a big, black handbag. "Put all my real-estate stuff in it and keep it right here by my chair. I can grab it and go."

I held up Old Yeller. "I keep my bag on the counter at home for the same reason. Hollis is lucky to have you on the job. With him not being here, I was wondering if I could use his cell phone. I'm financially distressed at the moment."

The light went right out of IdaMae's eyes, and she rested her head in her hands. "Oh dear me. How could Hollis end up in jail of all places? To make things even worse, his town house got broken into. Who would do such a thing? That nice caretaker came all the way over here to tell me. He changed the locks and dropped off the new keys. Plumb nice of him, if you ask me."

IdaMae took a key from her desk and handed it over, then pulled in a deep, ragged breath and forced a smile. "I'm sorry to be so down in the mouth. I just have these little worry spells from time to time is all. Hollis left his phone on his desk that dreadful day when they hauled him out in handcuffs." A tear trailed down her cheek. "I'll go get it for you," she said in a wobbly voice. "I put it on his charger to keep it up for when he comes home to us nice and safe."

"I'll get it." I started down the hall. "You finish up what you're doing." I didn't want to upset IdaMae more than necessary. She'd been through enough. I opened the top drawer of Hollis's desk to find business cards, envelopes, a carryout menu from Screamin' Mimi's pizza, a football schedule for the Georgia Bulldogs, the cell phone, and a .38 Smith and Wesson for those times when haggling over real estate went beyond haggling and someone had to restore peace and prosperity to the South.

The phone was one of those complicated phones with enough gizmos to get you to Mars and back and communicate with anyone you met along the way. I took it and the charger, thanked IdaMae, snatched two candies from the bowl, then called KiKi while walking back to Cherry House. I gave her Hollis's number and reminded her that under no circumstances was she to confront Baxter. I disconnected,

DUFFY BROWN

got home, threw in a load of laundry, and opened the Fox at ten sharp to three tourists who thought shopping at a Southern resale shop had to be the most fun in all of Georgia. God bless the tourists.

At noon I put a "Be Back at Three" sign on the door. This was no way to run a railroad. I needed regular shop hours, but I also needed to find Cupcake's killer. KiKi helped out at the Fox when she could, but she had a business of her own and Uncle Putter to tend to, in addition to now doing Savannah's version of *Murder, She Wrote* with me. Maybe the Abbott sisters would help out? I couldn't afford to pay them, but if I gave them 50 percent off what they bought at the Fox, which was my half of the profit from the sale, that might be incentive enough. Plus, they could gossip with all the customers.

I caught a bus up to Broughton. Usually I walked, but if KiKi saw Baxter with a bimbo, there was a distinct possibility she'd go ballistic on Trellie's behalf, and the SPD would have to call in the riot squad. KiKi had phoned earlier and told me she'd followed Baxter from his house to a garage, where he changed clothes and identities, picked up his truck, then headed to the Hilton Hotel on East Liberty. I got off the bus and found the service alley behind the Hilton, KiKi's out-of-place Beemer parked next to a van reading "Dan's Flora and Fauna." I slipped into the passenger side.

"What's up, Sherlock?"

"Nothing," KiKi said, "except I got to pee so bad I might drown. I'm willing to bet there's plenty going on with Baxter inside that hotel. Last time we saw him over at Marshall House; this time, the Hilton. That man's clearly up to no good. I never thought Baxter could be the killer, but the

~158~

longer I sit here and think about him, the more I realize I don't really know the man at all. He just sort of showed up in Savannah and got to be a regular on the benefit circuit, going to dinners at the Oglethorpe Club, parties at the country club and the Telfair Museum, and the like. He said he did some modeling in Atlanta, and before you know it, he and Trellie were making goo-goo eyes at each other over martini glasses, then running off to Vegas and tying the knot."

"You better go. The Petersons will have a conniption if you're late."

"Then the teens come in for cotillion dance lessons. The group I have this year can't dance for beans. How they ever learned to walk is a mystery to me. I'm leaving you the car, and I'll catch a cab out front. Let me know what happens."

"Get the cabbie to do a pee stop at Ray's BBQ, and pick up sweet-potato fries while you're there. Ray does great sweet-potato fries."

I watched KiKi head off, then got out and walked around the car, settling down in the comfy leather driver's seat to wait for Baxter. Five minutes later, he came out the service entrance, pulled his baseball cap low over his face, and jogged to his truck. He had on another pair of horn-rimmed glasses, and I watched him toss his case in the back of the pickup, then hop in the driver's side. I sank lower still as he motored out of the alley and hung a left. I brought the Beemer to life and followed at a distance. The BMW may be a really nice car, but it got noticed. What I needed was a silver SUV. Half the cars on the road these days were silver SUVs.

Baxter swung onto Bay Street, then circled around back of the Hampton Inn. This guy had one heck of a constitution and was headed for a lifetime achievement award of Wilt

Chamberlain proportions. Maybe that was the problem. Women panted after Baxter; I'd seen them do it. Trellie was older, and perhaps she simply couldn't keep up. The way this guy was going, no woman could keep up!

The service alley was tight with trucks and Dumpsters, forcing me to park at the entrance. I wasn't sure what KiKi and I were going to do with the information about Baxter. Tell Trellie? Confront Baxter with 'The jig is up, bubba; reform your philandering ways'? Have our obituaries posted in the morning news?

Someone knocked on the passenger-side window, and I jumped so high I cracked my head on the visor. Thinking about one's obituary can do that to a person. Recognizing the no-makeup look and the stringy mouse-brown hair that almost made my two-tone stripes look good, I powered down the window to Reverend Franklin's wife, Birdie. She was Hollis's cousin, so our paths had crossed a few times. "Uh, hi, Birdie."

She climbed in. "I know what you're doing here, and I tell you it's downright disgraceful. Do you have any idea how many lives you're going to ruin? Don't you have a conscience?"

"I'm not trying to ruin lives, I'm trying to find Cupca— Janelle's killer so an innocent man doesn't go to prison." *And I don't lose my house.*

Birdie nodded to the Hampton. "And you think that no-good cheater is the murderer?"

"Well, he's running all over town, slipping in and out of back doors, lying to his wife, sleeping with who-knows-how-many women, and getting blackmailed. I'm sure he wasn't happy about that."

"Oh dear Lord!" Birdie slapped her hand to her forehead and looked faint. "He's playing around with more than one?"

"The way I see it, Baxter is Hugh Hefner without the wrinkles and robe."

Birdie's face morphed from tortured to weird. "For pity's sake, who's Baxter?"

"The man I'm watching. Why did you think I was here?"

"To keep an eye on my Virgil, of course. I know he's fooling around on me with that snooty little deacon. I thought you were here to take pictures of the two of them together and get proof that Virgil had a motive for killing that Janelle woman and get Hollis off the hook. Virgil might be a gigolo in preachers' clothing, but he's not a killer. He's not that kind of man. He's a good man." Birdie bit back a sob. "He truly is."

"And why are you here?"

"I hired a private investigator, and he said Virgil and that bimbo meet here. I wanted to see for myself if it was true." She sniffed, her eyes watering. "Virgil never brings me to nice places like this."

The Hampton was an okay hotel but not a "nice places like this" hotel. It was a "Mom, Dad, and the kids on their way to Grandma's" kind of place.

"When Virgil and I go out," Birdie said to me, her voice bitter, "it's to those rallies and fund-raisers with rubber chicken, Stove Top stuffing, and no wine. I could do with a glass of wine served to me once in a while, something white. I'd love a drink with a little umbrella."

"You need to try the drinks with olives. I don't think your husband is a murderer, but he's not a good man either, least not to you."

Me giving marital advice was like Joan Rivers giving advice on facelifts, but if I stood by and let Birdie make the same mistakes I had, that wasn't right either.

"Look, if you know Virgil is messing around, and I know he's messing around, it's only a matter of time till all of Savannah knows. The way this works is that the guy gets the cupcake, and the woman gets the embarrassment and the heartache."

"But we were in love once. We have children. I don't know what to do." She bit back another sob.

Shoot the bastard was on the tip of my tongue, but I went with, "Tell Virgil he has to make a choice. Don't be stuck in the middle letting him make all the decisions for your life and his. I did that and nearly lost my mind. It's no way to live." I spotted Baxter's truck whizzing by and said to Birdie, "I have to follow that truck. That's Baxter, and he's messing around on his wife and clearly married her for her money. She could be in real danger." I started the Beemer and took off.

"Oh goodness." Birdie buckled up and gripped the dashboard. Hunched over in concentration, she peered through the windshield. "Don't be getting too close. I've seen those TV shows. You've got to hang back, or he'll spot us."

We took Habersham to Congress, and the truck swung in the alleyway behind The Planters Inn, which faced Reynolds Square. "Mercy me, this Baxter person sure has expensive taste. Is he really going after his wife's money?"

"If he killed Janelle to get her to stop blackmailing him, he could very well plan to knock off his wife for her money." Baxter got out of his truck, and I drove on past so as not to look too suspicious.

"Stop!" Birdie yelped.

"What? Where?" I slammed on the brakes, leaving the smell of burning rubber and two years' worth of tread streaked down the alley. Was there a cat? A dog? A kid? An adrenaline rush of perspiration trickled down my front. I didn't see anything, but Birdie flung open the car door and ran toward Baxter, her brown pencil skirt sneaking up her thighs, her jacket billowing out Batman style.

"I've had it with your kind!" she yelled at Baxter.

Good God in heaven, the woman had snapped! I ran after Birdie as she swung her purse over her head. "You two-timing good-for-nothing bastard, how dare you!"

Baxter held up his hands in defense, trying to ward off the blows. His hat few off, his glasses hit the ground, blood gushed from his nose, and he staggered backward.

"Make her stop!" Baxter pleaded. I grabbed Birdie, using all my strength to hold her. Note to self: *don't get the preacher's wife riled up!*

"He's one of them! They're everywhere; they're everywhere!" Birdie panted, struggling to get at Baxter again.

"What are you talking about?" Baxter used his sleeve to try and stop his bleeding nose.

"Men like you are what I'm talking about!" Birdie pointed a long, accusatory finger, as only a preacher's wife can. "You play around on your wife and think you can get away with it, and you don't care how much you hurt her or anyone else. Shame on you! Shame, shame, shame on you, Baxter!"

If Baxter didn't feel like he was headed straight for the fires of hell after all that, he was untouchable.

"You're nuts, a complete whack job." Baxter's eyes were already turning black and blue.

"We know you're cheating on Trellie," I said while keeping a firm grip on Birdie. "I've been following you around town, and we know about all the hotels, the sneaking, and going in through back doors."

"You're following me? Why don't you mind your own business, and for the love of God, I'm not cheating on Trellie. I wouldn't do that. I go to hotels because I'm an electrician, a master electrician. I take care of the high-voltage lines." He kicked his case, which he'd dropped to the ground. "Look in there if you don't believe me. It's all tools. No condoms in sight. You two should be locked up. You're both bat-crap nuts!"

Chapter Twelve

BAXTER was an electrician? "If you're innocent as the driven snow, why were you sneaking around?" I asked him straight-out. "Why the truck? Why the disguise? Why this?" I marched to the Beemer and pulled the horn-rimmed glasses from my purse. I waved them in Baxter's face. "Look familiar?"

Baxter's face went ashen. With his wild hair and black-and-blue eyes, if he'd had on a nightshirt and chains, he'd pass for Marley right out of Scrooge. This was a far cry from his usual yumminess.

"Where'd you get those?" he asked me, staring at the glasses.

"Where do you think I got them?"

Birdie looked from me to Baxter and back to me again, tennis-match style. "Somebody want to tell me what in the world is going on around here?"

Baxter snagged the glasses right out of my hand. "You were the one in the town house last night," he accused me.

"You were there trying to cover your tracks from being there before," I accused right back.

"I was looking for the information Janelle has on the people she was blackmailing," Baxter said to me in explanation. "I don't think anyone has found it yet, or they'd take up where Janelle left off, and I'd be back to forking over more money, just to a different person."

Birdie put her hand to her forehead. "Saints preserve us, never even considered the possibility of that happening. I figured that since Janelle was dead, the threat of being blackmailed was over and done with. It's not, is it? Virgil's a stupid fool." She scrunched up her face and studied Baxter. "But I don't understand about you. If you're not carrying on with another woman like you say, what did this Janelle person have that could hurt you?"

"Like I'm going to tell you so you can blackmail me. I should just start handing out leaflets and get it over with."

Birdie folded her arms. "Janelle Claiborne was threatening to blackmail my husband, the one and only Reverend Virgil Franklin, poster boy for family values, who is skipping around town as we speak, doing the deacon. Try and top that one."

Baxter let out soft whistle. "I think that wins the Kewpie doll."

"Blackmailers deserve to burn in hell for all eternity," Birdie said in an authoritative voice as someone who knew all about hell burning and what constituted admission. "I suppose you and my husband are in the same boat."

"Not really." Baxter said, running his hand through his

hair. "I love my wife; I truly do. At first I did marry Trellie for her money. Janelle knew that and threatened to tell Trellie if I didn't pay up."

Birdie said, "It's your word against Janelle's. Your wife would believe you, don't you think?"

"When I was in Atlanta, I'd married a woman there and divorced her and took her savings—well, half of it. I lost it in a real-estate deal gone bad, then came to Savannah to find another wealthy woman and do the same thing all over again. I fell in love with Trellie, really fell in love. I've been working to pay the woman in Atlanta back and pay Janelle to keep her mouth shut. I'm a pretty good electrician, and the people I work for don't travel in the country-club circles. They don't know me as Trellie's husband. I do the disguise just to make sure. Janelle knew my ex in Atlanta. Janelle knew a lot of people, like Dinah Corwin from WAGA, who's doing the interviews here in town. Janelle broke up her marriage and had to get a restraining order against Corwin. She went a little crazy."

Baxter gave me a look like Birdie and I belonged in the same category. He added, "I think one of the reasons Janelle came to Savannah in the first place was to bleed me dry when she found out I married Trellie."

"So you got tired of paying Janelle and killed her?" I blurted, then realized that may not be the wisest thing to say to a killer.

"Look," Baxter said to me, the part of his multicolored eyes that hadn't yet swollen shut looking sincere. "I'm trying to straighten out my life, not screw it up even more. I had an emergency electrical job over at the Bay Street Inn the night Janelle was killed. Trellie had a stomach virus, so we didn't make the party at the Telfair Museum. She went to bed early, and I took the job. Someone had backed into a pole and wiped out the electrical system to the kitchen. I worked six hours straight to get the inn up and running for the next morning. The manager paid me double. He'll remember the guy with the glasses."

"The glasses are a nice touch," I told him.

"The glasses are a necessity. I do some pretty tricky work, and connecting the wrong lines could be fireworks, if you get my drift."

"Guess it also helps with picking locks."

"I did what I thought I had to do. Did you find Janelle's stash of information? Are you going to tell Trellie all this or what?"

"I don't know where Janelle's stuff is on the people she's blackmailing, but you have to tell Trellie about Atlanta," I said to Baxter, Birdie standing at my side, nodding in agreement. "She'll find out. I did."

"Yeah, but you're a pain-in-the-butt snoop who's aiming to get into a lot of trouble if you keep digging around to find out who killed Janelle." Baxter ran his hand through his hair, making it look even scarier. "But you are right about Trellie finding out. Fact is, she'll probably get a registered letter straight from Janelle Claiborne."

"Uh, honey, Janelle's dead as can be. No worries there," Birdie said.

"Janelle's dead all right but not forgotten. Blackmailers are smart." Baxter had that defeated look about him, like someone fighting a losing battle. I'd had that feeling a few times myself lately. "Blackmailers have contingency plans to keep themselves alive and well. They leave incriminating evidence with a third party. In the event of their untimely death, this third party sends out that information to the police, government, press, spouses, or wherever it will do the most damage. This makes the people being blackmailed have second thoughts about killing their blackmailers."

He turned his attention to Birdie. "Have you gotten anything about Franklin's infidelity?"

"No, but the information could go to the church elders. I haven't heard any rumblings from them."

Baxter picked up his electrician's case and tossed it in the truck. He climbed behind the steering wheel and struck his head out the window. "Whoever has Janelle's contingency plan is going to act on it sooner or later. Usually that person gets a check every month. The month the money stops coming, the information goes out."

"How do you know all this?"

"Straight from the horse's mouth. Janelle told me."

IT WAS NEAR FIVE WHEN I GOT BACK TO THE FOX. KiKi sat behind the old oak that now served as a table I'd rigged for writing up sales. She was counting money. Lord be praised! Money! A pile of consigned clothes lay across two chairs waiting to be tagged and put out. Business was good, or at least it wasn't as pitiful as before.

"We're closed," KiKi said, still counting and not looking at me. "Come back tomorrow at ten. We have lots of new stuff."

"I parked your car in the garage."

KiKi's head jerked up, and she pressed her hands to her cheeks, looking relieved. "You're safe!" Then she hustled around the table and shook me, upset-auntie style. "Where in heaven's name have you been?" she demanded. "You never picked up your phone! I thought you were dead in an alley, bleeding from your eyes, until Elsie Abbott came in and said she saw you and Birdie Franklin in my car, flying up Bull Street."

"We were on a Baxter hunt." I locked the front door. "Thanks for opening the shop after your dance lessons, and you'll be happy to hear Baxter's not the killer. He's making a little extra on the side so he can treat Trellie well, and not just use her money. As for Birdie, Reverend Franklin is about to get his comeuppance."

"You believe Baxter is really innocent?"

"He's a man doing what he has to do to make things right for the woman he loves." I made a cross over my heart and held up two fingers. "I promise. All women should be so lucky."

Auntie KiKi did an ear-to-ear grin. There was no need to tell her about Baxter and his Atlanta life. That was between him and Trellie, and if they were all to remain friends, I wanted KiKi to think well of Baxter. "Baxter and I ran into each other when I was following him. He's an electrician."

"Electrician? As in sticking plugs into sockets?"

"Electrician as in those big overhead wires that get plugged into businesses and make them go. He had a job the night Cupcake was murdered. I met Birdie in the alley because she thought Virgil might be inside the hotel with Sissy. She knows he's cheating, and she's going to straighten him out."

KiKi kicked off her shoes and sat in the chair I'd slept

in the night before. I started hanging up the new clothes we'd gotten in that day. "I thought Baxter was a prime, grade-A candidate for Cupcake's killer, and he's not. Franklin's no saint, but I don't think he's the killer either."

KiKi handed me a skirt hanger. "Franklin doesn't have the cojones for murder." She let loose with a sassy smile. "Hey, I'm a woman of the world and traveled with Cher. I know what those things are. That leaves us with Raylene, Urston, Sissy, Dinah, and the others on Cupcake's blackmail list. It would be nice if we had that list."

I added a pink sweater to the rack of clothes. "Baxter filled me and Birdie in on the finer points of blackmail. Seems he knows someone who had an unfortunate experience with something of this nature." Sometimes a little white lie was all for the best. "Blackmailers have life-insurance policies. They leave instructions with someone that if they die, the incriminating evidence they have is to be sent out to where it will do the most harm. It guarantees that the people they are blackmailing will wish them a long and healthy life. The murderer could be someone Cupcake was blackmailing or not."

KiKi took a minute to digest this. "Actually it's kind of ingenious, if you ask me."

"As far as Birdie knows, no incriminating evidence has gone out yet, but it will. Janelle was a lot of things, but stupid wasn't one of them. You know she left evidence with some third party. She pays them each month, and when they don't get the money, people of interest get the dirt. What we need is Cupcake's checkbook, or address book, or something out of the ordinary that might lead us to the person Janelle's been paying. Maybe he, or she, knows who might have killed Janelle. We need to take another look at Hollis's town house.

This time we're not just looking for a list of names but anything a bit suspicious."

"First you need to put away your money." KiKi thrust a wad of bills at me. "And we need supper. I'm starved; aren't you starved?" She slipped on her shoes, then gave me a critical once-over, head to toe.

"What?" I asked, getting the feeling something was going on besides supper.

"It's been a tough day. I had Miss Annabelle do up a nice roast for me this evening, being as I was so busy and all. How would you like some mashed potatoes with that roast, little spring peas, and biscuits? Peach cobbler for desert? Doesn't that sound mighty good? I bet you could do with a supper of roast beef and cobbler."

I wasn't sure if a person could faint dead away from just thinking about food, but I was getting darn close to finding out.

"See you in a half hour, and put on that cute blue skirt you have and some lipstick. Lord knows you could do with lipstick once in a while, and a dye job would be in order, but there's nothing we can do to fix that particular situation right now."

KiKi turned to go, and I jumped between her and the door, flattening myself across the exit. "What are you up to?"

KiKi slapped a sweet-as-sugar grin on her face, which practiced Southern belles do without a moment's hesitation. "Me?" She rolled her eyes and placed her palm to her cheek. "Why, honey, would you think I'd be up to anything? I'm just having a little company over is all. One of Putter's doctor friends is in town, and with your pitiful day, this is just the ticket to set you to rights and—"

"And he's single, bald, lonely, and rich."

"Two out of four isn't bad, and I'm not saying which two, either, so don't be asking. The way Cher tells it, 'A girl can wait for the right man to come along, but in the meantime that still doesn't mean she can't have a wonderful time with all the wrong ones.' You need to start socializing, meet men, and have a little romance in your life. A woman can get crotchety if she doesn't get some romance once in a while."

I opened the door. "In case you've forgotten, romance is what got me into my current state of crotchety. I'll meet you at the town house. Leave the man; bring the cobbler."

After KiKi left, I switched laundry from the washer to the dryer and filled displays with the clothes KiKi took in. I hid the cash from today's sales in the freezer in an ice cream carton I'd gotten from the Abbott sisters' garbage. An ice cream container in the freezer was not exactly a rival for Fort Knox, but unless a burglar had a craving for Rocky Road, I was safe. I jammed the chair under the back door-knob, turned the lights on in my bedroom as if Reagan Summerside was home, dumped kibble out for Bruce Willis, then met up with KiKi and the cobbler on the front stoop of Hollis's place. I fished the new key from the bottom of my purse and opened the door. When we went inside, the place was still a shambles; no nice little cleanup fairies had come to the rescue.

After two hours, KiKi and I dragged a third garbage can to the Dumpster, and she said, "Unless we start tearing up the floorboards around here, we're out of luck finding Cupcake's collection of others' unfortunate deeds or the identity of that mysterious person she paid to keep her files."

We sat on the back steps watching the overhead security

light reflect off the big green Dumpster by the garages. If I kept having this much fun, I'd be tempted to take KiKi up on her next offer of bald, boring doctors.

"Do you think she could have hidden the files or maybe her checkbook at the real-estate office?" KiKi asked me.

"Not with IdaMae and Hollis having the run of the place. Boone was at the town house before me last night; he could have found Cupcake's list of those she was blackmailing. He could also be Cupcake's contingency plan, for all I know. He could be the guy she paid off each month. He's a lawyer, and he knew Cupcake."

"Maybe the reason he hadn't sent out the incriminating evidence yet was that it would interfere with Hollis's defense. The people being blackmailed were Hollis's friends, and that makes a mighty good motive for Hollis killing Cupcake if he found out and was ticked off." KiKi shook her head at her own idea. "But that's just plumb stupid. Hollis and Boone are friends. Would Boone really take on the job of sending out evidence against friends?"

"Urston, Raylene, and Sissy are possible suspects, and there are probably more. I have a feeling Boone knows who they might be. He knows things we don't; I'm right sure of it."

KiKi stood and stretched like a cat on a rainy day. "What are you going to do; ask that low-life rodent straight-out?" KiKi started up the back steps, talking to me over her shoulder as she went. "You can talk to him if you like, and I wish you luck 'cause you'll need it. I told Putter I'd meet up with him and tall, dark, and handsome at the country club for a nightcap."

We did a simultaneous eye roll at KiKi's visiting-doctor

description, which we both knew was a big Southern pile of crapola. "I'll walk to Boone's," I told KiKi. "It'll give me a chance to swallow my pride." I added the last part in an easy manner, finally getting the knack of lying though my teeth. "I'll see you tomorrow, and let you know what happens."

Unless you get a call from the police tonight and have to bail your beloved niece out of the clink on breaking-and-entering charges, I added to myself.

No way would I ask Boone anything. He'd tell me to go home and lock my doors. I'd simply take the information I needed. Boone said his office didn't have an alarm system. I knew Dinky, his secretary, the layout of the office, and about the staircase that had been walled over during office renovations. It was now in the back of a closet, and Dinky used it when running late to work and to sneak out for wedding-dress fittings in the middle of the day.

I needed to know who was on that blackmail list. Were they fed up enough to polish off Cupcake? Was there someone else whom Cupcake had pushed too far? Maybe all of them got together and pulled off a *Murder on the Orient Express* where everyone kills the bad guy. If that was true, why frame Hollis? Just toss Janelle's sorry butt in Ebenezer Creek Swamp and be done with the whole mess.

Someone somewhere had answers, and tonight my money—not that I had any—was on Walker Boone. I just didn't want him to find out.

Chapter Thirteen

I WATCHED Auntie KiKi drive away from the town house, then headed up Habersham. Boone's white-stone office was well over a hundred years old, with an elevated entrance off the sidewalk. It faced Columbia Square and was next to the Kehoe House, now a bed-and-breakfast and haunted by the Kehoe twins for the last century. Some kids can't wait to leave home; others you can't get rid of.

The live oaks in the square blocked the moonlight and confined streetlight to circles on the sidewalks. I found a vacant bench, and while waiting for evening strollers and traffic to subside, I tried to figure out how to get into Boone's office. Nothing came to mind, so I ducked into Screamin' Mimi's for a slice of salami-and-pepperoni pizza and had them toss on some anchovies since fish was brain food. If that didn't jar my thinking cells awake, nothing would.

I reclaimed my roost on the bench, the fragrant aroma

of the pizza keeping interlopers from horning in on my space. I took a bite of heaven and rummaged around in Old Yeller for something that might aid and abet my burglary. I came up with a flashlight, screwdriver, teasing comb, and black flip-flops to complement my burglar attire of jeans and an old Georgia Bulldogs T-shirt Hollis had left when he moved out.

The Second African Baptist Church chimed ten. I should wait another hour, but I was fidgety with wanting to get this ordeal over with. I wrapped up the last of the pizza and dropped it in my purse, then crossed the street to the white-stone building. Instead of taking the steps up to the porch and main entrance, I took the two steps down to another door below. Back in the day, this was the service entrance, where deliveries were made and servants entered. Now it was locked and dark.

I made the sign of the cross in hopes of not winding up damned for all eternity for being where I shouldn't, and I turned the door handle. It didn't budge. I turned it harder and shoved with my shoulder. The only thing that moved were my bones being squashed. Flipping on the flashlight, I tried to block the glare so as not to draw attention and studied the knob. It was big, brass, new, and solid enough to keep out invading armies and interfering ex wives.

"What you doing down there, white woman?" came a deep baritone voice from the sidewalk.

I yelped, tripped over Old Yeller, and landed flat on my behind. All I could make out against the darkness was a gold tooth, pristine white shoes, and bright eyes. "Big Joey?"

I scrambled to my feet as Big Joey took the steps down, making it very crowded in the very little space. We were toe-to-toe. I could feel the heat of his body seeping into mine, and he was sucking up all the oxygen. He grinned down at me. My head started to throb, my stomach rolled, and I couldn't breathe. I slid under Big Joey's arm and ran up the two steps to the sidewalk, gulping in deep breaths of air.

"You afraid of me, white woman?"

I shook my head and I pointed to where he stood. I tried not to hyperventilate. "No room. No air."

"Claustrophobia?" Joey grinned. "I read. I know." He leaned against the doorjamb, watching me pull myself together. "You and Boone got a thing going on? You sneaking in there to give him a little surprise?"

"The surprise part is true enough."

"You breaking in for something else?" There was a knowing laugh deep in his wide chest. "Scarlett O'Hara does Sherlock Holmes. What is that smell?"

"Leftover pizza from Mimi's. What are you doing in this part of town?"

"Heading for The Wall."

The Wall was a hole-in-the-wall place over on York Lane, which was still dirt paved. It had no AC, one bathroom so small you couldn't sit, and the best red-velvet cake, spiciest barbecue sauce, and sweetest iced tea in Georgia. It's where Savannah ate and the tourists couldn't find on their GPS receivers.

Big Joey turned around and took hold of the knob. Even under Big Joey's grip, the lock held. "You not getting in there without a key; Boone made sure."

"Why are you helping me?"

"Good deed for the day." He took my flashlight, which I'd dropped, and killed the beam. "What's Boone got that you need?" Big Joey gave me a suggestive wink. "Bet I can guess."

"Boone and I are after a killer, and I want to know what Boone knows."

"Lady, you never know what Boone knows." Big Joey hitched his head to the street. "Cops two blocks down don't much cotton to B and E; take it from one who understands this-here business. You being the judge's daughter could add drama." Big Joey took two steps up to the sidewalk, stopping next to me. "Look for a key. No scratches at the lock; door's not used much. No one carries the key for that door; they hide it."

"Are you going to tattle on me to Boone?" I asked as he walked off.

Big Joey turned back, his eyes lit with humor. "No need; Boone'll know."

I watched Big Joey meander on. "Thanks," I called to him, getting no response.

I didn't care if Boone did know I was here; I just wanted to have a look at his files. If they were on his computer, I was screwed—they'd be password protected. But not everything was on a computer. There could be notes, letters, a stack of incriminating evidence waiting to go out in the morning mail and ruin people's lives. I felt along the ground in front of the door, around in the dirt, and turned over a rock, and something scurried out. It if scurried onto me, there'd be a scared-stiff corpse under Boone's porch for the cops to find.

I was running out of time; I could see the cruiser with the bank of lights across the top approaching slowly in the curb lane, as if checking things out. There was no place to hide, and if Big Joey had seen me, the cops would, too.

I could feel my heart pounding in my chest. If I ran out from where I was now, the cops would see me for sure. Shaking, I felt over the doorframe again, and this time my fingers connected with a break in the stone, touching something cold, round, and metal. With two fingertips, I plucked the key from the crack. Because I was shaking so badly, I had to use both hands to jam the key in the lock. I let myself inside, closed the door, and heard the cruiser motor on by. If Hollis was really guilty after all this sweat and angst, I was killing the man dead myself.

I only knew about the stairway from Dinky bragging how she used it to outfox Boone. I twisted on my flashlight and aimed it up a flight of stairs that probably had "Condemned by the City Inspector" nailed to it somewhere. Holding on to the railing that wobbled under my hand, I took the steps one at a time, filling the narrow passage with creaking sounds. I got to the top, turned the handle, and stepped into a large storage closet. There were shelves of paper, ink cartridges, envelopes, and what had to be a five-hundred-dollar espresso maker that did everything from grind beans to dump coffee in the cup and serve it to you on a sliver platter. So, this is where my three-hundred-dollar-an-hour divorce settlement went.

I considered the coffeemaker in my kitchen, with its broken on-off switch and cracked lid, which I'd gotten at the Abbott sisters' yard sale. I swallowed back a growl, then opened the next door into the outer office. The closet was behind Dinky's desk, and I slunk across the room and into Boone's office—the snake pit. After months of divorce haggling that's pretty much what the place felt like. I had a bad feeling in the pit of my stomach that I was someplace I shouldn't be, and Big Snake would not be pleased.

I sat down in Boone's soft leather chair, put my purse on the floor, and held the flashlight in my teeth like they do on the TV shows. I tried not to think about the germ aspect, with my flashlight living in the recesses of my purse with my comb and other paraphernalia. Boone had a computer, not a laptop but one of those old ones, with the tower that sat under the desk. The man needed to upgrade. I hit the power button, and the screen came alive with a simple blue background, not even a big black Harley or badass fishing boat to liven things up a bit. I clicked on a folder just for kicks, but I needed a password to go any further. I considered trying "scum-sucking lawyer."

I rummaged through Boone's desk, finding the usual paper, pens, envelopes, and a gun. Most of the population of Savannah could give you the make and model of this particular firearm. I was more of the how-much-could-I-get-for-this-on-eBay mentality. It was heavy, older than dirt, completely untraceable. You can take the boy out of the hood, but you can't take the hood out of the—

"It's loaded."

I jerked up. The gun went off with a loud bang that scared the liver out of me. I dropped the gun and jumped out of the chair, the light in my mouth zeroing in on Boone hunkered on the floor. "Oh my God!" I mumbled around a mouthful of flashlight.

Looking none too happy, Boone said, "I told you it was loaded."

I spit out the flashlight, knelt down beside Boone, and grabbed his shoulders. "Are you dead? Where did I shoot you?"

Boone took the flashlight from the floor and waved it around to a blistered hole in some very fine cherry paneling that deserved better treatment.

"What are you doing here?" I asked in a high squeaky voice that I didn't recognize as my own.

"I think that's my line." Boone stood and lit the brass lamp on his desk.

"I could have killed you, and why didn't you ever offer me an espresso all the times I was here in this place?" My brain was oatmeal.

"When I saw the Colt in your hand, I figured the floor was the best place to be. You were going to be surprised no matter what I did. And I just got the espresso machine." He pulled out his cell.

"Who are you calling?"

"The cops."

"That's not very nice."

"I'm not a very nice guy."

Boone told the police that a gun misfired in his office and everything was okay and not to send a car around.

"They'll believe that?" I asked when he disconnected.

"It's my office. Things happen here. You're not helping Hollis, you know."

"All I want to do is find Janelle's killer, and I'm not having much luck."

"That's not my problem; you are." He closed his eyes and seemed weary. "What did I do to deserve you, and what is that smell?" Boone asked, his eyes tearing at the odor. Some people had no taste whatsoever.

"How'd you know I was here?" I asked him. "You don't

have an alarm system; you told me so yourself." I slapped my hand against my forehead, duh fashion. "Big Joey ratted me out, didn't he? I should have known."

"Big Joey doesn't rat." Boone pointed to a bookshelf behind his desk loaded with matching volumes of legalese. "Camera. I can check my office with my iPhone."

"And you happened to check it in the middle of the night to see if I was here?"

"You didn't find anything at the town house. I knew you'd come calling to see what I had, and ten thirty isn't the middle of the night. Breaking in here is what I would do, except I'd get away with it."

I sat on the floor cross-legged, looking up at Boone perched on the edge of his desk. "You think you're so darn smart."

"You got me beat in the little-black-dress department, but when it comes to finding evidence, it's no contest. Stick to being a shop girl." Boone's cell buzzed, and he checked the screen. "I gotta take this." He went into the outer office and called over his shoulder, "Don't move."

Yeah, right. I hooked my purse over my shoulder. Boone didn't know how I had gotten in, so getting out the same way had possibilities. I started to crawl off; then I remembered my leftover pizza, and I peeled off the salami, pepperoni, and anchovies and placed them on the CD tray (which no one used these days with flash drives around) on Boone's computer. I hit the close button and watched the smelly part of my delicious dinner slide away. Boone would have a great time wondering *Where's that smell coming from?* I crawled around the side of his desk, inched through the door behind Dinky's desk, slipped into the closet, and crept down the back stairs.

Now that I was out and free as a bird, I figured Boone probably let me go. I replaced the key in the crack and started to feel a little guilty over the pizza until I remembered his shop-girl crack. Hey, I was smart and getting smarter and making new important friends. Not everyone in the Victorian District had connections in the hood.

It was nearly midnight by the time I walked home. So much time spent tonight hunting around and so little to show for it. All I knew for sure was that Franklin and Baxter were off the hook, Cupcake had a contingency plan that would ruin a lot of people's lives, Walker Boone had his office bugged, and I'd probably get a bill for a bullet-hole repair job. I started up the walk to my house and listened for a thumping tail and looked for eyes shining at me from under the porch. Nothing. Bruce Willis wasn't there. He was on the porch, sleeping right by the front door. The trail of hot dogs had worked! I got my watchdog.

"What a good boy you are," I called, my flip-flops slapping against the wood as I took the steps. I clapped my hands so he'd jump up and come to me like he always did. He didn't budge. Bruce Willis just laid there, his back to me, very still. "I have a hot dog," I lied, feeling a little nervous at the no-movement thing. His tail didn't wag; his fur didn't move.

Terror shot through me. I dropped down beside BW and gathered his big mangy head into my arms. He opened his eyes, but it was a struggle. His breath smelled like . . . chocolate? There were wrappers by his paw, more by the door. "Oh no. Oh, please, God, no."

KiKi was at the country club; she couldn't take us to the vet. The Abbott sisters would be in a complete tizzy over BW and I'd have to call an ambulance and have three to worry about. Shaking, I fumbled through my purse and dug out the phone. I punched in Mamma's number. It went right to voice mail; she was probably at some political meeting this evening. I punched in the only other number I could remember.

"What?" Walker Boone's voice barked at me over the phone.

"It's Reagan. Don't hang up," I added in a rush. I was crying so hard I didn't know if Boone could even understand me. "Bruce Willis." I started to sob harder. "Someone fed him chocolate. I can't lift him. He's sick; he's so sick. KiKi isn't home, Mamma's not home, and—"

But there was nothing more to say. The phone went dead.

I didn't blame Walker Boone for hanging up. I had pushed his buttons too many times and had just shot up his office. The police. I could call 911. But if I told them that my dog ate chocolate, they'd refer me to the animal-something department, and those people would never get here on time. I started to cry harder. I wiped my eyes so I could see and ran for the street. I'd flag down a car, but at midnight on a little side street like East Gaston there weren't any cars—except for a red '57 Chevy, tires squealing around the corner and coming right at me, full tilt.

Boone slid to a stop and jumped out. Without a word, we ran up the steps. Boone scooped Bruce Willis up into his arms. Boone's dark eyes were stone cold, his jaw set, his shoulders rigid. I ran ahead and opened the back door of the Chevy and Boone slid Bruce Willis onto the pristine white upholstery. I knelt on the passenger seat and leaned over the back to keep watch. "He looks just awful."

"You would too if you ate poison." The big V-8 under

the shiny red hood came to life, and the Chevy launched forward. I had no idea where we were going and trusted that Boone did. I wasn't in the habit of trusting Boone on anything, till now. "Come on, Bruce; stay with me, boy," I soothed in a choked voice, stroking his fur.

BW stared up at me with sad doggie eyes that broke my heart, and I started to cry all over again. In times of crisis, I sucked. The Chevy jolted to a stop, and Boone killed the engine. A blue-neon "Emergency Animal Clinic" sign glared from the window outside, and Boone charged through the double-glass doors, sick dog in his arms. "We need some help here right now!" Boone yelled.

Three people in white lab coats rushed out into the waiting area and led us to an examining table in the back. I told them about the wrappers; then they made us leave the room. Boone and I sat on red plastic chairs in the waiting area lined with lots of red plastic chairs. We stared out the plate-glass window into the dark parking lot. "Who would do this to a dog?" I said to both of us. "Do you think they did it to scare me off looking for the murderer?"

"Or to get into your house."

"There's nothing in there but used clothes. Everyone knows BW wouldn't hurt a fly. He's a big fluffy marshmallow." My voice broke, and more tears trickled down my face. I wiped my runny nose on the back of my hand like a two-year-old. "Thanks for coming."

"You're welcome."

"There's salami, pepperoni, and anchovies in your computer."

Boone cut his eyes to me, his brows drawn together in one black straight line of disbelief.

"You said I belonged in a dress shop. I had leftover pizza. What's a girl to do?"

"Mimi's?"

"Who else?" I stood, glared at the closed blue door where they had Bruce Willis, and felt all my bones liquefy. I plopped back down in the chair and chewed my thumbnail down to the quick.

Boone took out his wallet. He opened it to a chunk of bills, fished around, and pulled out a mangled cigarette and one match. Ignoring the "No Smoking" sign, he lit up, took a deep drag, closed his eyes and had that same expression of euphoria on his face as I do when I eat peanut-butter pie.

"I didn't know you smoked."

He kept his eyes shut. "There are times."

Walker Boone was always cool, never ruffled; he never raised his voice; but right now, on the stress-o-meter, I figured we were both hovering in the red zone. I started on another fingernail. "Why did you come?"

"You got a dog with a good heart. He deserves a break." Boone reached out and ruffled my hair like I was ten years old. "And then he had to go and find you."

One of the lab-coat guys came out of the blue door and walked our way. I studied his face, looking for something positive—or God forbid something negative. I knew he'd tell us in a moment, but I looked anyway. Funny how every second seems like an hour when tragedy strikes.

"We think he's going to be okay," the vet told us.

Little black dots danced in front of my eyes, and I grabbed Boone's arm to keep from falling out of the chair. I couldn't talk, so I nodded as the lab-coat guy said something about inducing vomiting and swallowing charcoal to absorb toxins. We could see Bruce in a little bit. Lab-Coat Guy left without explaining what "little bit" meant, but I wasn't going anywhere so it didn't matter.

"You don't have to hang around," I said to Boone. "I'll let you know how he's doing."

Boone carefully snuffed out the cigarette, blew the tip cool, then put it back in his wallet between U. S. Grant and Benjamin Franklin. "I'll hang around for a while."

"But I'm here."

Boone leaned back, stretched out his long legs, and bent his head forward. "I'm tired. Someone broke into my office and made an unscheduled pizza delivery. I've had a bad night, and I've slept in worse places than this."

I studied Boone as he got comfortable, or as comfortable as one can get in a red plastic chair. He shut his eyes. Amazing! He really was going to sleep! After fifteen minutes, he pried open one eye. "You're staring."

"Are you Janelle's contingency-plan guy?"

Boone's other eye opened.

"The guy she paid each month to keep her blackmail stuff and to send it out if something unfortunate happened to her?"

"What happened to sleep?"

"Good grief. My dog's sick, and someone's after me, I can't sleep. So, are you Janelle's life-insurance policy or what?"

"That policy didn't work too well. I'm not the go-to guy for life insurance, but I imagine someone out there is. And before you ask, I haven't found Janelle's blackmail list or the evidence she had on everyone. I have no idea what she did with it. *Now* can we get some sleep?"

"It doesn't matter if we find the list or not. No one on it would have murdered Janelle. They knew if something happened to her, their secrets weren't secrets any longer."

Boone let out a resigned, sleepless sigh. "Janelle's murder was one of passion. She was whacked in the head by someone pissed off, who'd had enough of her for whatever reason and lost control in the moment. The murder wasn't thought out; it wasn't planned; it happened. That's why Hollis is a prime suspect, though the premeditated part is still on the table. He and Janelle fought that night, so he had preexisting motive. He had opportunity because she was alone in the house and Hollis knew it. The body was found in his car, and his fingerprints are all over the 'For Sale' sign. It was in the Lexus under the body. As far as the police are concerned, this case is closed. Now can we sleep?"

"If that's all you have, how do expect to find the killer? How do you plan on proving Hollis innocent?"

"I don't have to find the killer; I just need reasonable doubt. I need the jury to believe that someone else besides Hollis had motive and opportunity to commit the crime."

"Do you actually know that someone else met up with Janelle? Did the neighbors see another person?"

"The neighbors across the street were on their way to a movie and saw a single woman going into the house. Janelle's car was parked on the street, so she was already there."

"Maybe it was the person interested in buying the house?"

"That was a couple, and they arrived later. When the neighbors came back from the movie, they had wine on their porch and remember Hollis's Lexus going in the drive and circling around to the back. They went inside before it drove out."

"That's a big nail in Hollis's coffin." I hoped it wasn't literally. "Except Hollis is smarter than that; he wouldn't just drive up in his noticeable car and cart off a dead body. He'd wipe his fingerprints off the murder weapon."

"The police maintain Hollis was distraught and not thinking clearly. You and I know there's something else going on. And here's another interesting aspect: Janelle's purse is missing. The police searched everywhere for it. If Hollis is the murderer, there's no reason for him to hide the purse since his obvious plan was to ditch the body. Why not just drop the purse in the trunk, too? And why would Hollis wait till the next day to dispose of the body? Why not just do it that night and get rid of everything out in some swamp? It all seems a little off."

"Don't the police see that?"

"They see evidence. Usually it's a pretty straight line from motive to killer, but not this time. I think someone took the key from Janelle's purse, got the Lexus, and drove it over to the 'For Sale' house. He or she loaded up Janelle, then took the car and the body back to where Hollis parked it, framing Hollis while he sat fat, dumb, and happy in his office doing paperwork."

"So why *would* the killer keep a purse?"

Boone shrugged and yawned. "I don't know, and I don't care. My defense is that someone else besides Hollis could have done the deed, and I have an eyewitness willing to testify that a woman visited Janelle that night. She could have returned, gone in the back door after the potential buyers left, and killed Janelle. The obvious appearance of the Lexus at the house later on makes it look like a frame. I could drag the people being blackmailed up on the stand and question them, but they'll just deny everything. I need Janelle's blackmail list to prove I'm right and that others had motive."

"Do you think your case is strong enough?"

"I'm looking for the woman who visited Janelle at the 'For Sale' house. She wasn't there to see the house; there was no appointment in Janelle's book. That gives me my other person, and you know she went to see Janelle for a reason. I find her, I win the case."

I got an uneasy feeling in my stomach, the kind that said something else was going on here, and I wasn't going to like it. "Why are you telling me all this?"

"You have a right to know. You're putting your house on the line to prove Hollis innocent."

"Try again."

"You digging around ruffled some feathers. It's probably someone on the blackmail list, who could also be our killer."

"Our?" Now I knew how KiKi felt when I threw pronouns around.

"Go to the police about what happened to Bruce Willis. If you tell them you're poking around in your ex's murder, they will not be happy. A dog poisoning will make them keep an eye on your house. You need that."

"You think tonight is about someone trying to scare me off the case and whoever it is may very well come back? This gives a face to your theory." I thought about this for a few seconds. "You're using me, Boone. I'm bait? I'm nothing more than a fat old worm on the end of a hook for you to find the murderer."

"Hollis will be free, your house safe."

"If I live that long."

"Keep my number on speed dial."

I lunged for Boone, but the vet came in before I could strangle him. "Is everything okay here?" the vet asked, eyeing my hands around Boone's neck. "You can take your dog home tomorrow. You can see him now if you like. He's still a little groggy."

The vet handed me the bill, and I stuffed it in Boone's shirt pocket. "Consider it bait fee."

Chapter Fourteen

THE sun was turning Savannah from the pearl gray of dawn to sunny-morning yellow when Boone dropped me off in front of Cherry House. He told me to call if any new suspects surfaced. I told him to eat dirt and die. We'd stayed with Bruce Willis till the vet said Boone and I looked worse than the dog and threw us out.

I sat on the porch, feeling lonely without BW to keep me company and bad at the wretched night he spent at the vet. KiKi shuffled out the front door of her house in a blue-flowered robe and matching fluffy slippers, green cream on her face, eyes peering out raccoon style from the mask of goo. She sat down beside me, drawing close. I could smell the cucumber fragrance of the cream.

"What are you doing up so early?" I asked.

"Putter's off to a symposium in Atlanta for a few days, and I needed to help him finish packing. The man can't tell black from blue to save his life. And what are you doing, sitting out here at this hour?" KiKi nodded down the street. "I saw that spiffy red car driving off. Are you making time with the enemy? I hope it was good."

"Someone poisoned Bruce Willis, Boone took us to the vet, and now he's using me as bait to find Cupcake's killer."

Auntie KiKi looked at me as if I'd sprouted another head. "You're out of my sight for one little ole night and everything goes right to pot. Who in the world would hurt that sweet dog? How is Boone using you to find the killer? I thought that was his job."

"I think his job is mostly screwing me over. All Boone needs is to make the jury think someone other than Hollis had a motive to kill Janelle. He thinks the person who is after me is more than likely connected to Janelle's death. That gives Boone what he needs. I should never have told him about the salami, pepperoni, and anchovies."

"What's salami and anchovies got to do with any of this?"

"I sort of broke into his office and he caught me, so I left him a little present in his computer."

KiKi put her arm around me, the fuzzy part of her robe on my neck comforting. "Why don't you get a nice hot shower and come over for some eggs?"

"No bald doctors waiting in the wings?"

"No bald doctors, but you do have a dance lesson with Bernard at two."

Some days I got the bear, and some days the bear got me. I trudged inside, thinking that it was still early morning and I'd already been eaten alive. I started up the steps to my bedroom and stopped on the third step, a weird sort of creepy feeling pushing through my fatigue. Something in the house was off. I had no idea why I thought that, but I did. Maybe because I didn't just live here; Cherry House and I were a part of each other. I'd fixed rafters, plumbing, electric, floors: you name it, I had my fingerprints on it. Slowly, I turned and looked at the Prissy Fox from up on my perch. Everything in the store seemed the same, from the displays I did the night before to the checkout counter to the clothes I'd hung up when I came back from hounding Baxter.

I took the steps back down and went into the kitchen, dropped my purse on the counter, then held my breath and checked the freezer. Yep, the money was still there. This thing with Bruce Willis had me spooked, that was all. I picked up Old Yeller and started to leave, then stopped. The chair wasn't under the back-door knob. It was beside it.

I shut my eyes, trying to picture myself doing the nightly ritual of securing the place earlier in the day. It was like taking vitamins; you do it so often you can't remember exactly from one day to the next. Maybe I forgot the chair. Last night, when I went to the town house, seemed like a hundred years ago.

I was tired, I was hungry, I had eggs waiting, I told myself, feeling better at the thought of hot food until the curtain on the back door fluffed out from the frame. I walked over, my shoes crunching. I pushed the blue gingham aside to a broken window, glass on the floor. I felt cold, numb, violated. Even on the old marred wood, I could make out scrape marks where the chair was worked free from the knob and shoved aside.

Stooping down, I picked up shards, noticing a few drops

of blood there as well. Someone cut himself when he reached though the window. This was not a pro job but a person who wanted inside my house. Why?

I started to shake. The *why* was the same reason they poisoned my dog. Something besides fear stirred in my gut and snaked its way to my vocal cords. I slowly stood and planted my feet firm and put my hands on my hips. I wasn't exactly a Southern belle, but I'd lived in Savannah all my life and knew a thing or two about being fuming mad.

"I am not putting up with this foolishness any longer," I yelled. "This is my life, my house, my dog, and I'm telling you flat out—whoever you are, you're not getting the best of Reagan Summerside."

I looked around the Fox; there was nothing disturbed there. I stomped my way up the stairs as an act of courage, and also in case anyone was still hanging around. Maybe he or she would jump out the window. I grabbed a shower and pulled on a sweatshirt, jeans, and hiking boots from when Hollis and I decided to be more outdoorsy. That had lasted for all of an hour till we came across a Starbucks and regained our sanity. Today I needed to feel strong, determined, and in charge, and flip-flops weren't going to do the trick. I needed butt-kickers.

Ten minutes later, I opened the door to Auntie KiKi's kitchen and the aroma of biscuits, bacon, and coffee. Still in her blue robe but without the cucumber mask, KiKi scurried about, the Abbott sisters at the table, sipping coffee, a gift basket of pastries in front of them. No Southern woman worth her pearls made a morning social call without baked goods.

"Lordy, Lordy," Elsie Abbott cried when she saw me.

She dabbed her eyes with a lace-trimmed hankie. "KiKi just informed us about your poor doggie."

"What is this world coming to?" AnnieFritz added.

"I had to tell them," KiKi said, breaking eggs into a blue mixing bowl. "It's dangerous for all of us on this street when some ornery cuss is out hurting innocent animals."

"There's more." I took a seat at the table and reached for an apple fritter bigger than my hand. "Someone broke into my house last night. They busted out a window in the back door and unlocked it from the outside. I called the police and told them about BW and the break-in. As far as I could tell, nothing was missing. The police said they'd send an officer out later on and keep an eye on the street for us."

Jaws dropped. KiKi, Elsie, and AnnieFritz stared at me for a full five seconds without saying a word. Considering they were contenders for nonstop gossip awards, that was amazing. Finally AnnieFritz managed, "Things like that never happen around here since the Victorian District started renovations. Twenty years ago, homes were boarded up and sold for next to nothing. Then there were break-ins everywhere. But now that we've gone yuppie, everything is peaceful-like."

That every occupant had enough firepower to arm a small country didn't hurt either.

"This wouldn't have anything to do with you looking for Janelle Claiborne's killer, now would it?" Elsie asked, knowing everyone was thinking the very same thing. "We're all aware that you're trying to find out who did the woman in so you can get Hollis off."

AnnieFritz nodded in agreement and added, "Odds on the street are three to one Hollis is guilty as a priest in a whorehouse, but if you think different, honey, that's your business."

"Odds? As in betting odds?" KiKi's eyes were bigger than the yolks in the frying pan on the stove, the concept sinking in.

"Big Joey's the bank," Elsie elaborated. "He's sure Reagan will find the real killer. Big Joey says Reagan Summerside is a woman possessed, or maybe that was obsessed? Anyway, he stands to make what you might call a killing if she succeeds." AnnieFritz giggled. "I need to be more careful how I choose my words with Janelle gone and a killer on the loose and all. Have to respect those who go before us." Everyone in the kitchen made the sign of the cross for those already gone and in hopes none of us were next in line.

AnnieFritz said to me, "Sister and I have our money where Big Joey has his, and that's right on you, sugar. We figure he's street-smart and knows his stuff. He was at The Wall last night, and we happened to stop by for takeout after the Schiffer viewing. He remembered us from meeting up at the Holstead casket."

Elsie said to both KiKi and me, "All that crying and carrying on wears a woman out more than you can imagine, and Sister and I need to keep up our strength on account of we have a gig at a graveside at sundown. It'll be a two-hankie job for sure."

No wonder Big Joey helped me get into Boone's office. He was hedging his bets. Good deed? Ha! I took a gulp of coffee, wishing it was laced with something more than cream. Not only was I doing Boone's work for him, I was making money for Big Joey and the Abbott sisters.

"I know you've been having financial difficulties and all,"

Elsie said, handing me another fritter. "There's no chance you're moving, now is there? Since you opened the Fox, Sister and I have been dressing fine as peacocks, and business is booming. Seems classy women who know how to wear hats and use a hanky are in high demand these days. The young crowd is reserved and downright boring, not one gut-wrenching sob in the lot of them. No one goes home and talks about a boring funeral; they go home and say, 'Wasn't that a mighty fine affair, and ain't it touching how much Grandma's gonna be missed?'"

"How would you both like a job at the Fox?" I asked the sisters, hoping to take care of one of my own problems. "If you're betting on me to win," I said to Elsie Abbott, "I need time to work the case. I can't pay you—I'm barely keeping the place afloat—but I can give you 50 percent off anything you'd like to buy."

Elsie and AnnieFritz exchanged huge grins, their gray eyes sparkling. "You got yourself a deal," Elsie said, Annie-Fritz nodding in agreement. "We'll come over later on, and you can show us the ropes. Right now we're off to do our nails and then have our hair done up. We gotta look the part and all. Everyone will be decked out this evening on their way to the garden parties."

"And we need to find Big Joey and put another hundred on Reagan to win," Elsie added, and she and AnnieFritz hurried out the back door.

KiKi said to me, "Reagan, honey, they're betting on you just like a football game. How do you keep getting mixed up in these things?"

"I married Hollis, and the rest is history."

KiKi served me a plate of scrambled eggs, bacon, and

two biscuits so light they hovered. I took a forkful of eggs, and KiKi sat down and asked, "I suppose you're dressed like Sarah Palin because it's bear-hunting season in Savannah?"

I munched the bacon, thinking how much BW would love it. When he came home, we'd have a bacon fest. Maybe bacon wrapped around hot dogs—when I could actually afford bacon, that is. "I'm going to the crime scene and needed some courage to face the place. No one gets courage wearing flip-flops. Boone said the police have enough evidence to convict Hollis, and the case is ancient history. No one will be around."

"We're going to break in where Cupcake was . . . you know . . . killed?"

"You don't need to come. Hollis will have a conniption if you get caught."

"Your mamma will have a conniption if *you* get caught. I suppose they can have their conniptions together. Cher says, 'The only two people you answer to in this world are yourself and God,' and I'm sure the Lord wants to know what's going on around here as much as anybody. We need to get to the bottom of this, Reagan," KiKi added, sounding more serious than usual. "Whoever killed Cupcake isn't about to leave you be."

No longer hungry, I put my fork down. "That's what Boone said."

"For once the man's right about something," she said over her shoulder as she walked out of the room.

Fifteen minutes later, Auntie KiKi came back into the kitchen wearing a tweed skirt and tan blazer, her usually frizzed-out auburn hair pulled back in a tight bun, making her eyes crease at the corners. Arms held out, she did a little turn around and said, "It's a crime-solving outfit. Miss Marple. Very British. I wore it for Halloween a few years back. I think I'll make scones for dinner."

Except this was Savannah in April, but the scone idea had merit. If I could wear butt-kickers, KiKi could do tweed. She said to me, "I heard you talking. Did you call to see how BW is?"

"He's eating and still sleeping a lot. We can pick him up this afternoon."

"Bet that vet bill set you back a pretty penny."

"Boone paid."

"That was darn nice of him."

"Yeah, Boon's a regular Georgia peach." *Mostly the pits.*

We headed up Lincoln, the morning rush-hour traffic starting to take hold of the city. We turned onto East Hall, a quiet residential street with rehabbed houses and buyers hoping to make a tidy profit in a few years when the homes sold. KiKi pulled the Beemer in front of the "For Sale" house, which had yellow tape across the door. She kept the motor idling. The house was a teal Colonial Revival with black shutters, hand-turned spindles, peeling paint, and a collapsing roof. It needed love and money, lots and lots of money. "It's still decorated up with crime tape," KiKi said. "We can't just mosey on up to the front door and have you kick it in with your clodhoppers."

"These are hiking boots, and I was thinking something a little more subtle than kicking the door in. Let's park down the street and walk back this way. The house is on a corner; we'll cut in through the backyard."

"We could do this at night when it's dark, you know. It's

a lot easier to sneak around then without drawing attention."

"Do you want to look at Cupcake's blood on the carpet in the middle of the night?"

"Point taken." KiKi parked on the next block. We got out and strolled casually up East Hall. Birds chirped, flowers bloomed, and we were just two very strangely dressed women out for a morning stroll on a lovely spring day. When we got to the house, we took the side street, and KiKi casually followed me as I edged into the grass. The wood privacy fence across the back property line kept nosy neighbors from calling the cops on us. We made our way between two big hydrangeas that would really be something come May.

"Hi there," a man's voice called to us from across the street. It was too friendly to be the police, but we were busted all the same. "You ladies aiming to buy the place?" he asked us as he came our way. "Bet you can get a good deal on this nice, old place. It sure is sweet, don't you think? It's got original windows and hand-turned spindles. The inside's even better, with pocket doors and coved ceilings. Just needs a little TLC is all."

The man was sixtyish, with gray hair, and clearly more a lover of Southern cuisine and channel surfing than *Cooking Light* and sit-ups.

KiKi and I stepped back onto the sidewalk, and KiKi gave him one of her reassuring smiles that said all was right with the world and aren't we two of the sweetest women you ever did see.

"My daughter and I are looking to buy on this street," KiKi said, lying better than I ever could. "Such a nice area.

This house is a great fixer-upper and sort of caught our eye. Has there been trouble of some sort? We couldn't help but notice the yellow tape on the front door."

"An unfortunate occurrence," the man said in reverent, hushed tones.

"Occurrence?"

"Murder." His voice was barely a whisper. "I'm sure you can get the place right cheap because of it. You'll probably need to redo the inside, but that shouldn't be a problem for someone like yourselves."

He blushed. "I saw you park your BMW down on the next block. My wife and I live across the street and hope that someone who could afford this place would move in right quick and put an end to all the talk and gossip. Having an unfortunate occurrence on the street hurts property values, and the sooner we can put that behind us, the better for us all."

KiKi and I nodded in sympathy, and I asked, "Is there anyone else looking at the place? Like before the unfortunate occurrence? I mean, they might be after it at a low price as well."

"Well now, the very night the occurrence took place, a nice couple showed up, but JeriLynn—that's my wife, Jeri-Lynn—and I'm Tommy Lee—we knew nothing would come of it." Tommy Lee held out his hand, and we exchanged shakes. Then Tommy Lee went on, "We knew that couple couldn't pay what it would take to bring the place up to snuff. You can tell by the cars people drive if they can afford the house or not. That couple drove a Ford Minivan; that's not the kind of money needed for this-here rehab job. But there was a woman before them who took a look-see. Now she could afford to fix it up if she had a mind; I could tell right off."

"You knew her?" I asked, hoping for a clue to the mystery woman.

Tommy Lee shook his head. "She was dressed plain, nothing noticeable. I didn't pay much mind to her at first. Thought she was just another looker. But I think she dressed the way she did to keep the price of the house down so the real estate agent thought she didn't have much money and would take a low offer if she made one."

"How do you know she had money?"

Tommy Lee gave us a sly wink. "She drove a real nice car. Parked it way down the street, beyond where you parked today, and she walked all the way back. I didn't see her car at first, but I watched close when she left. That's when I noticed the Escalade, late model, white or maybe silver. It was getting dark so it was real hard to tell."

"Was she in the house long? I mean, do you think she was interested in the place?" I added the last part to sound less like the police grilling a witness and more like a friendly house hunter out for a nice chat and maybe saving property values.

"A few minutes or so is all. Guess she wasn't happy with the interior. I know it needs renovations. When she left, she kept her head down and kept walking, not one bit pleased about anything. After that, JeriLynn and I headed out to the movies. We wanted to catch that new Michael Moore movie. Jeri loves Michael Moore; she thinks he's the best director ever. The next morning, Frank—that's our neighbor to the right, in the nice big Queen Anne—told us about the Lexus he saw in the driveway."

Tommy Lee wrung his hands. "We all had such high hopes for the Lexus, figuring someone who made a late appointment like that at night must be serious about buying, and, of course, he had the right car. Then we went and found out it was the killer himself carting off the body. We should have suspected something wasn't right. Frank said the Lexus only stayed ten minutes or so."

Tommy Lee looked stricken for a moment, then forced a smile. "But now that the murderer's been caught, I'm thinking the lady in the Escalade might come back and get the house real cheap. Then again, if you beat her to it, you can get the place for a good price and fix it up fine and dandy. Everyone around here will forget about the unfortunate occurrence in no time. Everything will get back to normal."

I'm sure Cupcake would take issue with that *normal* part. We thanked Tommy Lee for his help and assured him we'd think seriously about the house. KiKi and I headed for the car. "Do you think Tommy Lee is watching us?" I asked KiKi.

"I don't think much happens on this street that he doesn't watch." We climbed in the Beemer, and KiKi turned the ignition.

Feeling tired to the bone from no sleep, I snuggled into the comfy leather seat. I hoped KiKi got stuck in traffic for a few hours, but the fact that we were five blocks from where we lived didn't make gridlock much of a possibility.

"You know," I said before I drifted off, "Boone told me a woman came to see the house where Cupcake was killed, but he never mentioned that she drove an Escalade. I don't know why he wouldn't tell me that when he's hoping I find her for him. The rat."

"Probably because Tommy Lee didn't tell Boone or the police about the Escalade." KiKi took a left onto Habersham. "Tommy Lee is a man fretting over his property value and what this murder means to his pocketbook. He wants that house sold right now, and he hopes the woman in the Escalade will come back and buy it. If she gets hassled by the cops or Boone, there's not much chance of her buying."

I sat up, suddenly not feeling so tired. "Tommy Lee withheld information from the police?"

KiKi waved her hand dismissively. "Not withheld so much as had a temporary lapse in memory brought on by angst and greed. He told us about the woman in the expensive car to make us feel pressured to buy the house quick out from under her."

"How do you know this?"

"Honey, it's what I and any other scared Savannah home owner might do in this uncertain housing market. It's hard enough to sell a big old run-down house these days, much less one that's connected to a homicide. Tommy Lee's looking out for his bank account. Now, who do we know that drives a white or silver Escalade?"

I felt my eyes start to close again. "Mamma has a white one. The parking lot at the country club has a good number of white and silver, but other than that, I got nothing."

"Raylene has a light silver Escalade." KiKi said, sounding thoughtful. "Let's see now, I do believe she got it last year, said it was better than any old BMW, of all the nerve."

"Raylene has Dior suits and Chanel bags, and Tommy Lee said the woman looked dowdy. Dowdy is not in Raylene's vocabulary. I'm going to sleep now; wake me tomorrow."

KiKi pulled into her driveway. I had my eyes shut, but I

knew from the little dip in the pavement that we were home. She killed the engine and said, "Raylene wouldn't dress in Dior and Chanel if she's off to have a chat with her blackmailer. She'd park down the street, and walk back to where Cupcake was so as not to attract attention or be recognized. That's exactly what we did. Maybe Raylene went to the 'For Sale' house and told Cupcake she was tired of paying her off, and Cupcake said, 'Well, ain't that just too bad for you.'"

"How would Raylene know Cupcake had a showing?"

"Cupcake and Hollis drove separately to the Telfair. I saw her car, and everyone knew she and Hollis had that argument and she left. Maybe Raylene followed Cupcake because she wanted to talk about the blackmail money. Raylene sees where the 'For Sale' house is, then goes to her house and changes so no one connects her with Cupcake. Then she drives back to the 'For Sale' house."

KiKi heaved a sigh. "This is too far-fetched. Do you really think Raylene could have that much rage in her to kill Janelle? A good old Southern gal hissy fit that we all succumb to now and then is one thing, but this is out-and-out murder."

"You saw her reaction to the tilted fountain incident, and that's nothing compared to people finding out that she's paying off Urston to win Best of Show. Raylene's fight with Cupcake was before the couple saw the house. Cupcake was alive then, and how does the Lexus figure into all this?"

KiKi drummed her fingers on the steering wheel, her eyes not focusing. This was Auntie KiKi deep in thought. "You know," she finally said, "Hollis's office is right around the corner from the 'For Sale' house. What if Raylene spotted the Lexus parked on the street?"

"There isn't one fight between Raylene and Cupcake, but

two," I added, following KiKi's idea and running with it. "One before the couple who saw the house, and one after they left. After Raylene whacked Cupcake, she took the Lexus key from Cupcake's bag and got the car."

KiKi fell silent then said, "I can see Raylene bashing Cupcake—had the feeling a time or two myself—but I can't see her stealing the Lexus and hauling a body. Raylene's a size 4; she could never drag Cupcake to the trunk."

KiKi looked at me the same time I looked at her. Together we said, "Urston!"

I added, "She calls, and he comes running. They wrap up Cupcake and wipe Raylene's prints off the 'For Sale' sign. I'm thinking she probably held it on the sides when she did the hitting, and Hollis held the sign on top when he pushed it into the ground in front of the house. Urston gets the car, they toss in the body and the sign, and Urston drives the car back to where Hollis left it parked. The whole thing takes under ten minutes, and Hollis takes the rap."

"Do you think that's really the way it all happened?" I asked KiKi, unnerved by the whole conversation.

"Some of what we have is probably right," KiKi said in a hushed voice. "Some wrong, but there's only way to find out which is which. We need to chat with Raylene Carter. Are you going to tell Boone what we're doing?"

"Yeah, when hell freezes over."

Chapter Fifteen

KIKI and I picked up Bruce Willis from the vet. We got him inside the house and comfortable on a blanket behind the counter. He may have been an outside dog before, but he'd feel safer inside and recuperate from his ordeal. Whoever minded the store could keep an eye on him. The vet talked me into buying more expensive dog food, and with nearly losing BW, I buckled to the sales pitch. That I'd be relegated to cereal and bologna for the rest of the week was a small price to pay for having my doggie back.

I called Boone to tell him Bruce was okay and that I had him home. I was still ticked off that Boone was using me as bait, but I figured I owed him the call for carting me and BW to the vet. I got his voice mail and left a message.

"Well, here we are, all gussied up," Elsie Abbott said, coming in the front door of the Fox, AnnieFritz following. "We're ready for Consignment Store 101."

The sisters had their hair set in big round Southern curls that made them a good three inches taller. They were primed for retail action in dark skirts and cream blouses. I showed Elsie how to write up sales and keep the books straight so consigners got their cut. KiKi introduced AnnieFritz to working the floor. Clothes in the dressing room needed hanging up and putting back out on the racks. Displays had to be checked for such things as blues getting mixed in with the black-and-white display and other retail catastrophes. Scarves, gloves, hats, and purses always needed straightening to make the place look boutiquelike and not like a yard sale. As for dishing out gossip and chatting with customers, that part the sisters had down pat.

Now that the sisters were onboard, I didn't have to close the Fox for lunch or for those inconvenient times when I ran around Savannah trying to catch a killer. Between the Abbott sisters, Auntie KiKi, and myself, we had the Fox covered and could keep it open regular hours. All I had to do was find enough customers to fill all those hours.

"You got that troubled look about you," KiKi said to me as we climbed into her car to pay Raylene a visit. "Worried about Bruce Willis?"

"And the store. Do you really think I can pull it off? I barely have enough customers to keep it going, and now I've cut my profits even more by taking on Elsie and AnnieFritz."

"If we nail Raylene as the one who did in Cupcake, the Fox will get a lot of free publicity. You'll be on TV and in the papers. Everyone will want to check you out. Business will be booming in no time. You need to get one of those charge machines to take credit cards."

"What if we're wrong about Raylene?"

"Well, then, it's like Cher says, 'Until you're ready to look foolish, you'll never have the possibility of being great.' If we're off the mark, then we've eliminated Raylene and Urston, and we move on to someone else. But we're not wrong; I can feel it in my bones. Everything fits. Raylene and Urston have motive and opportunity. I got Bernard to switch his lesson from two o'clock to three. That gives us time to rattle Raylene's cage before you get back here and dance with him. I think he's sweet on you."

"If Raylene and Urston are responsible, are you still going to make me fox-trot with Bernard?"

KiKi tossed her head back, let out a wicked cackle, and hit the gas.

"Maybe I should have called Raylene," I said to KiKi as she pulled up in front of Raylene's house. "Barging in like this could just upset her, and Raylene upset is a nightmare."

"Think of it this way: we'll catch her off guard, and she'll say something she shouldn't." KiKi got out, and I followed her up the brick steps. What do you say to a potential killer? Shame on you? What did I know about grilling a potential murderer?

KiKi seized the pineapple doorknocker and rapped it down hard. In Savannah, not having a pineapple door-knocker was akin to not knowing your grandma's biscuit recipe by heart.

"You didn't give me time to think," I stage whispered to KiKi. "I need time to figure out what to say."

"It'll come to you."

"Heartburn comes to you. This takes planning."

KiKi shrugged, and Raylene flung open the door, a scowl on her face. "Didn't you cause enough trouble the last time you were here? Polka dots? What were you thinking? People are still talking."

Gee, we were off to such a wonderful start. "Could we come in for minute?" I asked, trying for congenial and nonthreatening.

"You'll probably ruin something again. I don't want you anywhere near my house."

"We're here to discuss Janelle Claiborne. If you want to do that on your porch, where all the world can hear, fine by us."

"What if I just slam the door in your face?"

"What if I tell the world what I found in Urston's notebook?"

Anger lit Raylene's eyes, her upper lip curling into a snarl. For a split second there was a hint of conniving, bitchy Raylene, who manipulated her way into Savannah society. Then nasty Raylene vanished as quickly as she'd arrived, and Southern belle Raylene was back. "All I know is Janelle was your ex's fiancée, they had a fight, and he killed her. End of story."

"What about your fight at the garden party with Urston over paying Janelle? What about Urston's fight with Janelle at the Telfair Museum when he gave her money? That makes you both suspects as well."

Raylene straightened her shoulders and jutted her chin. "I have no idea what you're talking about. That's ludicrous, and you best mind your mouth, Reagan Summerside."

"Janelle realized what was going on with you and Urston," I continued. "Urston has a gambling problem, and you have a Best of Show problem. The two of you cooked up a way to fix your problems, until Janelle came along. She was blackmailing you."

"That is outrageous. You have no proof of this," Raylene growled in a low voice. "Not one little bit, and if you spread your lies around town, I'll haul your behind into court and sue your pants off, or worse. Much worse." Raylene slammed the door shut.

"Well now, that was interesting," I said to KiKi, both of us staring at the wood door.

KiKi grabbed my hand and hurried me back to the car. "Honey, this is better than fried chicken for Sunday dinner. We went and got ourselves a real death threat."

"Oh, gee, I feel so much better now, something to add to dog poisoning and house invasion." I got in the car, and KiKi fired it up.

"Raylene's guilty; don't you see?" KiKi pulled away from the curb and headed down Saint Julian. "No one gets that upset if they're innocent. But the old bat's right about one thing—we need real proof. We need to find someone who saw her come back to the 'For Sale' house a second time, and who saw Urston drive the Lexus. Maybe that Frank person next to Tommy Lee knows something. Tommy Lee didn't tell all he knew to the police, and I've got a feeling Frank did the same. They want this unfortunate occurrence to go away and that 'For Sale' house sold. They are not going to be forthcoming with information that stirs the pot, so you have to come up with a reason for them to tell you everything. I've got a private lesson out on Tybee Island this evening, but you can go visit Frank all by yourself."

"Since when do you make house calls?" I asked KiKi when she pulled up in front of my house.

"Since Corilla and Jack, the owners of the Crab Shack, offered me a fine low-country boil if I helped them brush up on their fox-trot. They have a wedding in Atlanta this weekend and want to do it up right."

"And you're not taking me with you to the Crab Shack?"

"You have a rumba lesson and a date with good neighbor Frank."

KiKi handed me the key to her house, then drove off. I could almost taste the low-country boil of steamed crab, shrimp, crawfish, sausage, potatoes, and corn on the cob. There was nothing better than sitting out on the docks at Chimney Creek under a full moon at the Crab Shack peeling shrimp and drinking beer. I let myself into KiKi's house, borrowed a pair of her dancing shoes to replace my hiking boots, and for an hour I wrestled Bernard around KiKi's parlor.

After Bernard left, I couldn't bring myself to stuff my throbbing feet back into my boots. I carried them and hobbled my way over to Cherry House. I stopped in the middle of my yard. There was a sign with "The Prissy Fox" scripted in green and pink, with a little brown fox in the lower right corner. What a nice surprise after a trying day of butcher-the-toes and catch-the-killer.

"Where'd the sign come from?" I asked Elsie Abbott as I came inside. A twentysomething lady had a dress draped over her arm, but that was it for customers.

"It's from your mother." Elsie tagged a yellow suit that had just come in for consignment. "She had it installed and everything. Said you better get yourself some permits and a license to keep on the right side of the law. Said the sign made your place official. She bought a black suit and some nice heels to go with it. I insisted on giving her a discount. I figured that's the way you'd want it. She has a benefit tonight. Word on the street is she's being courted."

"Courted?" Well, that knocked the air right of me. "My mamma? A man? Mamma's seeing someone." I felt dizzy. Not because mamma was with a guy but that I'd been so wrapped up in my own life I didn't know. I was a bad, bad daughter.

"Not a man kind of courting; they're courting her to be an alderman. They want Judge Gloria Summerside to run for city council. She'd be a right fine city councilwoman. I'd vote for her in a heartbeat."

Elsie dropped her voice to a whisper and eyed the lone customer. "Business has been kind of slow, but Sister and I did take in a lovely writing desk from Darlene Pritchard. No reason not to sell a little furniture. We'll talk the Fox up at the wake tonight."

"How's Bruce Willis?" I asked, coming around the counter. I plopped my purse on the floor and sat beside it. BW looked at me and added a pitiful whine.

"He's fine as frog's hair," Elsie said.

"He's just playing you like a well-tuned banjo for sympathy," AnnieFritz added, peering down at me. "Won't have a thing to do with that fancy food you bought him, but when I opened the fridge to put some sweet tea in to chill, he came running like his tail was on fire. Nearly knocked me down and parked himself in front of a pack of hot dogs on the second shelf. He wouldn't move till I fed him the last one. Your food supply's kind of sparse these days, honey."

I wanted more than anything to go upstairs and sleep. Instead I said to Elsie and AnnieFritz, "Can you watch the Fox for fifteen minutes more so I can run to the store for cheap dog food? BW really needs to eat something to get his strength back."

"And remember the hot dogs," Elsie added as I snatched

up my bag and pulled on the boots. I cut through KiKi's yard, then the next four backyards. This way it was a five-minute walk to Kroger's, and that gave me five minutes to shop. I dodged behind a red pickup and crossed Gwinnett just as a black car came right at me. It wasn't slowing down. It was accelerating! I froze for a second, doing the deer-in-the-headlights routine. Survival instinct kicked in, and I dove for the curb, hitting the pavement stretched out like a baseball player diving into home plate. Tires squealed, and I caught a glimpse of the car fishtailing around the corner.

I sat on the sidewalk and looked at my hands and knees, which had just started to scab over from the alley incident. A trickle of blood snaked down my leg. My pocketbook had saved my face from taking the brunt of a headfirst dive, and it didn't have a mark on it. You gotta love pleather. A man rushed over. "Are you okay?"

A woman came up, then another, and another. Savannah was not one of those cities where people didn't get involved. In Savannah, everyone got involved in everything all the time and never let go. Savannah was more of a dog-with-a-bone kind of city. I brushed off offers to call the police, an ambulance, a cab, and one for a date for Saturday night.

"I'll take her home," said a familiar voice from above. It wasn't God, though at times I'm sure he thought he was. I looked up to see Walker Boone hovering over me. "She's a friend," Boone offered in further explanation. "I'll give her a lift."

Boone hunkered down beside me, everyone else drifting away. "What happened?" he asked.

"I tripped."

"With those boots, I can believe it. Is there snow on the way that I haven't heard about?"

I was tired and cranky and really fed up with things happening to me. I wanted boredom, monotony, a plate of brownies in front of the TV . . . if I had a TV. "Nothing happened. I'm fine; go away. Stay away."

"I saw the car that tried to take you out."

That got my attention. "Was it an Escalade by any chance?"

"You're having problems with an Escalade?" Boone put his hand on my shoulder. "Who are you not having problems with?"

I stood, feeling a little wobbly. "I need to get home."

"It was a Ford Escape," Boone said, still sitting on the curb. He held up his hand with numbers and letters scribbled on the palm. "License plate."

"What were you doing here, anyway? Following me?" I poked myself in the chest. "Bait?"

Boone got up. "I was coming out of the Kroger parking lot, and the Escape that nearly sideswiped you almost did the same to me. Is it too hard to comprehend that I go to the grocery once in a while?"

I narrowed my eyes. "That's the best you got?"

"And maybe I was following you a little. What was going on with Raylene earlier? She was one unhappy camper. That woman is scary."

"I'm going home now," I said, hobbling. I'd twisted my foot in my butt-kicking boots.

"I can drive you."

I didn't bother to respond but limped my way back up Gwinnett. I didn't have dog food. What I did have was a can

of SpaghettiOs in back of the cupboard that I'd saved for a
dire situation. I glanced at my scraped knees and hands.
I bet BW would love SpaghettiOs.

I TOLD THE SISTERS THAT I'D TRIPPED. I DON'T
think they bought that version of why I was banged up any
more than Boone had, but they were far too polite to argue.
After they left, I closed the Fox early and fell asleep next to
BW behind the counter. I was suddenly wakened by someone licking my face and making little whiny sounds. Hollis?

Actually, it wasn't Hollis, and it wasn't sudden I realized
once my grogginess cleared. The house was nearly dark,
afternoon having passed into evening without me or BW
noticing because we'd slept for hours. I took BW outside for
a potty break. He seemed stronger, sniffing and lifting his
leg with usual doggie gusto. But the best part was that BW
went back inside with me. He was housebroken. Usually
that meant a dog went outside; for BW, it meant he came in.

We heated up the SpaghettiOs and had a quick dinner,
and I told BW I was going out and to mind the store. He
gave me a big yawn and fell asleep behind the counter.

It was later than socially acceptable to be out calling on
neighbors, but I needed to talk to Frank. If he had seen
Urston driving the Lexus, it went a long way in proving
Raylene and Urston guilty.

I rapped the pineapple doorknocker on the big Queen
Anne, and a gracious lady dressed in a peach linen dress
and pearls answered. I flashed one of Boone's business
cards, which I had from my divorce days, and said I was
with Walker Boone, attorney at law, and we were defending

Hollis Beaumont and trying to get all the facts. As soon as we did that, the police would take the crime-scene tape off the "For Sale" house.

Frank and his wife were jubilant to hear that the tape and the police wouldn't be around much longer. I chatted with them for ten minutes about the house and what they saw, and I realized they knew nothing. Yes, the Lexus drove up, but it was dark, and they didn't see the driver.

I left the Queen Anne and walked over to the "For Sale" house. I stood on the corner by the stop sign, looking at the dark, dreary Colonial Revival. Houses not lived in took on a sad, abandoned look all their own, as if no one loved them and cared for them. This place looked worse. Not only was it vacant, but tragedy had struck. It needed the *This Old House* people to come in, work their magic, and make it charming again.

What I needed in the way of magic was something more than Raylene's Escalade to prove her and Urston guilty. KiKi and I had never made it into the "For Sale" house to look inside. It wasn't likely the police had overlooked anything, but they didn't know Raylene and Urston like I did. There was a golden rule to snooping: do it often enough and something pops up—usually when least expected.

I cut around to the backyard and, with the help of a half moon overhead, made my way to the door. Using the Big Joey approach to breaking and entering, I found the key in a flowerpot with dead geraniums from last summer. Saying a little prayer Tommy Lee was busy watching something like *CSI* and involved in someone else's problems, I let myself in.

The outside of the house was spooky, the inside something out of Poe. Humid and musty, it smelled weird, like . . . death. My imagination was in overdrive, and if a heart started to beat under the floorboards or a raven swooped low, I was out of there. Fishing around in my bag, I found my flashlight. I twisted it on and crossed the muddy yellow linoleum in the kitchen to the dining room. My footsteps sounded downright thunderous in the big, empty house. Butt-kickers did not make good skulking shoes.

The carpet was beige, covered with plastic tracked up with a lot of footprints and debris brought in by lookers. A section of the plastic in the corner was cut away. It was the section used to wrap Cupcake.

I took a few deep breaths and slowly walked over to the cut-plastic area. I couldn't imagine Raylene killing Cupcake or Urston wrapping up her body, but somebody sure had. It was somebody no one suspected, or he or she would be in jail instead of Hollis, and I'd have Cherry House free and clear.

I directed my light to the floor. I could see the path where the body was dragged. I started to shiver, and I felt sick. This was getting me nowhere, and the place creeped me out. I looked around to make sure I hadn't messed anything up and swiped a handful of debris by the door that I tracked inside. I was ready to put the key back under the flowerpot but didn't.

What if I needed to get back in here and someone else took the key? I wasn't exactly a supersleuth, and if I could find this key, anyone could. I locked the door from the inside, shut it firmly, and stuffed the debris from the floor and the key into the front pocket of Old Yeller.

Taking baby steps across the yard, I slid between the two hydrangeas and right into Walker Boone, who was leaning against the stop sign at the corner.

"You have no life," I said to him.

"What I do have are pictures of the crime scene. Find anything interesting?"

"Why should I tell you?"

"Because I have something of interest for you. Sissy Collins owns the Ford Escape that nearly took you out. Guess she's not thrilled with you messing around in her love life. If she tried to kill you, she could have killed Janelle. Good chance she's my mystery woman who came here to see Janelle the night she was killed. Sissy didn't want her blackmailing Franklin."

"Sissy Collins is a twentysomething, lovesick husband stealer." I squeezed my eyes shut for a minute, giving in to complete frustration. "Then again, it wouldn't be the first time a twentysomething, lovesick husband stealer killed someone, would it? Until you showed up with the skinny on Sissy, I thought I had this case all figured out."

"Is that right?" Boone had that superior smirk in his voice.

"For the record, Raylene Carter is your mystery woman who came to see Janelle. Tommy Lee, your reliable witness across the street, failed to tell you about the Escalade he saw. He thought Raylene might be a potential buyer for the house, and he didn't want you upsetting her with a lot of questions about seeing a murder. But Raylene left the house before the couple who had the appointment showed up, meaning Janelle was alive then. I think Raylene came back later and killed Janelle, but I can't prove it."

"Or maybe Sissy came here after the couple left," Boone added. "She's infatuated with Franklin and would do anything to keep him for herself. Then there's Dinah Corwin.

We need to find the one person who couldn't take it anymore, someone who snapped. People kill for revenge, greed, love, politics. Why do you think Raylene wanted Janelle dead?"

Raylene had a kid and a marriage. Paying off Urston to win some stupid award wasn't right, but it wasn't worth ruining a marriage over, and the Carters would not tolerate a scandal. "I can't tell you why," I said to Boone. "If stuff got out and she's not the killer, innocent people get hurt."

"I can keep a secret." Boone did a cross over his heart. "You'd be amazed at the secrets I know."

"Like about your friends over on Seventeenth Street? Why aren't you with them? Why are you here?"

Boone rolled his shoulders in reply, meaning this conversation was over. He thrust a plastic bag in front of me, and I looked inside. "Dog food and a pack of hot dogs? How did you know I was out of both?" I shucked in a quick breath. "You broke into my house?"

"With the glass out in your back door, the breaking part's debatable. I was checking on our dog. No hot dogs in the fridge. An empty Science Diet bag of doggie kibble in the trash. I decided to make a donation."

"Our dog?"

"With that vet bill, I figure I own a leg and the tail. I have a window guy coming to your house tomorrow." Boone walked off toward the Chevy, hands in pockets.

"Did you talk to Sissy?" I called after him. "If you're following me around, at least you could make yourself useful."

"Hey, I got dog food; that's useful. I'll leave Sissy to you. You're the one on her hit list."

Chapter Sixteen

THE next morning at seven sharp the guy from the hardware showed up to fix the glass in the back door. BW needed an outside break, and Auntie KiKi needed to catch up on my world of lies, suspects, and murder. She waltzed across the front yard dressed in a yellow dancing skirt that fell below her knees and a red top with lots of ruffles. It was morning and salsa-lesson time in the Vanderpool parlor.

"What did good-neighbor Frank have to say?" KiKi asked me as she handed over a steaming cup of coffee.

We took a seat on the steps and watched BW mark his territory all the way around the yard. The dog had a bladder the size of a basketball. "Frank is no Tommy Lee. He's got nothing, so I ventured into the 'For Sale' house." I shivered at the memory. "Creepy, but not much there either. Just the plastic the body was wrapped in and the drag marks from hauling it outside."

KiKi's eyes rounded over her mug. "We should have gone in there together. That-there's no place to be alone."

"How was the Crab Shack?"

"The crab was dry, the shrimp overcooked, the mussels spoiled rotten. Worst meal I ever had in all my life."

I clinked my mug against KiKi's. "Thanks for that. How would you like to visit Sissy Collins with me this morning?"

"I'd rather go back to the Crab Shack." KiKi did a slow head wag. "Do you really think she has any part in this murder? She's just stupid and in love with the wrong man is all. It's like Cher says, 'Some women get all excited about nothing . . . and then they marry him.' That's Sissy to a tee. The girl would get hitched to Franklin in a second if she could."

"That girl tried to run me over with her car yesterday."

KiKi put the warm coffee mug to her forehead and let out a long audible sigh. "Lord have mercy. Just when I think things can't get any more bizarre around here, they up and do. I'll crank up the Batmobile."

KiKi headed back to her place, and I clapped for Bruce Willis to come to me. He did one last celebratory leg-salute, but before we got inside, a white Escalade drew up to the curb and stopped. *Uh-oh.* Raylene. For a second I had visions of drive-by shootings where the bad guy whips out a tommy gun and opens fire. Raylene got out, but instead of a gun, she had an armful of clothes, nice ones that would sell in a flash. She pranced up the steps and thrust them at me. "Open up an account with my name on it, and you and KiKi come to my house at nine tonight. The help has the night off, and Junior has a bank meeting. Our son will be at a sleepover. Park down away and come to the back of the house. Be discreet."

"What's going on?"

Exasperation pinched her lips into a tight pout. She spoke between clenched teeth. "We can't talk here in the heart of gossip town, and don't let that mutt near these suits. I want a fair price for them."

BW might be a mutt, but he was my mutt. Temptation to shoo Raylene off my property gave way to fundamental nosiness. "What's this about?"

"To get the Janelle situation straightened out once and for all," she whispered. "If you want to know, you'll show up. Don't be late."

"Maybe you'll just shoot me?"

"You're not worth the trouble and aggravation." Raylene pranced back to the Escalade and drove off. I went in the house, hung up the suits, and told BW if he had a snarl like Raylene's, our breaking-and-entering days would be over. I gave him fresh water, and when he refused to move from the fridge, I caved and got him a hot dog. I thanked the repairman, grabbed my purse off the counter, and met KiKi in her driveway.

"Was that Raylene here to do business?" KiKi asked as we drove off toward Sissy's. "I could tell that she gave you some nice stuff to consign."

"It was an excuse. What she really wants is to meet up with us at her place, nine sharp. We're to be discreet."

"I'll make sure my life insurance is paid up and leave Putter a note confessing it was me who dinged the front bumper of the Beemer and not him. No need to give Saint

Peter too much ammunition if we happen to meet up tonight."

"She wants us at her house. We should be okay there."

"It's the 'should be' part I don't much care for. You've seen that garden of hers. Easy enough to bury a body or two under that fountain you sold her, and no one would be the wiser."

We headed down Abercorn, and I told KiKi where Sissy lived, on State Street. After knocking on her apartment door with no response, we headed for Good Shepherd Church, on Whitaker. We entered the side door marked "Office."

A woman in her sixties with poker-straight graying hair and a Peter Pan collar blouse sat at a computer drinking tea, pinky extended. "Hi," I said as we walked in. "We're looking for Sissy Collins. Has she come in?"

The faux-brass plaque on the desk said I was talking to Helen Lenox. "Is this about joining the church? We have a mighty fine church here. We're very active in the community, you know."

There were a lot of reasons people got struck by lightning, and it seemed to me that lying about joining a church when you had no intention whatsoever of doing so was a guaranteed zapper. "We met Sissy at the family-values rally."

"Maybe Reverend Franklin can help you; he comes in around nine. I need to run to the church for a moment. If he's there, I'll send him right on over."

"If we could just speak with Sissy?"

Helen put her fingers over her lips as if squelching a sob. "She's in the back office." Helen's voice warbled. "And to tell the truth she may not be the one to talk to at this particular moment." A tear inched down Helen's powdered cheek, and she took a tissue from the crocheted daffodil dispenser on her desk. "It's so terrible. I'm afraid Sissy won't be with us much longer. How can this be?"

"She's dying?" KiKi asked.

"Moving to Charleston."

In Savannah, those two occurrences were pretty much synonymous. We thanked Helen as she left the office for the church, and KiKi and I headed down the hall to an open door at the end. Sissy was piling belongings in a cardboard box. When she spied us, her face reddened, and her eyes bulged.

"You!" she said and charged at me, waving a statue of Saint Francis surrounded by woodland animals. KiKi snagged Sissy around the middle, rumba style, and held her in place.

"I hate you!" Sissy spluttered, fighting against KiKi, dropping Francis and cracking him into chunks of plaster. "You ruined my life. I know you were the one who told Birdie about me. I saw you and her out in that alley, and now Virgil's chosen her. Not me. Her! He's ending it between us. How can he do that?"

Sobbing, Sissy sank into a chair, and I closed the door to the hallway. The only place that carried more gossip than a funeral was a church.

"We're in love. We're happy together," Sissy wailed, burying her head in her hands. "First it was that Janelle person making trouble for us. Virgil told me all about it, and how she wanted money, and how we had to be careful about meeting. She ruined everything. I'm glad Janelle Claiborne's dead. No one deserved it more."

"And then you tried to kill me, too."

Sissy looked up though watery eyes. "What do you mean, *too*?"

"You killed Janelle so your affair with Virgil wouldn't go public. Neither of you had the money to pay off Janelle, so you did what you had to do for the man you loved. Then you tried to kill me yesterday because you think I told his wife about the two of you, and I was getting close to finding out you were the real killer."

"I didn't kill Janelle Claiborne," Sissy's voice wobbled. "I didn't have to because someone did it for me. If you don't believe me, ask Virgil. We were together at the Hampton Inn the night she was murdered." Sissy sighed and rolled her eyes skyward as if expecting the clouds to part and angels sing. "Virgil brought me candy and flowers. We danced to Lawrence Welk on the PBS channel."

"You could have killed Janelle together," KiKi said, arms folded drill-sergeant style.

"My Virgil would never do such a thing. He's a saint. He only helps people and is an inspiration to everyone. I think that's why he's such a wonderful lover; he's pure of heart, mind, and spirit."

My stomach lurched, KiKi stifled a gag, and Sissy buried her face back in her hands, crying for all she was worth. She finally managed, "Are you going to tell the police I tried to run you over?"

"I'm not the only one who thinks you could have killed Janelle," I said to Sissy. "Franklin as your alibi isn't much of one, with both of you wanting Janelle out of the way. I wouldn't leave Savannah and take a job in Charleston just yet. Makes you look even guiltier."

"All Virgil and I did was fall in love. Two people who couldn't help themselves. Maybe Virgil and I will both be arrested and convicted. Lovers till the end."

KiKi and I left Sissy in fantasy land and headed down the hall. "What do you think?" I asked as we stood on the sidewalk outside by the magnolia with blooms bigger than my head.

"I think Franklin should be castrated and do the world a favor, and Sissy needs a shrink and lots of meds. She could have killed Cupcake. She's delusional and so blinded by love that she's dangerous to herself and anyone who happens to get in her way. That would be you and Cupcake, in case you were wondering. Sissy's a big girl and looks strong. She could have managed the body."

"If she got the car close enough to the back steps of the 'For Sale' house, she could have dragged the body out onto the little porch, down a few steps, and right into the trunk."

KiKi checked her watch. "I need to get back for a salsa lesson."

"Since I'm up this way, I'm going to get Hollis's mail and write a note to the post office powers-that-be to hold everything. Piled-up mail is a surefire invite to burglars, and we've already had our share. I should have done it sooner. I didn't think it would take this long to find the killer."

"They find the bad guys in an hour on TV, and that's including commercials," KiKi said. "I'll have the Batmobile ready at eight thirty tonight. We need to talk strategy."

"Strategy about what?"

"If Raylene killed Janelle, killing us won't be a problem. An exit plan is in order, and I don't mean in a body bag."

KiKi drove off, and I hoofed it over to the town house.

Using the new key I got from IdaMae, I jabbed it into the lock as a man in khaki pants and a blue polo walked over to me. I looked up into nice eyes, great teeth, and a big smile. Ted Bundy had nice eyes, great teeth, and a big smile.

"Hi?"

"Now, dollface, is that any way to greet a newfound friend?" He gave me a little wink.

"Cinnamon Sugar?"

He tugged at his shirt. "Conway by day, Cinnamon Sugar by night. You're just the lady I was looking for. I hear you opened a right-nice consignment shop over there on Gaston. Think you might have something for Cinnamon Sugar? Gets real expensive putting together outfits for the stage, and a girl needs to keep things fresh and interesting; you know what I mean?"

"I have a black beaded shawl that just came in."

"Honey, Cinnamon does not do black."

Since Cinnamon was probably a size 24 and about 240 on the hoof, my resources were limited. "I took in a rhinestone necklace you might like. There's a red-sequin purse that might work."

Conway's eyes brightened. "Now you're talking. Cinnamon does well with red, maybe a little turquoise now and then." Talking about himself in the third person was a bit strange until I considered the fact that Cinnamon Sugar was one person, Conway another.

Conway said, "I'll stop on by later this week. If you happen to see anything else that catches your eye for Cinnamon, you just put it aside now, you hear?" Conway hitched his chin toward the town house. "Your ex's, right?"

"I have to get the mail and check plants that I'm destined

to kill. Do you know anything about watering? Too much, too little?"

"Botany major at Ole Miss."

Conway/Cinnamon Sugar was a person of many talents. "Some things are meant to be," I said. I turned the key, and Conway followed me inside. I led the way over to the mini jungle by the window.

"Walker told me the place was broken into." Conway said, gazing around the living room. "This here looks like someone had themselves a holy fit and broke everything in sight. Least they didn't knock over your planters. These are some expensive palms you have here. Your ex has good taste."

"My ex doesn't know a rose from a daisy. These belong to his ex-fiancée."

"And someone murdered her?" Conway pulled a few spiky brown blades off the palms. "Who would do such a thing?" He held up the blades by the window to get a better look. "Honey, your fronds are stressed."

I didn't know if I should make another sign of the cross or offer an apology. "I take it that's bad?"

"They're brown, not pink like they should be." Conway *tsk*ed. "Too much water."

A six-foot-two guy *tsk*ing like Grandma Summerside over her petunias took me by surprise. Then again, if the situation of brown instead of pink warranted a good *tsk*, size and gender didn't matter diddly. Conway poked his finger around in the soil, saying something about rotting the roots. I only listened to this part with half a brain, the other half thinking about the palm that was the wrong color.

Before when I'd been in the town house, I'd been obsessed

with finding the blackmail files or picking up horn-rimmed glasses. "Are these the same kind of palms that are out at the Sweet Marsh Country Club?"

Conway laughed, his big, white, toothy smile cutting across his mahogany face. "Cinnamon Sugar is not exactly country-club material, if you get my drift. But these here palms are exotic, and I'm sure the country club gets the very best out there. Raimondo Baldassare has the palms at his nursery, the only place around as far as I know. Raimondo grows things no one else can. Word has it he's got a new rose coming out this summer that's just dynamite. That Urston Russell guy who judges the Homes and Gardens Tour is going plumb crazy trying to find out what it is. Raimondo has a green thumb, as they say."

"And a mighty fine butt."

"Amen, sister." Conway stuck the fronds in his pocket, just the way Raimondo did. When he noticed me watching, he said, "You don't want dead leaves in your soil. Messes with the pH balance. Wait two days to let them dry out, then water the plants good and leave them alone for a few more days. Now, I better be on my way. I've got a show to get ready for, and right now I smell like shrimp and scallops. I'm a chef over at the Pink House."

"Shrimp and tasso ham in cream gravy over cheddar grits is my favorite thing at the Pink House."

Conway beamed. "That-there's my dear auntie's recipe. Like I said, chef Conway by day and best-queen Cinnamon Sugar by night."

Since it was day, I thanked Conway for the plant advice. I told him I'd hold the necklace and purse for him at the Fox. After he left, I wrote a Dear Mr. Postman/woman note and emptied Hollis's mailbox of catalogs, flyers, and a few bills. I put everything on the kitchen counter so Hollis could take care of business when he got out of jail. By then, he might be ready for a free cruise, a five-dollar pizza, and a hearing aid. I caught the bus, and as it rumbled along, I wondered how Hollis and Janelle could afford exotic plants from Raimondo when they couldn't afford a security system. They were gone most of the day at the office. It was only common sense to choose security over palm trees.

I'D FINALLY REMEMBERED TO WIND MY GRAND-father clock, and it bonged ten times, the rich mellow sound filling Cherry House as I opened the door to let myself and customers inside. Business was steady enough to keep me hopping, and in between hops, I wondered what in the world Raylene wanted to talk about tonight. Maybe she'd confess to killing Janelle. Maybe hell would freeze over and winged pigs would fly over Savannah.

I was putting a straw hat tied with a teal scarf on the display table next to a nice Coach bag when IdaMae came in from the direction of the kitchen. She gave me a shy smile and little wave from the hall. "I was up this way showing a bungalow over on Bolton," she said to me as she walked over to the display. "What a great store you have here."

"And next time you can use the front door."

IdaMae got all red in the face. "You know how it is: friends in the back door, guests use the front. After all these years of us knowing one another, it seemed more fitting for me to come on in through the kitchen."

Bruce Willis trotted from behind the counter, tail

wagging, snout burned in IdaMae's dress where it shouldn't be. Dogs have no shame. IdaMae scratched him behind the ears. "Maybe I should get a dog."

"You sure get along with this big old guy, but Buttercup might have something to say about a canine in the house."

IdaMae looked around as if to make sure no one else was near, then whispered, "I came to warn you, honey. I hear you nearly got yourself run over by that Sissy Collins girl yesterday. Everyone's talking about it, and I couldn't sleep a wink all night just thinking about you in danger like that."

IdaMae got closer still. "I had to get myself over here and warn you. Sissy's not quite right in the head, if you know what I mean. Her mamma and I are neighborly, and I remember her saying that her Sissy is sweet as pie, but if she gets riled up, she can be downright dangerous. I was thinking if she tried to do you harm, she could have gone after Janelle. Now there's a woman with a real knack for ticking people off. Some say she was into blackmail." IdaMae put her hand over her mouth as if just saying the word was sinful. "Others say Sissy Collins had a reason to get herself blackmailed."

IdaMae gave me a hug. "Hollis has his troubles, and I couldn't bear it if something happened to you, too. You promise me to watch yourself." She cut her eyes back to the display table. "And since I'm here, I sure could do with a new hat and maybe a new sweater to replace this old thing I have on."

I wrote up the sale and thanked IdaMae for the warning. I told her not to worry and that I'd look both ways before I crossed any more streets. I closed up at six, straightened, and cleaned till seven. I took a long shower, shaved my legs, and moisturized. Just in case things went the way KiKi suspected they might go tonight, I put on good underwear and a nice yellow dress I wouldn't be mind being caught dead in. If I wound up on a slab at the morgue, I didn't want to embarrass Mamma. These things mattered in Savannah.

At eight thirty, I met up with KiKi, and we headed for the Historic District. "Given any thought to that strategy you were talking about?" I asked her as we tooled along.

"To tell you the truth, I took a lesson from Janelle's playbook."

"You're going to blackmail Raylene?"

"I wrote a letter and put it in my mailbox. It's all about how Urston and Raylene are in cahoots to fix the Homes and Gardens judging and how Janelle got wind of it and was blackmailing them. I said that we're on our way over to Raylene's house, and if this note goes out, come looking for us in her garden under the fountain."

"That should be enough for the police to investigate."

"Who said anything about the police? I sent the letter to Elsie and AnnieFritz. If we don't make it home, the letter goes out to them. One phone call from Elsie and AnnieFritz, and it will be all over Savannah what Raylene and Urston have been up to. They won't be able to lift their heads in this town ever again, and it will serve them right."

When we got to Saint Julian, we parked two blocks from Raylene's. "I suppose this is discreet enough," KiKi said and killed the engine. We got out and walked down to Raylene's, but instead of going up the elegant front main entrance, we took the gate to the side. A narrow path led to the garden, which was lit with little brass electric lights. Raylene sat at a wrought-iron table across from Urston, my fountain trickling in the corner.

"I'm not sure why we agreed to come here," I said to Raylene, KiKi and I taking the two empty chairs.

"Because you have no proof that Urston and I were involved in Janelle's murder, and you're hoping to get some information to save that husband of yours."

"Ex-husband."

"Whatever. Urston and I need to get this Janelle thing straightened out before you ruin us both, and in this town it doesn't take much. Junior has no idea what's going on, and he wouldn't be one bit happy if he found out. Winning Best of Show is nothing to him. I do declare, all that man cares about is his bank and whether Mother Carter called today and whether she was fairing well." Raylene cut her eyes to Urston. "Some men never do grow up."

"We figure you know about our little arrangement," Urston said, ignoring Raylene. "Belinda told me that you found my red notebook and the racing form when you were at my house. Doesn't take rocket science to figure out what we're up to."

"I'm not proud of what I'm doing," Raylene added. "But I'm the kind of person that when I want something bad enough I don't wait around to get it handed to me. I go after it, and nobody gets in my way."

I was okay up until that last comment. "And we're in your way?"

"You two are in everyone's way," Urston grumbled.

"Now you're going to kill us because we know too much," I said to Raylene and Urston, and KiKi rushed in with, "You should know we left a letter saying where we are and what's going on here. If we don't get home in one piece—"

"Oh, for crying out loud," Raylene said in her most

exasperated voice. "There's no need to kill you, though there are times when it's been mighty tempting, indeed. The truth is, Urston and I weren't anywhere near Janelle when she was murdered. You're right in that I went to see her when she was showing the house, but that was the last time I laid eyes on the woman. I needed to talk to her. With me giving money to Urston and Janelle these last few months, I was out of cash. In the beginning, it was simple—I just paid Urston—but then Janelle came along. If I went to Junior for more money, he'd ask questions. Having the wife of the bank president involved with blackmail and bribery would not set well with him and even less with Mother Carter. Junior may not divorce me, but things would never be the same between us; I know it."

"Janelle said she didn't care about your problems so then you killed her," KiKi said putting the obvious spin on the story.

"You're not getting this at all," Raylene huffed. "Janelle and I had a fight, verbal not physical, over my paying her. I couldn't afford it. She told me that was too bad and a couple wanting to look at the house was due any minute, so I left the place. I called Urston, and we met at Forsyth Park, in front of the fountain. There was a concert that night, and I had on some dreadful clothes that one of the maids keeps here at the house. Urston and I blended right in with the Savannah riffraff. We needed to figure out what to do about Janelle, but there was nothing we could do. Janelle held all the cards."

I rolled my eyes so far back that I nearly fell out of the chair. "And you expect me to believe that you then left the park and meekly went home."

"After my encounter with Janelle, I was dying of thirst and started to buy lemonade from a street vendor," Raylene continued. "Lola's Lemonade. She had a daughter, six or seven, who kept playing with the cups. I told the girl to stop touching everything with her dirty little grimy hands and that she needed a haircut and to wash her filthy face. She called me an old witch. I called her a street urchin. The mother and I got into it, and a policeman came over."

I felt bad for the little girl, the mother, and the cop, and it was unfortunate Raylene hadn't gotten tossed in the slammer.

"If you have any notion about telling Junior or the Homes and Gardens Committee about Urston and me and our arrangement"—Raylene went on—"realize it's your word against ours. You have no evidence of bribery or payoffs. You'll look like fools. And, of course, I'll have to sue you for defamation of character."

The looking-like-fools part was more bark than bite. Half of Savannah already suspected there was something going on between Raylene and Urston. Getting Best of Show three years in a row was suspicious as a hairpin in a bachelor's bed. "What did Janelle have on you?"

"Why do you need to know?" Raylene asked.

"It could help us find the killer, and that would get us off your back." Truth be told, it was a bad case of plain old Savannah nosiness on my part.

"This whole ugly affair is a result of Urston's big ego and small brain," Raylene quipped.

Urston straightened his bow tie. "Janelle played me like she played Hollis. She was young and pretty, and she and I shared a few bottles of Château Lafite. I told her I was an important person in this town and I was going to make Raylene win the competition. Janelle said I was fantastic, powerful, and handsome. She followed me around till she got pictures of Raylene paying me."

"Who knows where those pictures are now, but you sure don't have them," Raylene said to me in her snooty, high-pitched voice, irritating as nails across a blackboard. "In fact, you don't have anything on us." She stood. "Now go find the real murderer and leave us be." She did a little shoo wave as if KiKi and I were pesky mosquitoes who dared to invade her garden.

On our way to the Beemer, I said to KiKi, "I was so sure Raylene and Urston had something to do with Janelle's murder, and now we've got nothing."

KiKi gave me a devilish grin. "We got Raylene sweating, and that in itself is worth the price of admission. But I have to say, this makes Sissy Collins our gal." KiKi took the driver's side. "She must have been the one to visit Janelle after the couple left. She killed her and got the Lexus using the key in Janelle's purse."

"Can you really see Sissy doing that? Having the where-withal to pull it off?" I asked KiKi.

"Bet if I had a martini in my hand I could see it a lot better." KiKi headed up Bull Street to Jen's and Friends. The place had cheap drinks, was always crowded, and the decibel level made overhearing anything nearly impossible.

"How do you think Sissy got in the 'For Sale' house without being seen?" KiKi asked me once we had appletinis with more apple than tini, since we would have to drive home. We sat at one of the little outside tables on the side-walk, surrounded by other tables jammed close together.

"Same way I got in." I hunched over the drinks. "I snuck across the backyard. The privacy fence helps with the sneaking part. The night of the murder, Tommy Lee was at the movies and not out doing street patrol. Later, when Sissy came back with the Lexus, she'd want someone to see it because that would implicate Hollis. My guess is she drove real slow to give everyone a good look."

"But Sissy is so wrapped up in Franklin that nothing else registers with that girl, and the murder took some figuring out. If she is the killer, maybe she left something behind at the house," KiKi said over the rim of her glass. "I think we should go back to the house together and take another look around."

My skin crawled at the thought of revisiting the place where Cupcake died. KiKi asked, "So how did you get in the house, Houdini?"

Judge Gloria Summerside and Arthur-Murray KiKi Vanderpool were day-and-night different in some ways, but dead-on in others. George Clooney was their dream man, peanut-butter-chip ice cream from Leopold's their favorite food, and good-old Savannah stubbornness their life's blood. Reluctantly, I dug in the front pocket of my purse and pulled out the key to the "For Sale" house, still embedded in the fragments I'd grabbed from the floor to leave the crime scene as I found it.

"You need to clean that purse," KiKi lamented. "You're going to catch some god-awful disease they don't have a cure for and all your skin's gonna fall off," KiKi said pushing grass and leaves aside and reaching for the key.

"Wait a minute." I held my hand over the little pile of rubble in front of me. I plucked out a blade. It wasn't grass.

It was thicker, longer, distinctive, pointy, withered. It was pink. It was a frond. Yesterday I didn't know a frond from a cucumber. "This is a Tillandsia something-or-other. Someone else was in the 'For Sale' house the night of the murder."

"Right. Raylene was there, then Sissy."

"Besides Sissy." I held up the blade, pink, wilted, and interesting. "What do you know about Raimondo Baldassare?"

"How did Raimondo suddenly get into the picture?" KiKi asked me.

"That's exactly what I'm trying to figure out."

Chapter Seventeen

KIKI took the last sip of her appletini and wagged her brows, a sassy smile on her lips. "Well, Raimondo is always a fine topic of conversation, no matter what the reason. He's Italian, gorgeous, does up an incredible garden, and everyone knows he has the best butt in Savannah. Are you thinking about making a play for Raimondo?" KiKi gasped. "Is that what this is all about?"

Before I could answer, she grabbed my hand, her eyes dancing and not just from the tini. Auntie KiKi, Love Doctor. "Oh, honey, that's the best news I've heard all day. You're taking the plunge, getting back into the dating pool, and Raimondo is more delicious than strawberry shortcake at Sunday dinner. I'm plumb tickled for you. This is wonderful news. I never saw it coming."

This time I grabbed KiKi's hands and looked her dead in the eyes. "It's not coming. I don't want to date Raimondo;

I want to know what his plants are doing in Hollis's town house. Hollis has the same palms at his place that are at the country club, and we know the club spares no expense—the members wouldn't stand for it. How did Hollis get these expensive plants? More to the point, how did Cupcake?"

"And why do we care?"

"It's another big question that involves Cupcake." I twirled the frond around on the table. "Raimondo was at Cupcake's wake at the Marshall House. At the time, I thought it was a coincidence; the bar at the Marshall House is a popular watering hole for half the city, and he happened to be there. But now we have his plants at the town house. My guess is Cupcake put the squeeze on Raimondo, and not in a romantic way, and he gave her the palms. But why? What did Cupcake have on Raimondo?"

KiKi picked up the frond. "How do you know this is from Raimondo? How do you know someone else didn't drag it in that house?"

"When Raimondo prunes a bush, he has this habit of shoving the cuttings in his pocket so he doesn't leave a mess. Then he reaches in his pocket for his wallet for something else and the clippings come out, too. I saw it happen when I was at Raylene's garden party, and there were flower petals under his stool at the Marshall House. My guess is Raimondo was maintaining the palms out at the club, then came to see Cupcake the night she got whacked."

"Seems a little far-fetched. He could have been there anytime."

"That house wasn't shown all that often, and this palm isn't all dried up from weeks of lying around. It's fresh. From what the girls at the Cutting Crew and over at Shoes by

Sarah say, Cupcake was all about getting something for nothing. She coerced them into touching up her nails for free or new shoes or whatever else she can get away with. My guess is Cupcake had something on Raimondo and forced him into giving her the palms as part of the blackmail deal. He got tired of it all, paid her a visit, and killed her. He's a strong man; he could have easily moved the body."

KiKi downed the rest of her drink and mine, then handed me the keys to the Beemer. "Well, hang it all. We thought Baxter was the killer and that fell through, and the same with Raylene and Urston. My money's still on Sissy. What could Cupcake possibly have on Raimondo? He's not a sleazy hedge-fund manager; Raimondo plants pretty stuff in the ground."

"Tomorrow you should talk to Raimondo. Tell him you want to discuss plans for your backyard. I'll get Elsie and AnnieFritz to cover for me at the Fox, and I'll go to his house and find out what the Italian stallion is hiding."

"Honey, we all want to see what the stallion is hiding," KiKi quipped with a devilish smile. Then her brows drew down hard, and she folded her hands on top of the table. "If you get Raimondo all riled up and he cancels doing my yard next month, I'm going to be madder than a wet hen."

"Think of it this way. If I find nothing, Raimondo is off the hook, and you get a little one-on-one time."

THE NEXT MORNING I WAS UP EARLY, MOSTLY because Bruce Willis was up early. I could count on him to stay close to the house, unless a cat, squirrel, rabbit, or other furry creature invaded his territory in the morning, when he had energy to give chase. Territorial rights faded as the day wore on, and by noon BW was content to live and let live, and I could keep the door to the Fox open, giving the place a more welcoming appearance.

I sat on the steps and stifled a yawn as a scowling Auntie KiKi pranced across the front yard. She had on a yellow housecoat and matching slippers. Auntie KiKi, the princess of matching loungewear. "I'll have you know that when we got home last night I left a message on Raimondo's cell," KiKi said to me, without so much as a good morning or handing me a cup of coffee. "I asked to see him today and if he could pay a visit. Well, he just returned the call. He and his crew have two big jobs in town and he's busy as a one-armed paperhanger in a windstorm. He can't make it. That man didn't kill Cupcake; I can feel it in my bones. He's innocent of any wrongdoing, and this is just a wild-goose chase."

"Then come with me. We'll dig around out at his place and see what turns up." I winked. "Dig around? A landscaper? Get it?"

KiKi made a sour face. "I don't want to find Raimondo guilty of anything but taking off his shirt and making my backyard lovely as can be."

"You can find another landscaper."

"They're all fat and show their butt cracks when they bend over. It's downright obscene. Besides, none of them are as good as Raimondo. Take a look around this city; all the best yards are done by him."

"His nursery's out on Skidaway. Maybe the pink piece of palm is just coincidence."

KiKi waved her arms in the air and marched off, saying, "You're going to find something that's going to implicate

Raimondo, and here I am helping you do it. I should have my head examined for letting you talk me into these things."

At nine sharp the Abbott sisters arrived with peach jam, buttermilk biscuits, and cinnamon coffee. In no time, they were feeding BW bits of biscuit and deep in conversation with two early-bird customers about the likelihood of the mayor's secretary sleeping with the clerk of courts, and that our lovely UPS driver, Chantilly, broke up with her fiancée and was so distraught over the whole ordeal she was delivering packages to all the wrong houses.

"What's with the outfit?" KiKi asked me as we drove toward Truman Parkway.

I'd scooped my hair back into a ponytail and had on my hiking boots, brown shorts, and a tan T-shirt. "It's my blend-into-the-environment uniform. You know, like I work at the nursery."

"Have you looked at your front yard lately, honey? You're not fooling anybody." She glanced at my boots. "If I entertained any thoughts that you might be hot for Raimondo, they are now officially gone. You'd never get a man in that outfit."

"I don't want a man."

"Uh-huh."

The sky was overcast, a spring shower in the mix. "What are you looking for out at the nursery anyway?" KiKi asked when she got to the entrance ramp. "Raimondo works hard all day, then goes home and does more work. He's quiet, a man of few words in that sexy Italian voice that sends chills right through every female here in Savannah." She cut her eyes my way. "Well, most females in Savannah. My vote's still with Sissy being our main suspect."

"That's because she's not a lovely hunk of man in your backyard."

"There is that."

It was a twenty-minute ride out to Blooms by Baldassare. KiKi turned onto a gravel road, slowing the car so as not to kick up stones and ding the finish on the Beemer. The nursery was a flat stretch of land running alongside the river, with perfect rows of bushes and tress and flowers waiting to be planted in some lucky person's yard. The nursery was neat, orderly, well tended, and bigger than I expected, stretching on for acres. Business was good, very good.

"Turn there," I said pointing to a dirt road that led off the main gravel drive. "We'll hide the car back in the brush and sneak in the rest of the way."

KiKi pointed to the gas pedal. Her sandals were pink, strappy, with little buttons and bows, and I had an instant attack of sandal envy. "They'll get ruined if I walk in the dirt," KiKi said looking all innocent.

"You wore those on purpose."

"I'm not the one who wants to find Raimondo guilty. You go on foot from here, and I'll drive in like a customer. There's got to be men working here. I'll look around at plants, ask a lot of irritating questions that drive nurserymen nuts, and be the decoy. We'll meet up back here in forty-five minutes."

"That doesn't give me much time."

"That's all the decoy I can muster up for this project. Take it or leave it."

I got my flashlight from Old Yeller, then watched KiKi motor off. Taking the dirt road to the river, I faded into a line of river birches meandering along the bank. After a few minutes, I came to a clearing with a white frame house perched on one side and a cluster of red barns with white trim some distance away. Two greenhouses sat to the rear of the barns, windows wide open to let the spring heat escape. Even from where I hid in the trees, I could see hints of pink palms in the greenhouse. I figured the barns and greenhouses were business areas, the white clapboard Raimondo's own personal abode.

KiKi stood by her car, three men around her, looking a little befuddled. My guess is she was handing them some variation on the truth of Raimondo doing work for her and wanting to look at plants that might go in her yard. She pointed to a row of roses, then trees, and then a pile of landscape rocks. No one befuddled like Auntie KiKi. I crept over to the house, circled around to the back door, reached for the knob, and stopped dead. There in front of me as big as you please, was one of those blue-and-white ADT signs. Well, if that didn't beat all; Raimondo's house had a security system.

Then again, if I had a bunch of strangers wandering around my place and workers who came and went, I'd have an ADT system, too. Except so many times, people had them, got distracted, and forgot to set them. KiKi said Raimondo was really busy today. I crossed my fingers and turned the knob. No sirens, no flashing lights, no growling dog chewing on my arm. I was in!

The kitchen was neat, not crazy neat but light-years away from a messy bachelor pad. Dishes stood in a wood drying rack by the sink; three bananas sat in a basket on the table next to a stack of horticulture magazines. No crumbs, no spills, no dirty kitchen floor. I imagined Raimondo moving easily around his house, getting breakfast, sorting mail, drinking coffee, looking beautiful. I fanned though the magazines, gave the kitchen a final once-over, and spotted the end of a large, brown envelope sticking out from behind the toaster.

The rest of the mail was on the table, this envelope hidden away. It was addressed to Raimondo but handwritten, not one of those computer mass-mailing labels. It was from Estelle Smith, in Peoria, Illinois. Fan mail? Someone who knew Raimondo better than I did? Messing with mail in a mailbox was a big no-no, but it seemed to me that mail behind a toaster was more in the snooping category than federal-prison category, right? Then again, with all the other laws I'd broken recently, second-guessing a brown envelope was a waste of time. Pinching together the little brad on the back of the envelope, I pulled up the flap and slid the contents onto the table.

There were notes, drawings, and pictures of an incredible pink rosebush. I flipped through photos of people enjoying Christmas. Raimondo hugging an older woman with blonde hair, Raimondo with a middle-aged man and a woman, Raimondo opening presents and drinking a Miller Light. I always thought of Raimondo stretched out in one of those gondolas in Venice with a glass of wine and a sultry Italian beauty on his lap, not doing Christmas in Peoria. Who were these people?

I put the envelope back and started down the hall. The house was small; somehow on the outside it looked bigger. Raimondo's bedroom was a decent size with a queen bed not made, a nightstand, lamps, and a workingman's desk. I rummaged though bills, receipts, a phone number for Clark,

Dedmond, and Rice Accountants, and a postcard saying he was overdue at the dentist. I heard the back door open and close and nearly fainted dead away.

What happened to "no time to meet" and "busy as a one-armed paperhanger"? Heavy footsteps sounded in the hall, and I quickly crept into the bathroom off the bedroom and flattened myself against the white tile wall behind the door. The bathroom was neat and tidy. No dirty-clothes hamper to crawl into or shower curtain to hide behind. Raimondo had one of those new super jet showers that blasted the dirt right off.

I peeked though the crack between the door and the jamb. Raimondo wasn't in the bedroom, but I could hear him rummaging around in another room. When he came through the door, he wore skivvies and really nice muscles in all the right places. Sweet Jesus! Mamma never told me there'd be days like this, but she should have!

I bit my finger to squelch an appreciative sigh. Any lusty thing any woman in Savannah ever said or thought about Raimondo Baldassare was spot-on. Raimondo tossed his cell to the bed, then opened his dresser drawer and yanked out clean clothes. Raimondo was going to take a shower! From the odor drifting my way, I could understand why. What happened to the poor guy? Something with manure happened, that's what. Horticulture wasn't all pretty flowers and pink palms.

His cell phone rang, and he snagged it from the bed. He talked about a putting green. KiKi! She must have seen Raimondo come in, but her cell-phone diversion didn't work. I was trapped in the bathroom with no way out except through the bedroom. The only place to hide was a closet on the other side. I hated closets. I hated dead more. I crept carefully to the other side and opened the closet door just enough to squeeze though. I could hear more rummaging around in the bedroom and flipped on my flashlight to see if by some miracle granted by the saints of breaking and entering there happened to be a window and I could get out.

Except this wasn't a closet at all. It was a room with one of those fancy workout machines and a really nice tanning bed, which looked like a long space-age clam.

Footsteps came closer, going from carpet to tile. My heart was beating so hard in my chest that I put my hand over it to muffle the noise. Raimondo was in the bathroom. If Raimondo had killed Cupcake and he found me, I was toast. I thought of Bruce Willis without a doggie mommy, KiKi without someone to drive her nuts, and my cold dead body buried between the dogwoods and crabapples. I needed to hide, and all I saw was the clam. I started to hyperventilate at the thought of being wrapped up like a burrito in a tanning bed. I considered the alternative, which wouldn't have me breathing at all. I stretched out on the cool glass, pulled down the lid, and tried not to think how much this resembled a coffin. There was a four-inch gap between the top and the bottom of the bed. I clenched my teeth, focused my attention outside the shell, and turned off my flashlight. My heart raced; I could hear it. I was going to faint. At least I was lying down.

The door to the little room opened, and the overhead lights came on. I could see Raimondo walking around the room. He came over to the bed, his bare muscled leg right beside me. There was a click, and the lights in the bed blazed. I heaved a mental sigh of relief. Little spaces were easier to take when there was light.

His phone rang; this time it was the one out on the desk. I heard Raimondo walk out of the room. Shielding my eyes from the harsh glare, I could see him at his desk, pacing, still clad in his tighty-whiteys, and I would appreciate the view a lot more if it wasn't getting so freaking hot in here! So this was hell on earth; a tiny little space where I was cooked alive. My arms, hands, neck, face, and legs started to prickle, that dry, tingly feeling on my skin before I burned.

Raimondo's conversation went on and on. I couldn't get out of the bed. Raimondo would see me for sure. Minutes ticked by. I started to sweat. Reagan au jus. This was it; there was no way out. Raimondo would find me parboiled in his tanning bed, and I didn't even have on the cute yellow dress I wouldn't mind being caught dead in.

A loud banging sound came from the front door. Raimondo hung up, uttered a few expletives that weren't exactly Italian, and wrapped a towel around his waist. When he went for the door, I slid out of the cocoon. Creeping into the bathroom, I sidestepped a stack of fresh towels balanced on the edge of the sink and a bottle of Black Leather hair dye. I looked from the dye to the tanning bed to Raimondo. What the heck was this all about?

When I heard KiKi yelling at Raimondo about something, I crept into the bedroom, then the hall. My eyes connected with KiKi's for a split second; then I headed for the kitchen, with KiKi's voice escalating to keep Raimondo's attention on her and to cover my footsteps. Tiptoeing in hiking boots was tough. I opened the back door and ran for the river birches and didn't stop till I saw the gravel road. I hid in the brush waiting for KiKi, trying to catch my breath, feeling my skin crackle, sweating like a plow mule. When the Beemer came up the road, I ran for it, yanked open the door, and dove head first into the passenger seat. "Go!"

KiKi hit the gas, and the BMW lived up to the hype that went with the car. In minutes we were on the parkway and headed back to town. I finally got up the nerve to look at KiKi. "Guess this means Raimondo isn't doing your yard. You really lit into him back at his house."

"I'm writing you out of the will."

"Maybe there's another hot gardener around," I offered trying to salvage a great niece-auntie relationship. I expected KiKi to offer up another rendition of "There's no one like Raimondo," but instead a slow, sexy smile slid across her face.

"It doesn't matter," she said in a breathless voice. "Now that I think about it, I suppose I'll keep you in the will after all."

"Are you okay? Lordy, what happened back there?"

"I got to see Raimondo Baldassare in nothing but a little old white towel." KiKi's grin widened, and she fanned herself with her hand. "Life is good, honey." She looked a little dreamy-eyed. "Life is good, indeed."

"You do remember you're a married woman, right?"

"I promised to love, honor, and cherish, and there was not one little word about looking. I'm allowed to look."

KiKi was clearly in a state of Raimondo Baldassare euphoria, and I could relate. I could relate a lot better if I weren't cooked. "Do you know where Raimondo is from?"

"Florence, Rome, Naples, heaven—take your pick."

It was on the tip of my tongue to tell KiKi about the tanning bed and hair dye. I wanted to say there was something fishy about Raimondo. But I didn't. I couldn't. Raimondo wasn't just a superfine Savannah gardener; he was the resident pinup boy, the local eye candy, the man every woman in Savannah talked about at one time or another over lattes and martinis. He was Savannah's answer to Brad Pitt and Jude Law, and I had no right to take that away unless I had proof-positive Raimondo was the killer.

"Why are you so quiet over there?" KiKi asked, cutting her eyes to me. "What happened in Raimondo's house? What did you find out?"

"Nothing. I hid in the closet till you banged on the door and I could escape. That's it, a big waste of time."

"That's what you think." KiKi grinned again. "Since you didn't find any evidence that Raimondo's guilty, there's a chance he isn't, and that's good enough for me. My bet's still on Sissy; she's nutty as a Christmas fruitcake."

A tanning bed and hair dye didn't exactly smack of sanity.

When we pulled in the driveway to Rose Gate, the first big, fat drops of rain splashed against the windshield. I made a dash for Cherry House, the Fox emptying out quickly with the threat of an all-day soaker. Thunder rattled the city, and Elsie and AnnieFritz headed for their place to close windows and get ready for an afternoon viewing at House of Slumber. Bruce Willis sniffed to see if I had brought him food. Finding nothing, he settled in for sleepy time after an exhausting morning of eating biscuits. Morning business had been good, and the next time I went to the grocery, I would be able to fill one of those little plastic baskets. I wasn't up to cart status yet but beyond what I could carry in two hands.

I left the door open, listening to the rain beat a comforting rhythm against the metal porch roof. I didn't have any customers, so after lathering myself in aloe, I made a display in the front window with a navy suit, cream blouse, and a tan jacket. When I turned to add in a pink skirt for a little pizzazz to the display, I saw Birdie Franklin hurrying up the walk, huddled under an umbrella.

"You look good," I said when she stepped inside after leaving her umbrella on the porch.

"I got rid of the gray." She bit her bottom lip. "Mercy, honey, whatever happened to you? You look a fright."

I thought of my hair and my sunburn. "Which fright are we talking about?"

"You're red as an apple and your lips are swelling up like that Jolie person."

I ran my tongue over the fat, smooth, tight skin that used to be my average mouth. "It's allergies, bad allergies. What can I do for you?"

She blushed like a schoolgirl. "Virgil and I are going away."

"You're leaving Savannah?"

"Second honeymoon. Well, really it's the first honeymoon. We were broke when we got married. Virgil was in school, and we didn't have the money. I had an inheritance, but we wanted that for a house. Virgil says we don't have the money now, especially since I went and hired that private investigator. I told Virgil what a divorce would cost him, and he's starting to see things my way. That's why I'm here."

Birdie pulled a photo from her battered pocketbook. "I wanted to show you this so you'd know that Virgil didn't kill Janelle. I know there's been talk, and I wanted to set things to rights."

It was a picture of Virgil and Sissy, and Birdie explained, "The PI took it the night of the murder." Birdie pointed to the time stamp. "Isn't that a nice shot of my darling Virgil and his little harlot?" There were red devil horns drawn on Sissy. "So you can see that Virgil's innocent." Birdie snorted. "Well, we both know he's not innocent in some ways, mind you, but he's not your murderer."

And this picture proved that Sissy wasn't the murderer either. That pointed the finger straight at Raimondo.

"Now, with all that sordid business out of the way," Birdie went on, dragging my thoughts from Raimondo being a cold-blooded killer, "I feel the need to go shopping." She took down the suit I'd just hung in the window. "This is right nice, don't you agree, and just my size. I'll take it." She put the suit on the counter and gazed around the store as if it were her own personal paradise. She pulled a Visa card from her purse and tossed it on the counter beside the suit. "That's the card Virgil used for his tryst. I don't know what the limit on it is, but I'm going to try and see how close I can come."

By five o'clock I was exhausted, my skin was on fire, and my lips couldn't form words. Birdie Franklin shopped me out of everything in a size 8 and bought four purses and five pair of shoes. I gave her a nice discount and wished her bon voyage and happy honeymoon. She left, then brought me back a stash of popsicles for the swelling, a super economy tube of skin lotion, and a magazine, *Allergies and You*.

After she left, I sat on the porch, enjoying the cool of the evening on my toasted flesh and hanging out with BW. I sucked down one popsicle after another for dinner, sharing chunks with BW. We voted the blue ones best, followed by the red, then the orange. BW was great company. He didn't care that I had blotchy skin, that my lips were gross, and that I had two-toned hair that needed washing.

We decided Raimondo was not who he pretended to be. He had something to hide, and who better to extort money from him than Cupcake? It was a real shame he killed her, mostly because Raimondo provided great scenery for the local female population, and Cupcake had gotten what she deserved. Watching day drift into night, I let my eyes close, completely relaxed, and dozed off till I felt the porch boards sag.

I pried one eye open, thinking Bruce Willis was changing sleeping positions, except his big head was in my lap. I rolled my eyes up and zeroed in on a very ticked-off Raimondo Baldassare. He held up something long, thin, and silver. He gave it a twist, and the light came on, shining up to his menacing face, which looked demonic with all the weird shadows.

"I believe this belongs to you," he said without his sexy Italian accent.

Chapter Eighteen

"How do you know that flashlight is mine?" I asked Raimondo, trying to get my brain working.

"Mrs. Vanderpool was at the front door, and you were in my tanning bed." Raimondo shined the light in my face now. "And there's no use in denying it. You're a total mess. You got anything for that burn? You're going to blister and peel like old paint on a barn."

"Thanks for the warning. You can't kill me out here. I've got nosy neighbors. You have no idea how nosy. You'll never get away with it."

"Kill you?"

"Like you did Janelle."

"You think *I* killed her?"

"She knew you weren't Italian and was blackmailing you. Every woman in Savannah loves that you're sexy and exotic; if you lose that, you lose your business. I know you went to see her at the house that's for sale. You wanted to get her to stop demanding money from you, and when she wouldn't, you killed her, and if you come near me I'll scream my head off."

Raimondo turned off the flashlight and dropped it in my lap. "I didn't kill Janelle."

"Boy, if I had a nickel for every time I heard that line this week. I know you were at the 'For Sale' house, where Janelle was murdered. I found a pink frond from those exotic palms you grow. You're a neatnik. When you prune something, you stick the clippings in your pocket. The thing is, when you reach into your pocket, you pull out the clippings, and they go everywhere."

"I saw Janelle the night she was murdered," Raimondo confessed. He jammed his hands in his jean pockets. "I went in through the back door and heard her arguing with Raylene over money. Janelle just laughed when Raylene said she couldn't pay. Janelle threatened to tell Junior about Raylene bribing Urston. That's when I realized that Janelle was in the blackmail business, that it wasn't just me she was after, and she wasn't about to let anyone off the hook. So I left. I must have put my hands in my pockets, and the pink frond came out when my hands did." Raimondo took out his hands, tiny leaves of some plant coming along for the ride, proving his point.

"And you came back later on, killed Janelle, and framed Hollis."

"When I left, I went back to the Telfair. I had an interview with Dinah Corwin, that TV gal from Atlanta. She can vouch for me."

"An interview only takes an hour. That gives you time to get back there and do the deed."

"Dinah was running late because she spilled wine on her dress and I had to wait for her. Ask at the bar; they know me because I'm on retainer to take care of the indoor plantings. I didn't kill Janelle. In fact, after hearing Raylene and Janelle argue, I decided I was done with the whole ugly blackmail mess. I intended to tell Janelle she could shout who I am from the rooftops for all I cared. I was not paying her another cent."

"Who in the world are you?"

Raimondo folded his arms across his broad chest and leaned against my front door. The sexy smile was back. "Bob Smith, from Peoria, Illinois."

That took a second to digest. "Where did Raimondo Baldassare come from?"

"Desperation. I fell in love with Savannah when I went to art school here. My grandma had taught me about plants since I was old enough to walk, so I thought I'd open up a landscaping company. Nobody cared about another humdrum guy with a bunch of plants for sale. I left for a year and went back to Peoria. I bulked up, listened to Italian tapes, put on a white flowing shirt, dyed my hair and tanned my body, and came back as Raimondo. Image is everything, especially in this city."

"Why would you risk all that you've worked so hard for and not pay Janelle?"

"At first I needed the image to get the jobs, but now my work speaks for itself. No one's going to drop me because I'm not Italian. I do good work. My gardens are the best, and I have a new rose coming out that my grandmother and I developed together. It's going to knock everyone's socks off. I had no reason to kill Janelle. I was done with her."

"Then who did kill her?"

"You were at the wake at the Marshall House. There were a lot of people there that night, and it wasn't just a coincidence they were drinking and dancing."

"And they all have alibis."

Raimondo gave me a long steady look. "Somebody doesn't, or someone's lying."

He turned to leave and I called after him. "Will you still do KiKi's yard? It would mean a lot to her. I promise to stay out of your tanning bed, and Bob Smith is safe with me, I swear." I made a cross over my heart and held up my right hand, Girl Scout style. "I'm just trying to find who killed Janelle so my ex won't sell this house to pay his legal fees. KiKi is my aunt; she was trying to help."

"Tell Mrs. Vanderpool I'll call next week to set things up." Raimondo/Bob did the sexy smile thing again. "Seems to me your ex and Janelle deserved each other, and for heaven's sake get something on that burn."

Raimondo faded into the night. I was glad Raimondo-the-delicious was innocent and Bob-the-gardener was the toast of Savannah flora and fauna, but now I was out of suspects. If Raimondo was with Dinah, that meant *she* was with *him*. Everyone on my whodunit list had an alibi. There could be more suspects on Janelle's hit list of blackmail victims, but I didn't have that. I had nothing, zip, nada. The only thing I did have was a bad sunburn.

The killer was still out there. A time or two I must have gotten close, because my house had been broken into and I'd been grabbed and stuffed in the alley. I thought of that old Kenny Rogers song about knowing when to fold your cards and walk away. That's where I was. Tomorrow I'd pay

Boone a visit, tell him what I knew, and hope to heaven he had more information than I did.

When I lost Cherry House, I'd lose the Prissy Fox as well. Maybe I could find another location for my shop. Maybe I could move in with Mamma or Auntie KiKi and Uncle Putter for a while. Maybe BW and I could live in a cardboard box under the Talmadge Bridge. I considered my options. I always liked the Talmadge Bridge.

THE NEXT MORNING, BLISTERS HAD MORPHED INTO cracked skin. I brewed coffee, poured out two cups, and BW and I paid our favorite auntie a visit.

"What's this?" KiKi asked when she opened the back door. Today KiKi had on matching purples, from headscarf to velour slippers. Easter comes to Savannah. She gave me the critical-auntie once-over. "You got this from being out in the sun yesterday at the nursery?"

I couldn't very well tell KiKi about the tanning bed if I intended to keep Raimondo/Bob's identity a secret. "I've developed sun allergies. Birdie Franklin gave me a magazine; maybe it will help."

BW sniffed the kitchen for food, and KiKi and I sat at the table, which had been the gathering place for three generations of Vanderpools. What stories it could tell. "The good news is, Raimondo plans on doing your yard, and the other good news that is also bad news is that he is not the killer. He paid me a visit last night to return my flashlight, which I'd dropped at his place. He knew you and I are joined at the hip, and he figured if you were pounding on his front door in the middle of the day and acting loony, there was a connection between that and a strange flashlight in his hallway." A little white lie to preserve Raimondo's identity and KiKi's fantasy seemed like a good idea.

KiKi hunched over the table. "Raimondo really came to your house last night? Were you still wearing those god-awful boots? But I suppose with striped hair and peeling nose, boots are the least of your problems. Maybe when Raimondo does my yard, you can prance around in short-shorts and a halter top to pique his interest a little. You haven't done anything to mess up the rest of yourself, have you?"

"KiKi!"

"I'm just saying, is all. A girl could do worse than Raimondo Baldassare. Think of your kids with that lovely Italian skin and dark hair."

Wanna bet? I thought to myself, and took a big drink of coffee. KiKi went to her pie safe and withdrew a cinnamon coffee cake. Bank of America's safes had nothing on Auntie KiKi's.

I took down plates and got forks as KiKi asked me, "How do you know for sure Raimondo isn't the killer? I thought you had that pink-palm thing that put him at the scene? And if he's not the murderer, how does this translate into something bad?"

"The night of the murder, Raimondo visited Janelle at the 'For Sale' house."

KiKi gasped. "Mercy. He is a man of mystery. Raimondo has dirt? An ex? Kiddies? A handsome brother in the Mob?"

Lies were like that. Tell one, and you had to keep it up for ever. "I'm not sure about the dirt," I said, taking the easy way out. "But Raimondo had an interview with Dinah Corwin back at the Telfair Museum when Cupcake was killed, so Raimondo has an alibi. And Sissy has an alibi. Birdie

Franklin came in to the Fox yesterday and showed me a picture of Sissy and Franklin that the PI she hired took of those two together at the Hampton Inn. It's time stamped, and if a picture is worth a thousand words, Franklin and Sissy did not have murder on their minds."

KiKi slowly put down her coffee and slumped back in her chair. "I do declare. Raimondo didn't do the deed and neither did Sissy? Now what?"

"I'm headed over to Boone's to tell him what I know and hope he has more leads. I thought all night about there being another suspect, and I can't come up with anyone. I'm out of ideas."

"Jan from the Cutting Crew hated Janelle, and so did Sarah at the shoe store," KiKi offered up in desperation. "We need to talk to them."

"They're used to pain-in-the-neck customers driving them nuts. They may have hated Janelle, but if hair salons and shoe stores killed every nasty customer who walked though their doors, they'd have bodies piled high as the Forsyth Park Fountain and no one around to shop."

"You're giving up? We're giving up?" KiKi took my hand and looked sad clear through. "Oh, honey, this is plumb awful. You'll lose the house if Hollis goes to trial. The lawyer fees will be horrendous. I think you and Bruce Willis should move in with Putter and me; I truly do. Putter's always wanted a dog."

Only if that dog played golf and drank martinis at the club. "BW and I already have a place lined up with a good view of the river. We'll be fine."

KiKi and I finished our coffee and cake, talking about mundane things that didn't matter. Cupcake's murder had consumed so much of our lives this last week that it was hard to revert back to daily humdrum and be excited about it.

When BW and I got home, I changed into a skirt and blouse and put moisturizer on my face. I looked like a buttered russet potato. I told BW to mind the store and I'd be back by ten. I caught the bus and headed for town. When I got off near Boone's office, Dinky was unlocking the front door to Walker Boone, attorney at law. We stepped inside together, Boone following.

"I need to talk to you," I said to him.

"What happened to your face?"

"Hair-dryer malfunction."

"I've never met anyone else like you."

"Right back at ya."

Boone walked into his office, and I trailed along. "What now?" Boone asked from behind his big antique desk, which had probably belonged to Lee or Davis or Al Capone.

I looked to the wall, the bullet hole still there. "Aren't you going to fix it?"

"Great conversation piece. Keeps clients in line." He shot me a meaningful look.

I took a seat in a red-leather club chair, the same one I had sat in so often during my divorce. It still had my clenched finger marks embedded in the armrests. I parked Old Yeller beside me. "I thought lawyers wore suits."

"Have you ever seen me in a suit? You're stalling."

"Do you have any suspects for who killed Janelle?"

"And I should tell you so you can go mess up more lives? Sissy Collins was in such a state after you and KiKi talked to her that the church secretary had to call the life squad. It was some kind of anxiety attack. Sissy didn't kill Janelle."

"You want anxiety—she nearly ran me over with her car; now that's anxiety."

"Why are you here?"

"I'm out of the murder business."

"And the pope isn't Catholic."

"I'm letting you find the killer. I quit. The case is yours, all yours."

"You're giving up?" This time Boone sounded more serious. He let the words sink in for a second and raked back his unkempt hair, messing it even more. I doubted the man owned a comb. "About time you came to your senses. You don't have a clue what you're doing out there, running around looking for a murderer. The only thing you accomplished was to drive the killer underground and make finding him harder."

Teeth clenched, I leaned across Boone's desk. "I've been dragged into an alley, had my dog poisoned, my house broken into, been nearly run over, parboiled in a tanning bed, and will probably lose the roof overhead. I am in less than a good mood this morning, Mr. Attorney at Law. Do you want me to tell you what I know or not?"

Boone got a folder from the top drawer of his desk, and Dinky came into the office. "Mrs. McCoy needs to see you right away," she said to Boone. "Her husband just transferred their life savings to a bank in the Cayman Islands. I gave her a Valium and put her in the conference room."

"I have to take this. Don't hide pizza in my computer." Boone left. With nothing to do, I opened the file to pictures of Cupcake wrapped in plastic, her eyes wide open, vacant. I didn't think it would bother me after all that had gone on this last week, but it did. Death was never pretty, just sad.

The next picture was the trunk of the Lexus with the body in it, one without the body, a few close-ups of the "For Sale" sign with blood splatters, the dining room with the plastic cut out, and shots showing drag marks across the plastic. More shots of the back door, front door, the dirty floor with little yellow tent markers by a pen, black glove, used tissue, earring, and a blue sock—all left behind by potential buyers no doubt. Little wonder why real-estate companies covered carpets; they'd be trashed in no time.

I flipped the pictures over; there was just so much of Cupcake dead I could take before ten in the morning. I started to read the police report, but there wasn't anything I didn't already know, except that Detective Ross misspelled *chiffon*. I got to the part in the report about blood on the dress, which happened to be my dress that Cupcake bought at the Fox. Little gears in my tired brain start to churn, trying to make sense of what I saw in front of me. I stopped reading and flipped back through the pictures, stopping at the dirty floor. The blue sock thing threw me; who leaves behind a sock? I stared at the earring. It was black and beaded and dangly.

Holy mother of pearl! I bolted straight up in my chair. I knew that earring! I'd looked at the mate for fifteen minutes straight at the Fox trying to find a similar pair. That earring belonged to Dinah Corwin.

Everything fit like puzzle pieces falling together. Raimondo had the interview with Dinah, but he said he had to wait. Wait for what? Wait for whom? Why? This was before Cupcake's demise so there weren't all that many interviews because Cupcake spread those rumors about Dinah. And there was the little fact that Cupcake stole Dinah's husband back in Atlanta. Talk about a double motive. That first day Dinah came into the Fox, she said she'd spilled wine on her black dress. Raimondo mentioned it again when he said he was waiting for the interview. What if it wasn't wine but blood?

I grabbed the earring picture, stuffed it in my purse, closed the file neat and tidy as if all was right with the world, and walked out of the room. Dinky said Boone wouldn't be much longer. I said I had to get back to the Fox and told her to tell Boone something smelled really bad in his office and this time it wasn't my pizza.

I caught the bus, and by nine thirty, I was hurrying right on by Cherry House and heading for KiKi's. I banged on the front door.

"What's going on?" KiKi asked when I hustled inside. "You're all atwitter, honey. Now don't go getting yourself worked up this way; you can move right in with Putter and me. Everything's going to be fine."

"I'm not freeloading just yet," I said, trying to catch my breath as much from exertion as excitement. "I was in Boone's office looking at pictures of the crime scene."

"Honey, some people start the day with a walk in the park. You need to give it a try."

"There was a picture of the dining-room floor of the 'For Sale' house, and there was a bunch of stuff left behind by people who had gone through the house. There was even a sock. Who leaves behind a sock?"

"You're here to talk footwear?"

"An earring. It's black and beaded and it belongs to Dinah Corwin. She showed it to me at the Fox hoping I had a pair like it because she lost the mate."

KiKi led me to the kitchen table, where we drank coffee earlier. She pushed me down into a chair and pulled out the one next to me. "It's too much of a stretch to think you'd recognize a black earring. Savannah is loaded with them. You can't swing a dead cat around here without hitting a woman wearing a black earring."

"Dinah handed it to me herself and had me looking for a similar pair forever. By then I knew each bead by heart."

"Why would she let you look at an earring she left at a murder scene?"

"She didn't know she lost it there. How many single earrings do you have and don't know where you lost the mate? Dinah had no idea I'd ever look at crime-scene photos; she didn't know I was looking for the murderer. My guess is she lost the earring while trying to wrap up the body and drag it all by herself to the car. And the police can't find Cupcake's purse. I bet anything Cupcake was carrying the Gucci bag Dinah's husband bought for her in Atlanta, the one he took back from Dinah and gave to Cupcake."

KiKi sat still, hardly breathing. "Dinah got what was hers after she bashed in Janelle's brains." We both made the sign of the cross at the bashing part. KiKi confessed, "I have to admit, that's what I would do. Now what do *we* do? We don't have any real evidence to give to the cops, and that Detective Ross will never buy your black-earring story. That woman had on a polyester suit that must have been ten years old. Fashion is not that woman's thing at all. She'll never get it."

"So we make it her thing. Let's go find ourselves a Gucci handbag and a black earring."

"Where? How?"

"Dinah's staying at the Marshall House, and I have no idea how to get in her room." But the good news was that it probably wouldn't involve a tanning bed.

Chapter Nineteen

"I GOT Elsie and AnnieFritz to handle the Fox for me," I said to KiKi as I climbed into the Batmobile for another day of killer on the loose. "They promised to walk BW and not feed him any more biscuits. Seems I have a dog with fiber issues."

"How do you plan on getting the Gucci purse away from Dinah? Maybe she threw it away already."

"Would you throw away a Gucci purse? And this one has special significance for Dinah; it's her trophy."

"Like she won, and Cupcake lost," KiKi added as we did the stop-and-go traffic shuffle all the way up Abercorn.

"I've been thinking," I said to KiKi. "What if you take Dinah to breakfast, and I'll get into her hotel room?"

"Don't you think it'll look a little suspicious if I just ring her up out of the blue and say, 'Hey there, cookie, let's grab a bite'?"

"Tell her you've heard rumors that Raimondo has a new rose coming out this summer and thought she might be interested in it for her TV show in Atlanta. Say it's to make up for Savannah giving her the cold shoulder when she first got here. Take her to 17Hundred90; they have great Bloody Marys. Tell her about the Anna Powers ghost in room 204, make up stories, juggle, balance a ball on your nose, anything—just keep her entertained."

"We're both going to hell for all the stuff we've pulled this last week; you know that, don't you?" KiKi found a spot on the street so we didn't have to valet the Beemer. I said to KiKi, "I'll give you a half hour to get Dinah out of Marshall House, then I'm going in. Call me if you have a problem. Just think, if this works, I'll be living next to you forever."

"Right now I'm trying to decide if that's a good thing or a bad thing."

I pocketed my cell phone and some cash from my purse, then stuffed Old Yeller under the front seat in case a passerby had the hots for a yellow-vinyl bag and would be tempted to ravage the Beemer to get it.

KiKi walked off, and I looked up and down Broughton Street, hoping for inspiration. The Gap, J.Crew, and Abercrombie and Fitch were not inspiring. A Dan's Flora and Fauna van double-parked beside the Beemer. The driver, dressed in a green shirt and yellow ball cap, slid out, snagged a big bouquet, and hoofed it into the Gap store.

In Savannah, delivering flowers got you a free pass anywhere. All I needed was an outfit of some kind, flowers, and a big dose of intestinal fortitude to pull it off. I could do this. I found a tourist trap in City Market and bought a yellow cap with *Savannah* stitched in teal and a matching T-shirt.

I changed in the little dressing room and jammed my hair under the cap. I needed flowers, free flowers. The five bucks I had left would get me one rose, tops. I cut over to Hull Street and stopped in front of Colonial Park Cemetery.

KiKi's prediction of going to hell was about to take a serious turn in that direction. No one had been buried in this historical cemetery since 1850. That was a long time to be dead, but the soldiers there were not forgotten. The DAR made sure of that every Wednesday, when they had fresh flowers delivered to the center arch in memoriam. The random stuff I knew as a Southern history major was frightening.

I walked to the center, where a wreath of gorgeous daffodils, azaleas, daisies, and tulips stood on a wire stand. A wreath wasn't exactly what I had in mind, but it would have to do. "Look," I said in a low voice to all the dead people around me. "I'm just borrowing this. It's for a good cause, I swear. I'll have it back in an hour. What's an hour when you've been here for one hundred and seventy years, right?"

Getting no objections, I lifted the metal stand, then felt a heavy hand on my shoulder. "What's this all about?" said a voice with a deep drawl. For a second I thought it was God striking me dead for taking the wreath. Everyone knows God lives in Savannah because this is as close to heaven as one got on this-here earth in springtime.

I turned and looked straight into the face of Officer Dumont, so his nametag said. He was tall and thick and formidable, but he was not the Almighty. "I'm with Dan's Flora and Fauna," I said, lying to the best of my ability. "We delivered the wrong wreath here. This one goes to the Savannah's House of Slumber, over on Price. My mistake."

I held my breath and tried to keep my legs from shaking. Officer Dumont gave me a quick once-over. "Where's your van?"

Oh, Lordy, the blasted van. "My partner went to get the right wreath. I'm just going to walk this one over to House of Slumber, where it belongs, and make things right." I lifted the stand and started off. When I got to the corner, I glanced back, and Dumont was walking down Drayton in the other direction. I crossed the street, slung the stand over my shoulder, and ducked down an alley till I wound up in the lane behind Marshall House. Thanks to Baxter Anderson, I knew where the back entrance was, and I took the rear steps to the second floor. "I'm delivering this to Dinah Corwin," I said to a maid pushing a cart past room 210. "Do you know which room is hers?"

"Good Lord, did she up and die? Who would order such a thing for a living, breathing person? Miss Corwin's up in 312." The maid got close and dropped her voice. "She's a pain, that one is. Wants fresh towels twice a day, and the bed is never made up right to suit her." The maid glanced at the wreath. "Maybe someone's trying to send her a message."

I took the service stairs to the third floor. "I need to put this in room 312," I said to the maid doing up room 314.

"Sweet Jesus, are we having a funeral?"

"It's for Dinah Corwin."

"One can always hope." The maid gave me a hard look. "Flowers are to be left at the front desk, you know."

"It's on a stand. I have orders to put it in her room."

"Well, I'm not going to touch the thing. Bad karma." She slipped her handy-dandy universal open-door card into the slot, and turned the handle on 312.

"It'll just take me a minute to freshen this up," I said as I dragged the stand into the room.

"Honey, I'm here to tell you that you can freshen up those flowers all day, and they're still gonna look like they belong on a grave."

The maid shivered, made the sign of the cross, and left. I waited a minute, yelled thanks and good-bye, and then let the door slam shut, hoping the maid would think I was finished and left. Me and my intestinal fortitude pulled it off!

I searched the closet, then the drawers. The black beaded earring was right in with the pair of earrings I'd sold to Dinah at the Fox. I sat on the bed feeling weak and strong and happy and flabbergasted all at the same time. Dinah was the killer for sure; I had the earring to prove it. The whole ordeal was over, except for Cupcake being dead. Hollis would come home, and how much I owed Boone wouldn't be that bad, since Hollis didn't go to trial. Cherry House was mine!

I checked the door peephole. The maid wasn't in the hall, so I picked up the wreath, opened the door, quietly closed it, and crept down the back steps. I'd found the killer! My plan had worked!

"WHAT DO YOU MEAN MY PLAN WON'T WORK?" I said to Boone in his office an hour later. "I saw the earring that matches the one at the crime scene. Go to the police, get a search warrant, find the earring and probably Janelle's Gucci purse, arrest Dinah—end of story."

Boone had that patronizing glint in his eyes that made me want to rip all his hair off and throw him out the window.

"There's a glitch," he said to me in his know-it-all lawyer

voice. "You broke into Dinah's room, and from the looks of your outfit, I'm sorry I missed your performance. Anything you find because of the break-in is inadmissible in court."

"Tell the police you have a hunch the earring in the crime-scene photo is Dinah's."

"Oh yeah, the police just love that hunch stuff."

"Janelle had a restraining order out against Dinah in Atlanta. That has to count for something."

"So Dinah and Janelle didn't do lunch. The police can't ransack her room and her rights because of that. I need something more, something concrete to connect Dinah Corwin to this earring before the police will move on a warrant."

Boone looked at me, his eyes serious, his brain having a power surge. He tapped the picture from the crime scene of the earring I'd put down on his desk. "What we need is a picture of Dinah wearing this earring."

He got up from behind his desk, and I followed him into the large closet with the expensive espresso machine. He stooped down by a pile of newspapers. "We're here to look at your recycling?" I asked, the urge to strangle him stronger than ever.

"This is the week of the Homes and Gardens Tour, and Dinah Corwin has had her face plastered all over the newspapers. Maybe there's a photo of her with the earring. She dropped it when she murdered Janelle, so we're looking at papers dated before then."

I pulled off a handful of newspapers. Boone did the same, both of us checking dates.

"Here," Boone said holding up a front page of the *Savannah Times*. He pointed to Dinah with Baxter and Trellie Armstrong, smiling, holding drinks, looking very important.

"That's the earring!" I said, grabbing the paper right out of Boone's hand. I stood and did a yippee dance right there in the closet with Mr. Lawyer looking on as if I'd lost my mind. "We got her!" I threw my arms around Boone in a bear hug, realized what I was doing, and jumped back.

The corner of his mouth turned up in a slight smile. "You need to get out more."

"I get out plenty. What do we do now?" I said all breathless and exited. Finding that picture made me happier than I'd been in ages.

"*I* take the picture from the crime scene and the newspaper and go to the police, *they* get a search warrant, and *you* go home."

"Yeah, right."

We left his office together. Boone cranked up his Chevy and headed for the police station, and I hustled back to the Marshall House. I took a seat at the bar with a clear view of the double-glass entrance doors, the beautiful walnut check-in desk, and the winding stairway that General R. E. Lee supposedly took a time or two. With five bucks in my pocket, I ordered water.

Twenty minutes later, two uniformed police and Detective Aldeen Ross came in, Boone behind them. Ross flashed her badge and the warrant at the manager in a black suit, blue shirt, and yellow silk tie. Together the little party trooped up the circular stairway.

Boone spotted me. "That went pretty smoothly," I said to him when he took a stool next to mine.

"This is a nice place, but it's not the first time the Marshall House has seen a search warrant." Boone ordered a beer, and KiKi and Dinah Corwin came through the front door. KiKi mouthed, "What's going on?" behind Dinah's back, as Dinah said, "Well, I'll be. Here you two are together in the middle of the day. I think you're sweet on each other."

Dinah whispered to me, "But you really need to fix yourself up a little, honey. Walker here is a real catch, and you're looking kind of frumpy these days, if you don't mind me saying so."

Ross and two uniforms hustled down the stairs. Ross stopped when she spotted Dinah in the bar and pulled herself up to all of her five feet two inches. "Dinah Corwin," Ross said as she came our way. "You are under arrest for the murder of Janelle Claiborne."

"What?" Dinah looked ready to faint, and everyone within earshot stopped to take in the show. "You have the murderer!" Dinah declared.

Ross held up a plastic baggie thing that held the incriminating earring, and the Gucci bag.

"I didn't kill Janelle," Dinah said, her voice breaking. "She was already dead when I got to the house. I wanted to talk about the rumors she'd been spreading about me and tell her to stop. I might have done a little dance when I saw her beady little eyes staring straight up at me, and I took the purse, which was mine all along. Then I ran out. Well, I sort of skipped out, but I didn't kill her. I swear I didn't." She looked at Boone. "Can you help me?"

"Yes. Don't say anything more."

The police read the entire "can and will be used against you" mantra, then led Dinah out of the Marshall House in handcuffs.

"You're going to defend her?" I asked Boone. He tossed beer money on the bar.

"Why not? I sure didn't make much off you."

"This time you didn't make much. What about last time?"

"Yeah, there was last time. I'll get the paperwork going for Hollis. He should be out by tonight."

Boone left, and the rest of the hotel staff and guests switched gears back into a normal routine. KiKi hugged me tight enough to impede breathing. "That's it, honey," she cooed. "It's over. Lord be praised, you did it."

KiKi took Boone's stool and ordered us vodka martinis with blue-cheese-stuffed olives. "Now *this* is the way to begin a day."

I started in on the olives. KiKi started in on the martinis and asked me, "Why aren't you dancing on the tables?"

"Dinah looked totally distraught when Ross arrested her, not like someone who had killed and was glad that person was dead because she had it coming."

"Dinah was upset because she got caught. She thought she'd get away with it."

"Dinah and I had no use for Janelle, to be sure, but we'd both moved on, or so I thought. Why would Dinah risk that by killing Cupcake?"

"Because of Cupcake, Dinah couldn't get interviews, and she'd had enough of her; that's my take on this." KiKi finished off her martini and started on mine. "What are you thinking, honey?"

"I can't see Dinah pulling me into that alley, or breaking my window, or poisoning BW. I mean, why would she do those things?"

"I think there's two parts here," KiKi said, giving her martini-induced theory of the situation. "Yes, Dinah killed Cupcake for her own reasons, but when you went looking for the murderer, you got into a lot of people's business. The people Cupcake blackmailed got antsy you'd find out who they were and expose them and their secrets. They wanted you to stop, and scaring you is a good way to do that."

"I can't see Raylene or Urston breaking into my house."

KiKi held up a toothpick speared though an olive. "That sounds more like Sissy, if you ask me. Cupcake was out of the picture, Hollis in jail, and Sissy thought everything would die down and she and Franklin would go on with their hanky-panky. Then you came along, stirring the pot and riling everyone up again."

"That makes sense."

"Of course it makes sense. After a martini everything makes sense. Relaxes the brain, lets the little gray cells breathe free and unencumbered by problems."

KiKi finished off the second brain relaxer, and this time handed me the empty glass and keys to the Beemer, then caught a cab home. She needed to get back for a cha-cha lesson that promised to be very interesting with two martinis under her belt before noon. I wanted to tell Mamma about Dinah and find out if the running for alderman rumors were true. But instead of heading for the courthouse, I blew my last five bucks on milk and cereal and made a detour to East Macon. I parked in front of Hollis's town house. After a week in jail, having breakfast tomorrow in his own place had to be the next best thing to paradise. I was in a good mood, and I could afford to share a little paradise, even with my ex.

I put the milk in the fridge and dumped water on the plants like Conway said, except I dumped too much too fast, with dirt spilling down the side, leaving a muddy trail. I cleaned up the mess, fluffed up the dirt to even out the top, and noticed something sticking out where the dirt had been. It looked like the corner of one of those baggies Detective Ross used to protect Dinah's earring and purse. I slowly tugged on the corner, the bag sliding out of the dirt. There were papers inside.

My heart kicked up a notch, and my hands shook as I brushed off the potting soil and unzipped the top. There were pictures of Sissy and Franklin coming out of the back entrance of the Hampton Inn; Raylene paying Urston; Raimondo with his blond-haired family visiting Savannah; and Baxter with a woman who was probably his ex-wife in Atlanta.

There were names, bank-account numbers, and PINs. Welcome to the twenty-first-century method of blackmail: direct deposit. No clandestine meetings, no opening suitcases and counting cash in the back alley. More important, there were no other names on the list, meaning there were no other suspects, and everyone on this list had an alibi. I'd had a few niggling doubts about Dinah doing the deed, mostly because I liked her, but this tied everything into a neat little package. Tomorrow I'd give everyone on the list his or her information. Case closed.

I felt the universe shift into place, peace settle into my bones. I had my life back, my house back, and I had a dog. What more could a girl want?

It was three when I returned to Cherry House after visiting Mamma. She was running for alderman all right, proven by the campaign button she pinned on my yellow *Savannah* shirt. I walked into the Fox, and KiKi, AnnieFritz, and Elsie threw confetti at me and blew silver noisemakers left over from New Year's. Bruce Willis barked and ran around in circles.

"Oh, honey," AnnieFritz gushed. "KiKi told us everything. We've been on the phone for the last hour spreading the word how you connected Dinah Corwin to the earring at the crime scene. Glory be, you are the berries."

"And that I won you a boatload of cash doesn't hurt," I added.

"There is that," Elsie said and snatched up her purse. "Tomorrow night we'll have a nice supper, my treat. Right now we got to get ourselves ready for the Steller funeral. It's going to be a whopper. Clyde Steller was president of the Oglethorpe Society for years, and then he made that hole-in-one out at the club back in 2001. Hard to tell which will bring in the most viewers."

KiKi gave me another hug. "After the wake I'm meeting Putter out at the club. He's taking me dancing, which means he bought another expensive golf club while in Atlanta and is feeling guilty as sin about it. I have such a good time when Putter's got a bad case of guilt." KiKi followed the sisters out the back door, and I went and got the broom for the confetti.

"Good news," I said to BW as I tried to sweep up pieces of plastic confetti that stuck to everything like little magnets. "We're not relocating."

I finished straightening, then very quietly opened the fridge to check the dinner menu, knowing that if he heard me, BW would come charging in and not leave till he got his hot dog handout. Some dogs responded to a whistle; for Bruce Willis, it was the fridge. He was all guy. If I still had a TV, BW would probably have a remote taped to his paw.

I cooked up two dogs and SpaghettiOs, and we dined al fresco on the front porch with the cherry tree in full bloom and a half moon hanging over the spire of Saint John's. Hollis called to say he'd stop by around nine to pick up his keys and cell phone and that the crime-scene people finished processing the Lexus so it was ready to go.

I locked the front door, and BW fell asleep behind the counter. I put the day's take into the Rocky-Road carton, then dumped my purse on the counter to pull out Hollis's wallet, key ring, and the new key to the town house. I slipped the new key on the ring next his Lexus key. For a second I wondered how Hollis would get the Lexus home with me having his keys here till I remembered the Lexus was hauled off by the police, my key still in the ignition.

Except it wasn't really my key that was in the ignition, of course, it was Hollis's key. I was tired, not thinking straight, but this wasn't right either. I'd sold the fountain to Raylene, needed the Lexus for the delivery, and IdaMae had given me Hollis's key. But she couldn't have, because here it was, right in front of me on his key ring.

There were two keys to the Lexus. Hollis had one, and the other key I gave to Cupcake. I remember watching her snatching my keys and dropping it in her Gucci bag before picking up my chiffon dress.

If I had Hollis's key here in my hand, it had to be Cupcake's key at the station. IdaMae didn't give me Hollis's key; she gave me Cupcake's key, and the only way she could have done that was if she had taken it from Cupcake's Gucci purse the night she was murdered.

A chill snaked up my spine, and I felt lightheaded. Dinah Corwin didn't kill Cupcake. Dear God, IdaMae killed Cupcake!

I gasped at the realization and dropped the keys on the

counter. My head snapped up, my gaze fusing with IdaMae's, who was staring at me through the kitchen window. She should be home, having tea, petting Buttercup, going to the library. She didn't go to the library the night Janelle was killed; she went to the "For Sale" house and killed her! I lunged for the kitchen door to lock it, but IdaMae was faster. Her two hundred pounds shoved against the door hard, knocking me backward. Her eyes were dark, threatening. Her lips were thin and set in a straight line. There was no trace of a proper belle anywhere. *Good God, she looked like she came from Chicago!* She locked the door behind her and took Hollis's .38 from her pocket.

"Why couldn't you just leave things be?"

Chapter Twenty

"YOU should have let Hollis rot in jail," IdaMae said to me in an angry voice I didn't recognize. "He cheated on you, divorced you, treated you bad."

"Rot in jail? Hollis was going to sell this house to pay legal fees. I worked my behind off to fix it up. I redid the entire upstairs, including the bathroom, by myself. It's Irish cream and celery green; let me show you." I was scared and babbling.

"Stay right where you are, and don't move." IdaMae waved the gun, then picked up the key ring I'd dropped on the counter. "Everything was fine till Hollis put this in your purse. My plan was for him to give me the keys when he got arrested, not you. I was supposed to be there when the police came, not you. You hadn't been to the office in months."

"You weren't upset over Hollis getting arrested. You were upset because he gave me the keys. You wanted to water

Hollis's plants so I wouldn't use his keys and maybe spot the Lexus key. It's all about the keys. You dragged me into the alley to get at my purse, and you broke in here looking for it."

"I tried everything to get these keys," IdaMae snarled. "After the break-in at the town house, I had the locks changed. I wasn't worried after that, till Dinah got arrested." IdaMae wagged her head. "Hollis would be let out of jail and coming to get his things. I knew you'd put it all together." She bit her bottom lip. "I just knew you would. I even told you that lie about going to the library the night Janelle died. Why couldn't you just run your store and be content with that?"

"Why frame Hollis? He's family. How could you?"

"He chose her over me." IdaMae's eyes sparked with rage. "He was going to fire me. Janelle wanted to take over the office and wanted me gone. Hollis was going to do it; she told me so that night at the house. I offered her cash to leave Savannah. She laughed at me, said she had a lot of pigeons here. She knew dirty little secrets. Reverend Franklin was good to my mamma when she was at the nursing home. I wasn't going to let that two-bit hussy do such a thing to that fine man. She was mean and hateful, and Hollis was no better."

Her voice cracked and a tear trickled down her cheek, followed by another. "How could Hollis up and fire me after all these years? This here is the South. We don't treat family that way in Savannah."

"Hollis was blinded by love, honey." And IdaMae was blinded by hate and revenge. They all needed therapy.

"Janelle and Hollis had it coming," IdaMae declared. "I wrapped that little witch in the plastic, knew she had your

Lexus key because she'd been driving that fancy car the day before. I got the Lexus after I bashed in Janelle, and when I came back, her purse was gone. Someone had been at the house. I was worried at first, but no one said anything. I figured whoever took that purse was glad Janelle was dead. She was a mean, hateful woman. He was poison for you, Reagan. Pure poison for us all."

Poison. The word bounced around in my brain. "You tried to kill Bruce Willis. You're the one who fed him the chocolate. You even have it on your desk. That's why he liked you so much when you came shopping here at the Fox. He never did anything to you. He's just a sweet dog."

"He's a mutt. He's just like Janelle. No breeding, no family name, no old money or fine home. If he'd barked, he'd have given me away. I needed to get inside and look for that key."

"If you shoot me, KiKi and the sisters will come running."

"Everyone's at Clyde Steller's funeral. No one will hear anything. I'm going to shoot you with Hollis's gun here. When he comes in, I'll shoot him. He called me to say he'd been released and would be at the office tomorrow. He thinks everything will be like it was before. But it's too late for that. It'll look like the murder-suicide of a deranged man. His fiancée is dead, his business nearly bankrupt, and you won't sell the house for the money he needs. Everyone knows you had a messy divorce and hate each other."

The grandfather clock let out the first chime for nine o'clock. IdaMae slipped the key ring in her pocket. She was going to get away with murder. Make that three murders, and she'd poisoned my dog. Suddenly I was gut-cramping, hair-frying, foot-stomping, hissy-fit mad. There was something about a full-fledged hissy that cleared the brain and stiffened the Southern spine. I picked up the ice cream container. "I need to put this away. It's chocolate. I don't want BW to get sick again."

I opened the freezer door, then slammed it shut. Immediately, I heard the telltale scratch of nails on hardwood, and BW bounded around the corner in full gallop. Startled, IdaMae turned, and I shoved her backward as hard as I could, the gun going off, scaring the liver right out of me. I half ran, half stumbled into the dark front hall, remembering too late that I'd locked the door and now couldn't get out. I dove under the rack of evening dresses, trying to think of a plan besides being scared and throwing up.

"You can't run from me, Reagan." IdaMae's voice came from the hall. "I know you're in here."

For a second I panicked that BW would follow me, thinking this was a game. But no game compared to hot dogs. BW was rooted to his spot in front of the fridge, waiting. I didn't have a gun, but I did have home-court advantage. I knew every creak and groan of the old floors.

"I'm going to find you in here, honey," IdaMae sing-songed. "There aren't many places to hide." Her steps got closer. "Hollis will be here any minute, and then I'm taking care of you both."

The floor squeaked, then creaked. Hangers slid across a wood dowel. IdaMae was searching for me by the blouses. Footsteps and then a double creak put IdaMae by the skirts now. More hangers parted. She took two steps to the coat-rack, where I'd just finished a display of denim and red jackets. It crashed to the floor. Footsteps came closer, stopping in front of the little black dresses where I hid. I back-crawled out the other side till my foot touched the wall and my hand connected with the grandfather clock.

IdaMae shoved aside the dresses, and I stood, flattening myself beside the clock. I had nowhere to go. Faint moonlight backlit the windows, and IdaMae's silhouette moved away from the dresses.

Come to mamma, I mentally pleaded. *Just a little closer to the clock.*

"Reagan!" Boone shouted from the hallway, nearly giving me a heart attack.

Stupid man! He'd get himself killed on my account, and then I'd have to feel bad about it.

IdaMae turned toward Boone's voice, and I shoved the clock hard. It crashed to the floor, missing IdaMae but offering one heck of a distraction. I jumped over the clock and did a headfirst tackle, flattening IdaMae facedown in the hallway, knocking the wind right out of me and jarring every bone in my body.

"Get the gun!" I gasped as it skittered across the floor, but Boone was already stooped down beside me, gun in one hand, holding IdaMae's wrists behind her back.

"Let me go," IdaMae sobbed. "Let me go. You're ruining everything."

I sat on the floor, gasping for air, listening to IdaMae cry, trying not to shake so hard and wondering if I'd broken my elbow.

"This is not funny!" I said as Boone ruffled my hair.

"The Falcons need a linebacker." He snatched a belt from the floor and secured it around IdaMae's wrists.

"What are you doing here?" I pushed Boone backward,

knocking him off balance. Even in the dark I could see him grinning as he landed on his butt.

"Looking for you—thought you might need some help."

"You knew IdaMae was the killer and didn't tell me?" I socked his arm and his grin broadened.

"I wasn't sure till I saw the gun in her hand."

"You're enjoying this, aren't you? You're crazy as a waltzing pig. We could have been killed."

"Yeah, but we weren't, and it's always fun to nail the bad guys."

I sat back and wrapped my arms around my knees, trying to pull myself together and not shake myself apart. "Hard to think of IdaMae as bad."

"She's a long way from good, sweet pea," Boone said, his voice dead serious. He touched my lip, which I didn't realize was coated with blood. "She was going to kill you, Reagan, without a second thought. There's noting good about that."

"How did you figure it out?"

Boone leaned against the wall, looking comfortable. Sirens sounded a few blocks away. "It bothered me that Dinah didn't have the key to the Lexus. If she was the killer, it should have been somewhere. She had the purse and the earring; why not the key? Hollis said you had his keys. When I got the Lexus out of hock, there was the other key, the one you used. Your key had to be the one the killer used, and that pointed to IdaMae because you said she gave it to you."

"How'd you get in here? IdaMae locked the back door."

"You need better locks."

Sirens stopped in front of Cherry House. I turned on the

lights and opened the front door to red and blue strobing cruisers, four uniformed cops, and Detective Ross, who looked none too thrilled to see me. Boone gave the quick version of what happened, which didn't satisfy Ross one bit. She gave us the quick version of how we were not the police and needed to stay the heck out of their business, then added a few choice phrases straight off Seventeenth Street.

I watched Ross escort IdaMae out of my house and wondered how this all happened. A lot more was ruined around here than my marriage. I fed BW his hot dog and hitched a ride with Boone to the police station. "What are you going to do for fun now that this is all over?" Boone asked me as he drove the Chevy. He had the top down, displaying the meandering live oak branches overhead.

"Stay as far away from you and Hollis as possible."

EARLY THE NEXT MORNING, I DRANK PECAN COFFEE as Auntie KiKi stomped back and forth across her kitchen, little circles of smoke curling from her ears. "I go dancing one little old night with my honey, and look what happens— I miss everything. Who found Cupcake's body in the trunk?" She jabbed herself in the chest. "Me. Who was there when the coroner carted off the body?" She jabbed herself again. "Me. I have finder's rights. This is not fair."

KiKi picked up the *Savannah Times* with IdaMae's picture on the front and waved it in the air. "You're mentioned in here, Boone's mentioned, and even that Detective Ross. But am I? No. Every good gossip deserves press time once in a while to keep up her credentials. This was my one-and-only chance at a little fame."

"Maybe there'll be another murder?"

KiKi made the sign of the cross. "Saints preserve us. I don't need press time that bad, and all I can say is that you better have the Fox ready for business at ten sharp. Everyone's going to want to see the place, with it being in the papers and all. Too bad there's not blood on the floor. The place would be swarmed if there were blood."

I agreed about the blood but held high hopes that the smashed clock and bullet holes in the kitchen ceiling and dining-room wall would be enough to entice shoppers. Only in Savannah.

I told KiKi I needed to tidy up the shop. I returned to Cherry House and changed into my business uniform of navy skirt and cream blouse. I ratted up my hair to hide the stripe effect, then hitched up Bruce Willis. I snagged my purse off the counter and locked up the place. I was off to play Santa Claus before the Fox opened. I wanted to hand out the information from the blackmail list. I didn't tell KiKi, figuring this was between the people being blackmailed and Janelle. I was just the middleman, setting things right.

BW and I strolled up Abercorn, past Calhoun Square, with Savannah's most haunted house at the corner; past Lafayette Square, where the Saint Patrick's Day parade began each year; past Oglethorpe Square, named for our dear founding father even though his statue was over on Chippewa Square. Then again, General Pulaski's monument was at Monterey Square and not Pulaski Square. Next was Reynolds Square, ablaze with azaleas and tulips and named after a governor in the seventeen hundreds who robbed the city blind. Go figure.

BW and I turned down Saint Julian and took the front

steps to Raylene's. I rang the bell, and her majesty herself opened the door. "Well, I do declare, if it isn't the town troublemaker. What do you want now?"

"Can we talk for a second?"

"You're not bringing that mangy mutt into my house. It's bad enough Priscilla Annabelle has gotten herself sick today, and I'm all alone here and have to answer the door, and now you want to talk? I don't have time to talk. Go away."

I was tempted to just toss the information in the trash and forget Raylene, but I wanted something. "It's about Janelle."

Raylene huffed and *tsk*ed and rolled her eyes till I saw only the white parts before she finally stepped out. "What?"

"Here," I said thrusting an envelope at her. "I found Janelle's list, if you know what I mean. It's not a good idea for you to win Best of Show this year."

Raylene put her hands to her hips and hissed. "And why not?"

Because the whole city was sick to death of Raylene, and it was time for a change. "There's still certain information out there that Janelle left with someone. If it fell into the wrong hands, it could be embarrassing if you won and then it got around that you were actually paying for the privilege."

"Are you threatening me?"

"I'm just saying there's information out there, is all."

"Wait right here," Raylene said with more confidence in her voice than I liked. She left me standing on the porch, then retuned a minute later with a white folder. "You mean *this* information? Walker Boone delivered it to me himself yesterday. He's such a nice man, not like some people in this-here city." She gave me the *Some people* look. "He said he came across Janelle's blackmail list, and returning the information she had was the right thing to do. Guess I can win Best of Show or Best of the Whole Planet if I have a mind to." Raylene snapped the folder from my hand, stepped back in her house, and slammed the door in my face.

I was rooted to the spot. Boone! Blast his no-good, cheating, conniving hide. He was the life-insurance guy after all. Cupcake's contingency contact person! He lied to me straight-out, told me he knew nothing, and all along he knew who was on that list. He knew everything. He had all the information. He knew they had motives to kill Janelle but didn't expose them. How nice for them. How rotten for me. I was going to kill Walker Boone dead as Janelle and bury his pitiful hide in my weed-infested yard.

When BW and I got to Boone's big house on Jones Street, I rang the bell over and over and banged on the door with both hands and even kicked it a few times.

Boone opened the door, a happy-as-a-pig-in-mud smile creeping across his face. "Took you long enough."

"You're pond scum, you know that? You played me, Boone. You lied to me. You let me stumble around and find out why everyone was being blackmailed. I looked though Urston's closet and touched his gross shoes. I followed Baxter down alleys. I sweated in Raimondo's tanning bed. This has not been fun. Why did you get involved with Janelle Claiborne in the first place? I don't mean that literally."

"I told Janelle I'd do her dirty work so it didn't fall into the wrong hands. I had the information; I had control. She thought because I'm of questionable origins I'd do anything for a buck."

I mentally reddened at the accusation because I had thought the very same thing about Boone.

He added, "I didn't have the right to tell you. Besides, you're the one who found all the alibis, and I really didn't know who murdered Janelle."

"I did your work for you," I growled.

"Look at all the money you saved. Your legal fees are next to nothing."

"They're probably in the thousands."

"Probably."

"Thousands are not nothing!" BW sat on my foot and gave Boone his paw. I folded my arms and glared. "This isn't over, Boone. It's you and me, and this time there's going to be a humdinger of a fight."

He grinned and ruffled my hair. "I'm counting on it. I truly am."

Indigo Tea Shop owner Theodosia Browning finds herself in hot water when a body surfaces at the grand opening of Charleston's Neptune Aquarium—her ex-boyfriend Parker Scully . . .

FROM *NEW YORK TIMES* BESTSELLING AUTHOR
LAURA CHILDS

AGONY OF THE LEAVES
• *A Tea Shop Mystery* •

When Theodosia notices what look like defense wounds on Parker's hands, she realizes that someone wanted him dead, but the local police aren't keen on hearing her theory. She knows that if she wants Parker's killer brought to justice, she'll have to jump into the deep end and start her own investigation . . .

Includes delicious recipes and tea time tips!

laurachilds.com
penguin.com